Uprising

Ellen Fritz

Uprising
By Ellen Fritz
© 2016 Ellen Fritz

Swartz Creek, MI 48473
Cover design by Clarissa Yeo

Tell-Tale Publishing Group, LLC
5471 Peri St.
Swarz Creek, MI 48473   TT Imprint

CHAPTER 1

Gretchen Wagner died for no reason. Detective Ted Peterson re-read the report on his computer screen and blocked out the noise of the officers in the surrounding cubicles. The autopsy told him nothing. There were no signs of injury, no drugs, no alcohol, no trauma. She had been a healthy twenty-two-year-old Pennsylvania girl. Might have lost a baby recently, but there were no problems or complications. She had died right outside her home, and the doctors couldn't find anything.

He'd drawn the case this past winter and couldn't get it out of his mind. Gretchen lived in a cheap apartment in Pinehurst and worked at the local dollar store. Her body was found on the sidewalk by four strangers who were questioned, but knew nothing. They just happened to be driving by.

Although Gretchen's case wasn't classified as a murder, it was clearly a suspicious death. Suspicious death usually ended up being murder. If he could figure out how she died, he'd most likely find out someone caused that death. He'd searched for anyone she might have been involved with, but, even though she had been pregnant and seemed to have lost that baby, that didn't mean she had a steady boyfriend. The people she worked with were barely more than strangers. None of them admitted to seeing her socially or knowing anything about her.

The only suspicious thing he found was her credit card record. A one-way bus ticket from LeGrand, Oregon to Pinehurst didn't make much sense. Nothing told him why she'd been in Oregon or even how she'd gotten there. She didn't have a car. There was no record of her going on a bus, train, or plane, and no record of her staying in any hotel. People living on her small salary didn't usually take vacations. Someone else was involved in that trip, but Ted had no idea who that might have been.

"Peterson." Charlie Roth's voice jerked Ted out of his contemplation. He looked up and saw Roth and Greg Rudawski—known as R and R—leaning on his office doorway wall.

"The Celtics started ten minutes ago. What are you doing?" Rudawski asked, stroking his mustache. Before Ted could answer, Roth said with a smirk, "You're working on that cold case again aren't you? I thought the Lieutenant assigned you to the Stone House case."

Ted shrugged. "The Wagner case bothers me. Young healthy girls just don't die for no reason."

"Yeah, like you know anything about the female of the species," Rudawski teased.

Ted smirked back, hiding the pain from that barb. "Are you saying they're the same species? I thought they were all aliens— or maybe that was just the ones you date."

Roth rolled his eyes and tapped Rudawski in the arm. "We'll be at Play It if you change your mind."

Ted sighed as they moved off. Maybe he should go to the bar, watch the game, be the third wheel and drown his sorrows in public. He shook his head and reminded himself of his borrowed motto: "Don't let them see you sweat."

R & R had worked with him on the case at first, but other crimes happened and Gretchen's case slipped down to the bottom of the priority list. There was just something odd about the circumstances that made him go back to it. Tonight, he reviewed the four people who'd found her. A college professor, his accountant wife, and two college students weren't likely suspects, but they were all he had left.

The first time he'd questioned them that cold night outside Gretchen's apartment, their reactions had seemed odd. Finding a body on the street would be pretty upsetting for anyone, but he could somehow feel their anguish as he talked to them, especially the girl named Alexa Collins. She seemed really torn up by Gretchen's death. Maybe she knew more than she admitted.

Out of curiosity more than any real suspicion, Ted checked police records, work records, the standard stuff he'd done a million times, to get any information about those four strangers. All of them checked out. Adam McLane had been in several foster homes after losing his parents, Erik Ander was born in England, Aricia Ander in Greece, and Collins was from right here in Massachusetts.

He checked with the university and had periodically driven past their homes. He noticed right away that, even though McLane was registered as a dorm student, he seemed to be living with Collins. Not unusual. The Anders had a place off campus, but all four of them spent a lot of time together.

The different voices of the night shift reminded him that he should probably be going home - not that there was anyone to go home to. He reluctantly saved his notes, closed the files, and turned off his computer. Gretchen's mystery would have to wait another day for a solution.

Jacob's Steakhouse caught his eye as he drove home. A steak sounded better than a frozen dinner. Ted shook his head no at the hostess when she asked if he was waiting for someone else and ignored the implication that he was a loner when she sat him in the back corner at a small table that would be intimate for two but was less conspicuous for one.

After ordering, he watched the other customers as he waited for his salad. Gretchen's ghost or some higher power must have been looking out for him, for sitting at the table closest to him were his four good Samaritans. He'd noticed them right away, but they didn't seem to recognize him. Maybe that was because they were in the middle of a serious conversation.

All four of them talked quietly, whispering at times. Ted could periodically pick out a word or two, but nothing he could connect to Gretchen Wagner. He sipped his beer and considered that perhaps they were just what they'd said they were— innocent passersby. Perhaps he just needed to let it go and focus on the case he'd been assigned.

After his salad arrived, he studied their profiles. Alexa Collins blonde hair and chirpy voice fit her perfectly perky appearance. Adam McLane, obviously smitten with her, looked like a body builder. Erik Ander, the Londoner, had a hipster thing going on with this shaggy brown hair hanging in his eyes and his tall, skinny physique. His soft accent made his words harder to hear than the others. He probably had all the sorority girls signing up for his class. His Greek wife, Aricia, looked exotic with her short dark hair and her olive complexion. He couldn't tell if she had an accent or not because she didn't say much. They mentioned a couple unusual, maybe foreign, names. Then they mentioned something about Oregon.

He closed his eyes to concentrate on their voices. Their mention of Oregon wasn't proof of anything having to do with Gretchen Wagner, but he'd learned not to trust coincidence. Then he caught the word *abduction*. That got his heart beating faster. He strained to hear details, but they were even quieter than they had been.

Then came one of those moments that often happens in any group of people. That moment of coincidental quiet when everyone in the room stops talking except one person. In this moment Mrs. Ander clearly said, "... disappearance at State College ..." and "Gretchen's murder."

McLane added, "They might take someone else. Sindri..."

Ted's steak arrived, and he missed the rest of the conversation. Who was Sindri? What happened at State College? While he tried to hurry his suddenly attentive server off, the group got up to leave. Alexa Collins glanced his way, and he hid his face, wiping his lips with his napkin. He sure didn't want them to recognize him now. There was now no doubt that they knew more about Gretchen.

They knew that she was murdered.

CHAPTER 2

Ted got his steak to go and hurried out. The parking lot showed no sign of the group. Had they driven together? Were they headed to the Anders' or Alexa Collin's apartment? He considered having a patrol officer cruse by one while he checked the other and then thought of explaining to his lieutenant why he was wasting Pinehurst's limited resources on a cold case instead of working on his current assignment. Had they gone somewhere else?

He'd noticed that McLane had carried a bunch of flowers out with him—so perhaps they were celebrating something? Like duping the slow detective six months ago? He snorted in self-depreciation, and hopped into his Crown Victoria. He paused at the lot exit and went left toward campus.

The Anders had a modest house in a quiet neighborhood just south and west of the campus. He didn't see a car in the drive and the porch light seemed to indicate that no one was home. He waited for a few moments outside, just to be sure. The neighbor's side door light flicked on and a young boy took the trash out. He glanced at Ted's car, idling across the street, and went inside. The light flicked off.

He did a three-point turn in the Anders' driveway and headed for Collins' apartment. Maybe he'd catch them there, dropping the students off, and he could question them as a group before inviting them individually to visit the station.

He passed McLane and Collins' place of employment— Sean's Coffee Shop—on the way to the apartment. The shop had lots of college students hanging out, studying or socializing, but no sign of his quarry.

He remembered they mentioned a disappearance at State College. He looked up disappearances in State College, Pennsylvania, on his onboard computer. Yes, someone had gone missing. Another young woman. Why would college students abduct and, presumably, kill other college students? Anders and the others hadn't gone out of town recently as far as he knew. Maybe it was some sort of slavery ring?

He spotted the Anders' car on Collins' street. It wasn't good police procedure, but his curiosity got the best of him as he parked and walked around to the rear of Collins' apartment complex. She lived in the rear apartment on the first floor. The front door faced the alley and a small patch of woods. He looked around, but no one seemed to be out enjoying the evening. Before knocking on the door, he decided to peek through the window. He needed to get an idea of the layout, but mainly he'd see how they interacted with each other.

He could see the living room, down a short hallway, and partially into the kitchen. The flowers McLane had earlier sat in a vase on the counter next to a nice looking cake. At the sight of it, his stomach reminded him that he had skipped most of his dinner. A moment later, the four of them gathered in the living room and stood in a circle. They held hands and smiled at each other in obvious affection. He almost looked away, embarrassed at the thought that maybe they were swingers. But like seeing a car wreck on the side of the road, he had to look.

The hairs on the back of Ted's neck stood straight up as if lightning were about to strike. He blinked his eyes a few times and pinched himself. Erik Ander was the first to change, then his wife. McLane followed and finally Collins turned into something tall, thin, with lavender skin and long pastel-colored robes. The one facing the window had eyes of deep, deep blue with spots of light twinkling in them.

A second later, all four disappeared.

* * *

Lexi grabbed Adam's hand as they went into the kitchen, sharing her excitement in the mental space that only the two of them shared through their bond. She didn't need the squeeze of his hand to know that he felt the same. The call to teleport to New Mira had come. All four of them stood in a circle and dropped their Human disguises, smiling as they saw each other's true Miran forms. Delight circled through them and they mentally reached out. The response from the others, over half a world away, mirrored their feelings and welcomed the group to New Mira.

They materialized in the room she'd seen several times, but it continued to strike her with its beauty. The deep turquoise of the granite walls and ceiling, the veins of cream and silver that reflected light around the room, and the pale lavender skin of all the gathered Mirans were sights that she would always love. This was the area occupied by the Originals, the eight Mirans who were the only survivors of their crash landing on Earth.

Sindri, Balere, Nereus, Adam's direct ancestor, and the other five Originals greeted the group with hugs and welcoming words as they all moved into the modern conference room. She knew the ten of them would be the only ones in the meeting, but their discussion concerned all Mirans and everything they said would be communicated to the community.

Once everyone made themselves comfortable around the conference table, Sindri, their wise and graceful leader, began.

"The Dabih records that Lexi recovered have been incredibly difficult to translate. Their language is very different from any other we know, but we've made some good progress. We've concentrated so far on the earliest records, most of which are reports and simply factual.

"We've learned that the Dabih–this is the name they use for themselves throughout the records–didn't crash on Earth as we did. There is evidence that they were looking for what they call a 'water planet,' and Earth seemed to be perfect for them. Water is mentioned quite often and is very important to them, but we haven't determined why.

"There is mention of a war on their home planet, but not many details. One thing is very clear. They abandoned their home planet and brought their whole surviving population here. We've translated a reference to fifty thousand and we assume that is their original number.

"From what we can determine, the Dabih are amazingly different from us in temperament, philosophy, and values. Most of the passages mention division and fighting among themselves. Reports of attacks and even murder are shockingly common. We found one section that we think describes a group overthrowing the established leader. Another part seems to be describing the role of the leader which appears to be a kind of dictatorship.

"Several other small passages have been translated, but they make no sense out of context. What we have so far has given us a very different view of the Dabih than what we previously thought. Actually, what we knew before was mainly assumption. We assumed they were like us, but we were very wrong."

She paused, the room completely silent. Emotions skittered across the group, ranging from curiosity to fear. Lexi'd heard the hate and anger in Terazed's voice and now understood it better. Hate and anger might be a way of life for him and all the Dabih.

"Sindri," she broke the silence, "this all makes sense when I think about some of the things Terazed said to me. His superiors had no idea he was working on the device he used to block my powers. He said he would be richly rewarded when he demonstrated it to them and had it kill me."

"When I threatened the other Dabih with death," Erik added, his soft accent making his words seem formal, "it didn't make much difference, but when I said we'd protect him, he told us where to find Lexi. He also said that they were out of favor with their superiors for letting Gretchen escape. It's as if they live in more fear of each other than of us."

"There is still so much to learn," Sindri shook her head, "but we've had some important new insights. My greatest fear is that they won't allow us to deal with them peacefully and may eventually force us to destroy them. The most important thing we can do now, though, is to continue gathering information."

Everyone's nods of agreement echoed her hopes for an easy resolution. More than that, though, they could all clearly read each other's emotions. All Mirans could.

"However, the Dabih seem to have backed off. No hunters have been detected for the past ten days."

"No hunters? Anywhere?" Lexi asked, her astonishment matching those gathered around the table.

"Lexi, I'm still hoping that Dabih calls you again," Sindri said. Her voice conveyed her apprehension, because she recognized that would put Lexi in the middle again. "He called to make sure we knew he wasn't the one that took you. If we've started to reach him, maybe he can convince others that we can work together."

"We can hope they've decided to go the peaceful route, but I won't hold my breath on that one." Balere said, crossing his arms. The lights in his eyes swirled and gave off little flashes indicating his annoyance.

"I agree," added Aricia. "If they've changed tactics, odds are it will be something worse than what they've been doing."

"Or they've finally found a way to breed here," Lexi whispered. Her dread spread across the table like a shadow.

Sindri gestured at her. "Be calm, child. We know Gretchen's death and your abduction still haunt you. Surely after all these hundreds of years, the Dabih have not solved their breeding problem."

Lexi nodded and controlled her emotions. "You're right. Terazed made it sound like they were nowhere near a solution to breeding. Odds are good they didn't suddenly find an answer."

"I sure hope they didn't," Erik said seriously.

Balere looked very thoughtful as he added, "I've been thinking about all the things that have been happening in recent months. Gretchen's escape from the Dabih and subsequent murder, our visit to their caverns in Oregon, Lexi's abduction and escape, all might have caused them to want to stay out of sight for a while. We watched once for centuries while they stayed hidden. They might have gone back into hiding."

"That would follow their usual pattern." Erik nodded and added, "But I also think that they might have just changed where they're hunting. There are other places to find young women besides a college campus. They could target shopping malls, clubs, even prostitutes walking the street."

"You're right, they could be hunting almost anywhere," Adam said, reaching out to hold Lexi's hand.

"And we'd never be able to keep all the possible areas safe," Sindri said, her sadness swirling around the room. "All we can do is keep watching. We'll get word to everyone to keep patrolling, but we'll have to widen the scope. If there's an area like a mall nearby, we'll have to check it, but I'm afraid many areas will be missed. I'd like you four to check out State College and then concentrate on the areas near your home and around Boston."

Lexi and the others nodded understanding. The Originals expressed their ideas unemotionally, almost coldly, but she could sense the same fear and dread that the younger Mirans were feeling. It was more than speculation to her, though. She'd heard the terror in Gretchen's voice; looked into Terazed's eyes while he explained the details of his plans to kill her.

"In the meantime, we'll continue to translate all we can of their records. We'll contact you when we have more to tell you." Sindri ended the meeting, and the four from Pinehurst were teleported back to Lexi's apartment.

CHAPTER 3

Ted just stood outside Collins' apartment, staring at the empty kitchen. A barking dog startled him. The night went on and no one noticed his presence. He walked slowly to his car, opened the windows and sat there. He needed air, he needed to try to think about what he'd seen. He literally shook himself to get his brain working and took a drink of the cold coffee that had been sitting in the cup holder since early morning.

Two options came to mind. He might have been hallucinating and suffering from some serious mental illness or he'd really seen four people disappear into thin air.

People? They sure didn't look like people when they got all tall and lavender. If they didn't look like people, then what? He didn't want to think his next thought. Didn't want to admit even the possibility because they looked like something alien. Not another country alien, another planet alien.

The whole concept of aliens from outer space had always made Ted think of one word, *crap*. Flying saucers, sightings on lonely back roads, Area 51, alien abductions, all a load of crap.

"Oh, my God," he whispered out loud. Alien abductions. Had Gretchen been abducted by aliens? The idea just spun through his brain. He couldn't make himself believe in such things. Could they just take someone and then leave a body on the street with no evidence?

Thinking of the crime scene started to bring back his logic. He knew he wasn't nuts or hallucinating. He had seen the four of them change into something else and disappear, and humans couldn't do that.

His logic led to only one conclusion.

"These guys aren't human", he whispered as if whispering would keep it from being real. He put both hands over his face and tilted his head down toward the steering wheel, rocking slowly back and forth.

So what did he do with this? What was his next move?

It seemed obvious if they'd killed Gretchen without a mark on her, they could just as easily kill him. He suddenly felt like he'd narrowly escaped the biggest mistake of his life. He'd come so close to confronting them and trying to get them to give up evidence that they were involved in Gretchen's death. If he'd let them know that he was suspicious, they probably would have killed him. Except for lucky timing, he could be dead now, and the other detectives would be investigating his disappearance.

It wouldn't make much sense that four aliens land on Earth to settle down in Pinehurst. They seemed so human, holding down jobs, going to school. He'd done background checks. McLane and Collins had perfectly normal birth certificates, school records, everything. He hadn't gone as far with the other two because they weren't born in this country, but maybe he needed to look closer. If they were aliens and could cover their tracks so well with human records, then this could be huge. There could be a lot more of them.

His stomach tightened, but not with hunger. This was way too big for him, but he couldn't ignore what he'd found. He needed to keep his cool, keep watching, and see what he could dig up. He took a deep breath and reached for the key to head home when he saw Erik and Aricia walking around the building from the rear of Collins' apartment. A glance at his watch showed him he'd been there much longer than he thought. It was already 11:20.

The two of them were holding hands, smiling and laughing. Erik opened the passenger door, and they kissed before she got in. He got in the driver's side, they both put on their seatbelts, and drove away.

"So damn human." They looked like any happily married couple, genuinely in love. But they were aliens. Could aliens fall in love? After what he'd seen tonight, he would never again think anything was impossible.

The next day he pondered what his next move should be. But then, he'd thought about it all night, too. Following them around town wasn't going to get him anywhere. He needed to get to know them better to see if he could establish some kind of pattern, or find some evidence of what they were doing. The simplest thing he could think of was to go to the coffee shop where Collins and McLane worked.

"Earth to Peterson," Rudawski's voice made him blink. He realized he'd had frozen, his coffee cup halfway to his mouth. They were sitting in his car, observing the comings and goings of people out of a small house where a suspected smuggling ring might be operating.

He grunted in wry appreciation and sipped his coffee. Rudawski got more comfortable in his seat and went back to watching.

That afternoon, he used the excuse of the notoriously poor coffee at the station to make a run to Sean's Coffee Shop. It looked like any other coffee shop, a few tables and a large counter showing off pastries along with a chalkboard with the day's special coffees. Alexa Collins was behind the counter. The busy shop made him change his mind on asking her about Gretchen Wagner. He'd wanted all four together so he could catch them unprepared. At least he'd find out right away if she knew him.

"Can I help you?" Her name tag read "Lexi" and had a flower sticker and a smiley face on it. He asked for his coffee plain, black, no muss no fuss. The lieutenant had wanted some sort of mocha thing, R and R both took theirs with cream. He took a table, and she brought his order to him in a few minutes. Thanking him, she gave no indication that she knew who he was.

He lingered over his coffee, watching her while his takeout order got   cold. She went about her work in a cheerful manner and seemed well liked by her coworkers, who obviously had no idea she turned into a tall purple creature with sparkling eyes on her off hours. A small, bouncy red head came in, obviously looking for someone. Collins asked her for her order but the red head ignored her.

"Emily, Adam isn't here. Do you want a coffee?" Obviously the red head was a regular.

The red head pouted but ordered a fancy coffee. Collins gave it to her in a to-go cup. The red head left, less bouncy than before.

The boss, whose name tag said Betsy and had a cat sticker on it, joined her at the cash register.

"Not that I..." Collins started to say something else but changed it to, "Is Sean still looking to hire additional help?"

Betsy snorted and wiped the counter down. "Not that one, I assure you."

Collins nodded and went to clean a table.

The other customers trickled out, and the shop grew quiet. Fearing that he'd be stuck there—empty cup in front of him—he got up to leave, but paused when he heard Collins talk to her boss.

"Have you ever been hiking in the Berkshires? The weather is so beautiful right now. I just love spring," Collins said. We were thinking of going hiking tomorrow."

"The Berkshires are beautiful, alright," Betsy said. "But Adam works tomorrow night, so you won't have time."

"Oh, you're right," Lexi shook her head. "I forgot Adam's schedule. We'll save the hike for another time."

Aliens went hiking to enjoy the weather? Too bizarre. Collins was obviously covering up something. But why would she ask her boss about the Berkshires? The Berkshires were four hours away. Maybe they were going to "beam" there. How ridiculous. He shook his head and left her a tip.

The bustle at the station hid the fact that he'd lingered. The lieutenant and both Rs were in a meeting, so he left their drinks on their respective desks. Settling at his own desk, he tried to concentrate on the case before him, but couldn't. From Collins chatter with her boss, it had seemed like all four of them planned on being gone most of the next day, which happened to be a day off for him.

He had a thought. It was unethical, against police procedure, and would never hold up in court. It was downright breaking and entering, but putting a bug in Collins' apartment might be the only way he could get concrete information. He could watch them forever and not learn anything more than he already knew. They acted so human and did such normal things. Even if he saw them disappear again, so what? It wasn't like he could follow. Besides, he didn't want to see that again. If he could get in the apartment when he knew they were gone, he could hide a wireless microphone in no time at all. Then he'd be able to listen to every word, every plot, every admission of who they really were and what they'd done to Gretchen Wagner.

CHAPTER 4

Ted left his house about 9:00 Saturday morning, figuring that would have given them plenty of time to leave on their hike or wherever they were really going. He went past Anders' first and found their car in its usual place. Maybe the other two had picked them up. He pulled to the back of Collins' apartment so he wouldn't be seen walking around the building and her car was there. He drove slowly down the alley but stayed within sight of the apartment.

She usually had the bedroom and kitchen curtains open by this time in the morning. Looking around more carefully, he noticed that mail was sticking out of the box. She would have collected that by now, too, so maybe they weren't home. Damn, maybe they did "beam" away somewhere. How could he do surveillance on people who traveled like that?

He parked and pulled a small case out of his backseat and shoved it in his pants pocket as he made up a cover story. He'd ring the bell. If they answered he'd ask if they knew the people living in the front apartment, pretending there was some issue with them. If they didn't answer, he'd go in and get the job done. Simple, but his stomach gurgled.

He'd "borrowed" the listening devices, listing them as a part of his current investigation. Once he had his information, he'd retrieve the bugs and no one would be wiser. He rang the bell again just to be sure. They didn't answer.

Learning to pick a lock was an incredibly useful thing, but he'd never done it to actually break into someone's home. He didn't feel good about it, but he got into the apartment without any trouble and without leaving any sign of his break-in.

He put one microphone on the inside of the couch leg. Even if they moved the couch, they wouldn't find that. The other one would be good in the kitchen, but finding a spot for it was more of a problem. He finally spotted the narrow slot between the refrigerator and the counter and carefully placed it there.

When he left the apartment, he drove several blocks away before parking again to check his laptop. This was a great system with sound activation so he didn't have to listen to hours of nothing. It would record right to his laptop so he could listen when he had time, and he'd have exactly what he needed.

As he sat in his car, he thought back to his years with the Boston PD - the times where he sat listening, watching, waiting for other information to come so that he could solve other cases. The thing that led him to police work was that he wanted to help people. He wanted to have the opportunity to make a difference in the lives of victims and get criminals in prison. Plain and simple.

He loved the detective work, and he was good at collecting the evidence, trying to figure out the criminal mind, and putting together a solid case that would lead to a guilty verdict. But he hadn't felt very successful in Boston. He found Boston just too big, too impersonal. His caseloads were horrendous. The overwhelming paperwork took up too much of his time, and the victims became faceless case numbers because there were just too many of them. The detective position in Pinehurst opened up so he went for it.

Maybe it was a stupid move. Pinehurst was a small college town with all kinds of activities for the students, but not much for the adult community. It was small enough that there were only three detectives on the force. They were friends, often worked cases together, and supported each other, so that helped. But R and R were married with kids, leaving him the odd man out. The lieutenant had a new girlfriend every other week it seemed.

A memory of the Anders kissing as they left Collins' place made him scowl. Maybe he'd meet someone to share his life. There were plenty of college kids around, but he wasn't interested in a girl. He longed to find a woman. Someone more mature, more serious about life. Someone who wanted a future like he did. A woman who would give him children and grow old with him. He shook his head and drove home. After three years in Pinehurst, he hadn't met anyone that inspired more than one date, so that hope was fading.

Part of him felt guilty about putting illegal microphones in someone's home. He was always the one arguing that the end didn't justify the means and would never do this in any other situation. Although he felt bad, he didn't have any other choice. This was something outside of police procedure, outside the situations that the laws covered, outside of his usual moral judgment. This was beyond Gretchen Wagner's murderer. These were aliens who were abducting and killing human women. He might be on the trail of saving thousands. Maybe the whole human race was in danger.

At home, he worked on some paperwork to get his mind on something besides the aliens, but he kept the laptop open. Finally, the microphones were picking up some sound. He listened carefully. A giggle. Something hitting the couch. Great, they're making out and whispering. Like he needed to listen to that. After a while, real conversation happened on the kitchen mic, McLane talking about his college ambitions.

"I'm not interested in wrestling anymore," Adam said. "I'm going to tell the coach tomorrow.

"Why are aliens talking about wrestling?" Ted grumbled, but then grabbed his notebook and quickly wrote, "Be here to protect me," and "The whole dah-bee thing." What did that mean? He'd never heard the word dah-bee and had no idea how it might be spelled, but he'd try to find some reference. And what did Collins, an almost seven-foot alien who could disappear, need protection from?

He heard them say goodbye—Collins must have been leaving for work—before the loud music started. He groaned and poured a cup of coffee. Great, now he had hours of music or TV to listen to. Eventually he would hear something important, he hoped. Something that was real evidence. He still didn't know what he would ever do with the evidence, but he was determined to get it.

By 9:00 p.m. that night, he was going a little stir-crazy and had to do something. McLane would be walking home with Collins at midnight, so he could follow them. Maybe they'd meet the other two, or maybe not. It didn't matter. They might talk about something important once they got home. Mainly, sitting in his apartment listening to McLane's choice of crap music was making him tense. Maybe he'd sleep some if he got out for a while and got some fresh air.

He parked about a block away from Collins' apartment and waited for McLane to pass on his way to Sean's Coffee Shop. He'd follow him there on foot, then follow the two of them home. Simple and probably a waste of time, but at least he was doing something besides sitting, staring, and thinking about how dangerous these aliens could be.

CHAPTER 5

Ted rubbed his jaw, irritated with his surveillance of McLane and Collins. Finally, they left the coffee shop with their arms around each other. To be honest, he admitted that he was irritated with himself because he was becoming more and more obsessed with the aliens that he wished he knew nothing about. Maybe he was crazy. He imagined presenting his evidence to the lieutenant.

"Aliens? Really, Ted? " He could hear the lieutenant's raspy voice and laughed to himself, picturing Rudawski taking him in for possession of an illegal, labeled as mentally disturbed and advised to seek legal help. His old partner in Boston would get a kick out of that.

About a block in front of him, they stopped in a shadowed area to make out. He wanted evidence, but kept getting this lovey-dovey stuff. Mid-kiss they broke apart and started to run. Not toward Collins' apartment, but into the campus.

He ran after them at a distance, trying to be as quiet as possible, and followed them into the commons area. There were quite a few students around, which meant he could maybe get closer without being noticed. What had made them break that kiss so abruptly and take off like that? Were they late for something?

They passed a group of students and walked straight toward some man in a brown coat sitting on the steps and stopped in front of him like he was their reason for being here. Ted had to get closer. Looking around, he spotted one of the huge pillars on the entry to the library just a couple feet from where the man sat. If he could get behind it, he could listen.

As they stopped, Ted passed them and went up the steps. He curved his path like he was heading for one of the library doors at the far end. Their view of him would be blocked by the diameter of the pillar. He stopped behind it, tried to look casual to anyone else coming or going from the library, and listened.

* * *

Lexi gasped. "Terazed."

The Dabih stared at them as they approached. He looked relaxed, but they could feel his power. They summoned their power, standing shoulder to shoulder in front of him. They were ready to strike a deadly blow, but hopefully didn't need to do anything in front of so many Humans.

"This is much braver than I would have expected from you, Terazed," Adam said with a growl.

"I face you alone, Lexi, and you bring one of your body guards. Maybe you're not so confident of your powers anymore," he answered with a wide grin.

"Remember me?" She let the sarcasm be obvious in her voice. "I'm the one who could have easily killed you, but chose not to. Never doubt that it could still happen."

"Idle Miran threats," he said, dismissive and arrogant. She wondered if that was a characteristic of all Dabih, or just Terazed.

"I would think you'd take Miran threats seriously. Don't you remember telling me we'd already killed most of the Dabih? I guess I was right when I assumed you were lying."

He turned to Adam. "Do all Mirans have such a nasty attitude, or just the females?"

"You haven't begun to see Miran attitude, yet, Dabih," Adam answered, flexing his muscles, "but keep taking and killing Humans and you'll see plenty of it."

"This has nothing to do with Humans." He spat out the word *Humans* like it was a bad taste in his mouth.

Adam glared at him. "Everything between Mirans and Dabih has to do with Humans. The day you stop killing them, we stop killing you, and we can share this planet in peace."

"We don't share, Miran." Terazed glared back.

"Why are you here?" Lexi snapped at him.

"I want my device back." His voice was more forceful and she could sense his anger.

She laughed. "Why would you expect to get it back?"

"I offer you a deal, Lexi Collins." He tried to make his voice persuasive but his eyes were cold. "I will never again use it against you, including your body guard here if you want, and I will make another for your use and teach you to use it effectively."

"For my use?" She shook her head in confusion.

"Yes," he said stretching out the word making it sound like a snake hissing. "Think how far you could go if you could control your superiors with my device? You're young, it may take some time, but you could have anything you want. Any position of authority you want. Anything."

"You expected that I would want to use your device against other Mirans?" She was shocked and didn't try to hide it.

"How could you think that?" Adam added, his own shock apparent.

"Don't pretend you haven't already tried, but you gave up because nothing happened. You see, the power source is rather tricky. I'll have to show you how to get it to work."

She took a deep breath. "Terazed," she said, now calm, "you don't know us at all. We don't fight against each other. We have no positions of authority because we work together on everything. All Mirans have one common goal. To live in peace. We only fight you to stop your genocide of the Human race. Our only wish is that Mirans, Dabih and Humans will one day share this planet peacefully."

He stood, glared at them. "Share," he snarled. "That will not happen. You stole my device and my records, but I'll make another. This planet will belong to the Dabih, and Mirans and Humans won't even be a distant memory to us."

He stalked off. Once he was around the corner of the library building, they sensed him teleport away. Lexi sat on the steps, slowly releasing her power. Adam sat beside her, putting his arm around her shoulders.

"We have to go to New Mira tonight," he sighed, "but, man, I am so tired. I could fall asleep right here."

"Me, too," she said and rested her head on his shoulder. "Holding my powers ready that long just about wiped me out."

"You're not kidding, but Erik says that gets easier after a few decades."

"And here we are handling this craziness," she added with a little aggravation. "I'm three months, and you're a year old."

"A year and a half, thank you," he smiled trying to dispel her anxiety.

"You old man," She smiled back and pretended to punch him in the stomach.

He laughed and hugged her. "Let's crawl home and find someone to teleport us."

"Okay," she said with a yawn.

* * *

Ted had wanted something to happen and it had, but things started really getting weird. Before the conversation even started, he felt something. Some kind of buzzing in his head, subtle but definitely there. For a moment, it made him feel dizzy like he'd been upside down and righted himself too fast. When the dizziness passed, the buzzing radiated through his whole body, like an electrical charge through the air.

He tried to ignore it as he listened carefully. He knew right away that this wasn't a buddy. This was an enemy. A deadly enemy that, in other circumstances, could lead to death for either side. From what they said, it had led to death before. Gretchen Wagner's death?

The guy walked away and within a few seconds the buzzing stopped. Ted slumped against the pillar, which made him realize that his whole body had been tense and rigid. He felt like he'd just finished a tough workout.

McLane and Collins sat on the steps. What did they mean by "holding powers?" What was New Mira? Is that where they went when they disappeared? But the conversation between the two of them was secondary. Ted didn't follow the aliens home. For the first time in his years as a detective, he felt like he had too much information and couldn't take anymore. His body felt like a heavy wet blanket. It was all he could do to drag himself back to his car.

CHAPTER 6

Adam called Erik and Aricia as they walked so they could meet at their apartment. As soon as they got home, they dropped their Human disguises and reached out to New Mira. They waited, arms wrapped around each other. Instead of sensing the Mirans welcoming them to New Mira, as normal, Sindri, Erik and Aricia suddenly materialized.

"Sindri, we were on our way to you," Lexi said with surprise.

"We sensed your exhaustion and didn't want you to use your weakened powers to come to us." She could sense Sindri's concern as she spoke.

"Are you two okay?" Erik asked, also concerned.

"We're fine," Adam nodded. "Just tired."

"What happened?" Aricia asked.

Adam did most of the talking. She could sense their surprise at the deal she'd been offered. When he finished, Sindri looked into both their eyes with compassion.

"First, I hate that you two had to go through all this. You're too young to have to use your powers like that. You need to stay in your true forms and get as much sleep as possible tonight. You should feel fine by morning.

"Second, you are both incredibly strong and determined. I'm proud of the way you handled Terazed."

Lexi sighed in relief.

"Now," Sindri continued, "The business of the Dabih device. We did test it. Balere volunteered to have it used on him. I don't know whether Terazed is a terrible liar or just incredibly stupid."

The were all surprised by Sindir's statement.

"He told you it was tricky. It took some minor adjustments, but our technicians had no problems. It worked perfectly to block Balere's powers, but only took him a few minutes to break through it. He was impressed, though, that you were able to overcome it," Sindri added with a smile. "Your powers are strong."

For some reason that embarrassed her a little. "Thank you, Sindri," she answered. "I sensed Terazed really believed I'd tried it, but why would he tell me it was tricky when that was such an obvious lie?"

"Exactly. It makes no sense. But we've carefully studied the pictures you two brought back from Oregon, and it looks like their technology is very old. Old by even Human standards. It's no wonder they haven't been able to use science to help them breed. They don't seem to have the equipment to do adequate DNA or stem cell research. We're starting to believe that they are nowhere near us in science or technology, and they might not have the skills to do what they've been trying to accomplish."

"So," Erik hesitated, "where does that leave us? What can we do?"

Sindri shook her head. "There's not much we can do, but our engineers did get curious about that power-blocking device. They think they can build something simpler that will work against the Dabih. They're hoping such a device could even keep them from teleporting and they're designing a hand-held tool that could be used on an individual or a group. I'm not sure how we'll test it, but I'll let you know when they get something accomplished."

"Wow," Lexi said, "that could make a real difference. We could block their powers and keep them there long enough to talk to them."

Sindri nodded. "And ours won't have a function to inflict pain. That was just barbaric of them."

"Sure was," Adam whispered as he looked in Lexi's eyes. He took her hand and cradled it next to his heart. She could feel that he hated that Terazed had used that device on her and still felt guilty that he hadn't been able to protect her.

"We'll leave you young ones to your sleep, but I'm afraid that you two probably made him pretty angry. He may be back. Stay alert and be careful. You will be the first ones to get the new devices when they're ready."

She hugged them both and teleported back to New Mira. Erik and Aricia stayed a few minutes longer, reassuring them that they were just a phone call away.

* * *

By the time he'd driven the few miles to his small house on the edge of town, Ted was feeling a little better. He'd never felt anything like that buzzing and didn't remember ever hearing of someone having that kind of reaction to anything. It felt a little electrical, but not exactly. It was maybe more like being hit with a Taser, but much more subtle. He'd been a volunteer guinea pig in Taser training and didn't ever want that feeling again.

He changed his clothes, got a beer out of the refrigerator, and sat on the couch.

"So that was a dah-bee," he muttered and took a sip. According to what he heard, not only was there a group of aliens on Earth, there were two: Mirans and Dabih. This new guy, the

Dabih, was abducting and killing humans. The Mirans were trying to save humans. The Dabih were trying to take over the planet, and the Mirans were trying to share it.

"What the hell have I gotten myself into?" he said aloud before draining the bottle in his hand. Was he the only person, the only human anyway, on the planet that knew about any of this? All the sightings and reports of abductions that he'd dismissed, had they been real?

He noticed his open laptop and the signal that something was being recorded. They were going to that New Mira place, so the recording shouldn't last long. But it did. He should probably listen, but frankly couldn't face learning any more about aliens. He wished he'd never started any of it.

He had spent his whole career gathering information to get to the bottom of things. Well, he'd gotten his answers. That guy on the library steps was most likely the one who'd abducted and killed Gretchen Wagner. If that were true, his case was solved. But how could he ever do anything about it? There was no way he could tell anyone else. Even if they didn't have him committed, he had no physical evidence. And this was so much bigger than one murdered girl. How many had been killed over the years? How long had it been going on? How many aliens were on the planet?

He reached for his empty bottle and saw that his hand shook. He could feel the horror running through him like that electrical current when he was behind the library pillar. If any of them found out that he knew about them, they'd kill him. Or worse, he could be the next human trapped on some space ship while aliens conducted horrible experiments on his body and mind.

He had to forget about the whole thing. No more following, no more listening. He had to pretend he'd never started this investigation, let Gretchen Wagner rest in peace, and go on with his normal life. Thank God they hadn't seen him and didn't know he'd been watching them.

Closing the laptop, he felt a small sense of relief. He started to get up to head for bed when he thought of the hidden microphones. The realization that he'd have to get the bugs out of Collins' apartment caused a moment of dread that made his stomach hurt. If he left them, chances are Collins would never find them, but the next time someone did inventory at the station, Ted would be busted. If he got caught trying to get the bugs back, he'd be alien toast. If he didn't, his career would be toast.

CHAPTER 7

It was barely light when Ted left for work Monday morning. The cloud-covered sky said it would be a dreary, drizzly day. Spring was beautiful, but rain and the lack of sun depressed him. Like he didn't have enough to be depressed about.

He'd spent Sunday hovering outside of Collins' apartment in hopes that she and McLane would go somewhere, but the lovebirds were only interested in nesting that day. So he went to Plan B, which was to leave the bugs and hope that an inventory didn't happen or that no one needed them.

Determined that he was going to put all the alien stuff out of his mind and just go on with his life as if aliens didn't exist, he plunged into his current case and tried to concentrate on solving that and helping those victims.

When the lieutenant's request for Ted to join him in his office came, Ted's mind instantly snapped back to the bugs in Collins' apartment.

"Sir?" he asked as he sat down.

"Are you okay, Peterson? I noticed you missed the meeting with the DEA agent."

Ted controlled the urge to cuss. That's where they'd been when he returned with the coffee that morning.

"Sorry, sir. I got caught up in an Adam 2 at the coffee shop." Ted knew the lieutenant wouldn't mind if he'd stopped to help someone. Pinehurst PD was all about community relations.

The lieutenant didn't comment on this but stroked his chin.

"Rudawski tells me you've been distracted lately. And, frankly, you look like hell. Are you sure everything is all right?"

He doesn't know. No one knows. It seemed so unreal.

"I need you to be focused on the Stone House case," the lieutenant continued.

Ted nodded, not trusting himself to lie outright to his superior officer.

"In fact, I want you to go in and set up some listening devices on in the suspect's car."

"The '68 Camaro?" His smile matched the lieutenant's. The suspect in the case drove a wicked sweet silver hot rod.

"I'm all right, Lieutenant. I promise."

The lieutenant believed him and he believed it himself until he got to the equipment room and realized he didn't have the bugs. Cussing under his breath, he pretended to get the listening devices from the shelf and then modified the date on the log to match the correct day and time instead of last Friday night.

By lunch it was a struggle to concentrate on his work at all. He'd hardly slept for three nights while watching those damn aliens. Maybe he should claim illness and go. And then the lieutenant would be all over him for not being forthcoming. And he still had to break into Collins' apartment to get the microphones back.

Every so often when it was fairly quiet, he could hear the Dabih's voice saying coldly, "This planet will belong to the Dabih." He chased that sound from his head, but it kept coming back. His only hope, he decided, was that time might help. He'd get the bugs, listen to the human suspect in his current and entirely logical case, and keep doing his best.

McLane appeared to be at home when Ted cruised by Collins' apartment. That kid had enough muscles that Ted doubted the other aliens would have a chance to torture him before McLane beat him down. He went to his house, frustrated.

After eating a frozen dinner he sat down on the couch to watch some basketball or something distracting. He noticed the laptop on the coffee table and remembered he'd never listened to the conversation recorded after Collins and McLane got home.

The detective part of him wanted to listen. But the other part of him wanted to forget everything he knew, couldn't stand the thought of what else he might learn. He didn't need to have more information that he'd have to try to put out of his head.

He erased all the recordings he'd collected and put the laptop in the den. No more, he thought. He'll get the bugs tomorrow and it would be over.

After hours of staring at the TV screen, he finally went to bed. By 2:00 a.m., he had only been asleep for about an hour when he woke up to his phone ringing. Caller ID told him it was the night shift captain, so he answered quickly.

"Sorry to wake you up, but I've got a situation here that might be related to the Gretchen Wagner case you were working on."

That got him wide awake. "Gretchen? What is it?"

"I remember you saying you had some evidence that she might have been kidnapped. I've got a girl here who walked in saying she was kidnapped and just escaped. I thought you might want to be involved in this."

"I'll be right there." He dressed as quickly as he could and ran to his car to get to the station. He hated that some girl was the victim of an abduction, but was glad that he finally had something that would get his mind off aliens. Pulling into the parking lot, the thought struck him that she might have been taken like Gretchen. What would he do if she said she was abducted by aliens? A week ago, he would have laughed and said she was a nut case. Now, he'd have to listen.

He gave the girl a hot chocolate and poured himself a cup of coffee. They sat at the conference table instead of in the interview room because the chairs were softer and Ted wanted this girl to be comfortable and forthcoming.

"I was heading for my car at the mall just after dark. Two guys who seemed to come out of nowhere grabbed me. I don't know what they did to me, but everything went blank. I woke up in a room with fifteen other women."

"Fifteen?" Ted raised his eyebrows.

"I counted, twice," she said, earnestly.

He asked her to describe the room.

"Not very big, like a bedroom in any house, and we sat on the floor. Two men came in the room and took one woman out, locking the door as they left. About ten minutes later, they came back and took another."

He asked her how many they might have taken before. She saw them take three.

"I was placed along the wall by the door. When the guys came in again, I scooted back farther hoping they wouldn't select me. They left the door open. When the girl they were taking started to fight and scream, I saw my chance while they struggled with her. I crawled through the door and into the hallway.

"The hall was dark, but I found a closet and quickly hid inside. The girl who was screaming suddenly went quiet, and I heard the men dragging her down the hall in the opposite direction. Once I realized they were gone, I got out of the closet and found a bathroom with a window. I climbed out and ran as far as I could."

"They didn't notice?"

"I didn't stick around to find out and I walked in the shadows. I don't know what happened to my cell phone and didn't want to flag down a car, so I just walked right to the station."

Her story was incredible. Such things didn't happen in small towns like Pinehurst, but she was obviously telling the truth, since he was the third person to hear her account and she never wavered. This girl was sharp. She'd kept her head and didn't let her fear keep her from taking advantage of the opportunity to escape.

She finished giving him a description and location of the house as her parents got there. She was sent to the hospital to be checked out even though she said she wasn't hurt, just scared and tired.

Ted and a group of officers set off into the pre-dawn gloom. They soon discovered the abandoned two-story house on the edge of town by the old railroad tracks where she'd been held, but they were too late. The kidnappers must have realized she escaped and immediately moved the rest of the girls away.

The crime scene techs arrived and he joined them in looking for evidence. How many girls, why did they take them, why leave with one at a time? Were these local crazies or someone who'd just picked a random mall?

Once inside, he felt slightly dizzy.

"Man, I've got to get some sleep," he mumbled. As he went down the hall, the dizziness changed to a subtle buzzing in his head. The buzzing spread through his body, and he felt his muscles get tense. No, he thought, this can't be happening.

The buzzing was gentler, probably because they weren't around anymore, but it was the same. Just like that guy outside the library. It was the Dabih and they'd been in this house very recently. They'd snatched those girls just like Gretchen Wagner. Had they killed them yet?

There wasn't one mark on Gretchen's body, but he knew they didn't bother taking them just to kill them. What else were they up to? He shivered. He knew the horrors humans were capable of. What might aliens do?

After a few minutes, the buzzing was tolerable, so Ted went through the motions with the other officers and looked for evidence he knew they wouldn't find. No tire tracks, nothing left in the room, no fingerprints. Nothing. And that just made him mad.

All those innocent girls. The tortured families that could only pray that they'd be returned. He had to think of something. As he drove home, the first ray of light broke through the trees. He knew in his gut there was only one thing he could do. He had to go to the Mirans.

CHAPTER 8

That evening, after a long day of answering phones and paperwork and a nap, Ted watched as Collins left the coffee shop about 6:00 p.m. McLane hadn't come in. Those girls had been gone almost twenty-four hours and he didn't have time to hesitate any longer. Once they were both home, he'd knock on the door to have a conversation that could either end his life, or save the lives of all those terrified girls.

He parked his car in the alley again and watched. The calls had come in and the families of missing girls he'd talked to all day needed to get their daughters and wives back. They expected his best effort. They deserved his best effort. What they didn't know was that his best effort might mean sacrificing himself.

Finally, he forced himself out of the car and walked toward the apartment feeling like a death-row inmate heading for his execution. He stopped in front of that innocent-looking door, took a deep breath, and knocked.

"Hi, um, I'm Ted Peterson. The detective you talked to the night you found Gretchen Wagner's body. Could I talk to you two?"

"Sure, come on in," Adam answered as he stepped aside. "Have a seat. Lexi, this is Ted Peterson, that detective we talked to that night."

They'd both sensed that it was a terrified human outside their door even before he knocked. They had no idea what his appearance might be about, but Lexi's concern was that he was close to being as terrified as Gretchen had been. What could be scaring him so much?

"Hi," she said sweetly. "You've been in the coffee shop, haven't you?"

"A couple times." Ted looked around at the nice little apartment he'd glimpsed from the window. He could see in his mind the four creatures that had stood in the kitchen and disappeared before his eyes. The knots in his stomach felt like they'd grown spikes. The two of them were pretending to be the innocent humans that went to school and work every day and they were so good at their game. How had they learned to act so human?

He could chicken out. He could simply ask them some unimportant questions about Gretchen and leave. Then he heard the voices of the mothers who had called to report missing daughters.

"What can we do for you, detective?" Adam was saying. He had a curious look on his face. "I'm not sure if…"

"Look, I have to tell you something," Ted interrupted. His knees suddenly felt week and he sat clumsily on the couch as they stood looking at him with curious expressions on their faces.

"I've been like, watching you. And I've heard some things," he stammered. Say it—get it over with. He looked up at them. If they were going to kill him, he wanted to see it coming. He saw their confused looks.

"The thing is, I know you're aliens—Mirans—and I know about the Dabih. I need your help to save some girls the Dabih took last night."

CHAPTER 9

"I don't know what you're saying, Detective," McLane's voice was amazingly calm.

Collins excused herself and walked into the kitchen. Ted could hear her calling someone.

"Yeah, you do know," he said, turning his attention back to McLane.

"I thought you were going to ask us about Gretchen," Collins said, returning to the room with a cup of coffee and a plate of cookies. He appreciated the gesture, but couldn't stomach anything with the thought of his impending death on his mind.

"This is way beyond Gretchen."

At that moment, Ander walked in, looking like he was ready to fight. Ted stood up, ready to fight back. Ander looked him up and down and then deliberately turned to McLane, "What's up?"

"You don't have to pretend that she didn't call you," Ted said. "And you could have beamed into the living room 'cause I've seen it before."

"What are you talking about?" Ander asked, his eyes narrowing.

"I've been watching all four of you, I've heard about the Dabih trying to kill humans, I've seen you disappear into thin air, and I've seen what you really look like. You know, tall, lavender skin, sparkly eyes. The Dabih kidnapped at least fifteen girls last night, probably more. I need your help to get them back. I'm the only one who knows about you and the Dabih, so I had to come here." The words flew out of his mouth.

The aliens froze, stunned looks on their faces.

He added, "So are you going to help me or kill me the same way the Dabih killed Gretchen Wagner?"

They exchanged looks and silent communication, he guessed. Ander gave him an intense look and a wave of exhaustion washed over him. He wanted to say "No," but didn't get a chance.

* * *

"What did you do?" Lexi demanded.

"Hey man, that's a police officer," Adam objected.

"It's just a light stun," Erik said, putting his hands on his hips. "This is a disaster. How the hell did he get that much information about us? We have to get in touch with New Mira."

"We can't just leave him here." Adam started to pace.

"I'll go to New Mira. I think Sindri might want to talk to him here or maybe take him there. I don't know. I'll be back as soon as possible." Erik reached out to New Mira and, within a moment, he teleported away.

Adam and Lexi were left standing in the middle of the room staring down at the unconscious police detective.

"God, I hope he doesn't wake up until Erik gets back," Adam whispered.

"How on Earth did he get all that?" She whispered too, afraid to wake the man.

"He must have been watching us since Gretchen's death. How did he hear us and see us teleport?" They were both too shocked to come up with any answers.

"Oh, Adam, I just don't know what to think. What will the Originals do?"

"Beats me. I don't think this has ever happened, at least not in modern times. I don't know what they'll do."

They waited, unconsciously adding to each other's shock and confusion. It seemed like forever, but it was actually just about ten minutes before Sindri, Balere, and Erik materialized in Human form. She'd never seen Sindri as a Human before and she was gorgeous, with fawn colored hair and emerald colored eyes, but it seemed strange. She was born with her Miran form and that seemed right. Balere's Human form seemed drab next to Sindri's, yet she was sure he'd be mistaken for a movie star in public. The Originals had thousands of years to choose a Human form that pleased them, so of course they were attractive.

"Erik's told us everything this man said," Sindri said in her usual calm voice, but inside Lexi could tell she was feeling the same shocked disbelief.

"He's afraid we're going to kill him," Lexi stammered. They had to do something about this human detective, but what? Her thoughts bounced around her head. Had this ever happened before? What was the policy? Would they kill Detective Peterson to protect their secrecy? No one wanted to kill humans, but could it come to that?

Sindri put a hand on Lexi's shoulder, giving her a fuller impression of her love and compassion. "We'll question him and see if we can do anything about his claim that the Dabih took all those women. It's not like them, but it could be the change we knew might be coming."

"Poor man. It may not be easy to convince him that killing him's the last thing we'd do," Balere said sadly. "Humans have a great fear of other beings."

"We should probably sit down to make him more comfortable," Sindri said as she looked around. Adam pulled chairs from the kitchen and they sat in a circle around the couch.

"Wake him, Erik," Sindri said.

Detective Peterson slowly opened his eyes, looked around at all of them, and jumped to his feet, his hand going to his gun. No one moved.

"What'd you do to me?"

"I lightly stunned you," Erik answered calmly. "Not enough to harm you, but we had to make some plans before we chat."

"Ted Peterson," Sindri spoke gently, "I'm Sindri and this is Balere. We are not going to harm you. Please sit down so we can talk comfortably."

The detective took a long moment while, presumably, he worked things out. He sat on the edge of the cushion nearest the exit, obviously ready to bolt.

"So why isn't Mrs. Ander here? I thought you four were always together," he said after he cleared his throat. She could sense anger warring with relief from him. Probably relief that they hadn't immediately killed him.

Erik actually laughed a little as he realized how well the detective knew them. "She had a business meeting in Boston today and won't be home until late."

"You guys are good at this human stuff, aren't you? Even have business meetings, huh?"

"Most of us live among Humans, as Humans, so I guess we are pretty good at it," Sindri answered him. "How did you find out about us?"

"Before I answer any questions, I'd like us to make some kind of a deal," he answered. They could still feel his fear and his determination to sound assured and in control.

"What do you have in mind?" Sindri asked, willing to let him lead this discussion.

"You need to know that I will never tell anyone about you or the Dabih. I only came here because I need help, and you're the only ones who can help me. I also know you're really powerful and could kill me very easily. Probably as easy as he knocked me out." He tilted his head toward Erik and everyone felt the flare of his anger. He clinched and unclenched his hands and continued, "So, if I swear I'll never tell, will you swear not to kill me or send me to your space ship or anything?"

"Detective," Balere answered quietly, "you need to know some things about us. We've been on this planet for thousands of years. Long before your recorded history. Our ship was destroyed when it crashed on Earth, and we would not have survived if it wasn't for your planet and your people. We have never killed a Human and never will. So, yes, we will make that deal gladly."

The detective snorted. "And your recorded history is detailed enough that you know you've never killed a human?"

"No, we're not depending on history. We know because we were there."

"You're telling me that all you guys are thousands of years old?" He shook his head.

"Not all of us," Balere smiled. "Sindri and I are two of eight Original Mirans that survived, so we are many thousands of years old. Everyone else here is much younger."

The detective eyed Sindri for a long moment, his face blank but his feelings whirling. They went past so quickly, Lexi couldn't sort out what he really felt.

"Why are you telling me all this?" he asked.

"So you'll understand who we are. You don't need to make a deal with us to make sure we don't harm you. And we know you won't tell anyone, otherwise you wouldn't have come to us alone. Beside, how many people would believe you?" Balere's smile radiated sincerity.

Finally, the detective gave a brief smile in return. "They'd have me committed."

"So, tell us. How did you find out?"

CHAPTER 10

Detective Peterson stretched out his long legs, ran his fingers through his dark hair and told them how it all started with a desire to get some answers about Gretchen's death and everything he'd done. He ended his story by reaching under the couch and pulling out a small metallic disk, a microphone. He said there was another in the kitchen. Through all these revelations, he spoke apologetically, letting them know that he'd done some things that he wasn't very proud of.

They were astounded. The detective had bugged Lexi's apartment, which made her angry and embarrassed. Adam, sharing her outrage via their bonded space, moved his chair forward as if to place himself between her and the detective.

He ended his story with the girl that escaped and the other fifteen girls that she had to leave behind. She sensed his disgust with the Dabih that had taken them.

"You are a very resourceful man and obviously an extremely good detective," Sindri told him with a sense of wonder in her voice. "But I'm still confused about one thing. How do you know that it was the Dabih that abducted these women?"

"That buzzing feeling. I felt it in the abandoned house just like on the library steps. It was more subtle at the house, so I figured that was because they'd already left."

Shock swirled around the group. He could sense the Dabih, even after they'd left an area. Only the Originals could sense where they'd been.

"What does the buzzing feel like?" she asked.

"Don't you guys feel it?" His forehead wrinkled in confusion.

"Yes, we do, but Human's don't. You have a very rare talent, Detective, so please describe it to us."

"Well, I feel kind of dizzy at first, then this buzzing starts in my brain and spreads through my body. It makes my muscles tense, especially at the library when I was close to him. After that, I was tired and felt like I'd had a hard workout. At the house, it was the same, only milder."

"Amazing," Sindri said and Lexi could tell she was thinking very carefully. "You know, Humans have more mental ability than they give themselves credit for, but I've never known one who could sense the Dabih. You don't sense us?"

"No," he shook his head. "I don't feel anything around you guys."

"Ted, can I call you Ted?"

He nodded.

"We want to help you find the abducted women, but there is a problem. We don't know where the Dabih are or where they might have taken the women. They have hidden from us for centuries. Does anyone here have an idea how we should begin a search for them?"

"Terazed," Lexi offered. "We could go back to San Francisco and try to get some information from him. If he's still there."

"Terazed?" Ted asked with surprise. "The arrogant ass from the library? He's still around?"

"It's doubtful he's still here." Lexi smiled at Ted's perfect description. "He kind of works, for lack of a better word, in San Francisco. He teleported here to talk to me."

"Teleported," he said, obviously thinking carefully. "Like you guys. They could have taken those girls anywhere, couldn't they?"

"Yes," Sindri answered, "and that's the problem. I think San Francisco is our best option though. Who wants to accompany Lexi?"

Adam, Erik and Balere immediately spoke up. Lexi don't think any of them could have been forced to stay behind, and Sindri knew that. Lexi appreciated that she took it for granted that she would head for San Francisco.

"When could you go?" Ted hesitated.

"It's about 5:00 p.m. on the west coast. This would be an excellent time."

Ted was amazed. "You mean right now?"

"As soon as I ask one more question," Sindri said with a faint smile on her lips. "Would you be willing to go also?"

"Me?" Sindri felt his determination to go mixed with distrust that they'd somehow do something to him.

"Yes, but I'm not sure what help you'd be. You'd certainly be able to identify the kidnapped women. Perhaps you could run a couple of experiments for us.

"First, I'd like the chance to test your sensing powers. Don't worry, Ted, we can protect you," Sindri said in response to the look of wariness on his face. "We can kill with a thought, and we have killed Dabih. But I'd also like to give you a weapon to test for us."

"A weapon? I have a gun and a Taser."

"This would be more like a Taser, but designed to block Dabih powers. Didn't you hear the conversation we had about it in this room after Lexi and Adam talked to Terazed?"

"No. I got something recorded that night, but erased it without listening. I erased everything I had."

"Thank you for that. It's good to know that none of our conversations are floating around cyberspace," Sindri said and smiled. "The weapon we've recently developed should block Dabih powers. It doesn't stun, though, because it was designed to be used by us. The Dabih would still be conscious and possibly still physically dangerous. Would you be willing to test it for us?"

Ted hesitated for a moment, looking around at all of them and obviously thinking. "Sindri, you've got me curious, and for some reason, I'm willing trust you. I don't know. I mean, you could be using some kind of mind control on me, but for some reason I don't think so. Yeah, I'll go."

"Will we go directly from here?" Erik asked. "I should leave a message for Aricia."

"Yes, but with four of you going, and one a Human, we'll need extra help from New Mira. I'll go back and arrange things. Expect a call that we're ready in about ten minutes."

"We'll be waiting," Balere said.

"It was very nice to meet you, Ted." Sindri smiled. "We'll talk again." She teleported to New Mira. His eyes were a mile wide as she disappeared.

Erik went into the kitchen to call Aricia and talk privately. Lexi was sure he was telling her what he could, but being in a hurry and on a cell phone, he'd be careful not to say anything too incriminating.

"Wow, she doesn't mess around, does she?" Ted commented once Sindri was gone. "What is she, your queen or something?"

Through all the revelations, Lexi could easily sense that Ted seemed to be most impressed with Sindri. She didn't blame him.

Sindri was way impressive. The surprise, though, was that Sindri had seemed to be impressed by Ted. She thought she'd sensed Sindri's attraction to him as she said goodbye, but maybe she'd misread her.

"She's our leader," Balere answered.

"You have elections, or take turns, or what?" He seemed more at ease.

"She's the leader because those are her natural skills and has been leader since we arrived. I also have a leadership role, but my skills are more tactical, where hers are managerial and motivational."

"So, you're her general."

Balere nodded. "In Human terms, I guess so."

"Well then, General ..." Ted started to ask.

"I'd rather you called me Balere. We have no titles."

"Okay, Balere," he continued, sounding businesslike, "If the women aren't in San Francisco, where do we look next?"

"If they're not there, that's the information we need to get from Terazed. If he's there. We've only known of two Dabih settlements, and the other was destroyed in an earthquake."

"In Oregon?" He looked like he finally found an answer he'd been looking for.

"How did you know about Oregon?" Adam asked.

"Gretchen's credit card records showed a bus ticket from there."

"It was the earthquake that gave her the opportunity to escape," Lexi told him. "She was so brave and really resourceful." She knew everyone could hear the sadness in her voice.

"The ones that escape always are," he said with unexpected compassion.

"Balere," Adam said, "how are we going to teleport Ted when he can't sense us?"

Ted looked at Balere as well.

"He'll have to hold on to one of us. I suggest Lexi because she has the smallest mass, and the two of them together would be more easily handled. We'll all have to keep our awareness of him, though."

"When Adam was blocked, you couldn't teleport him. How is this different?" Lexi asked.

"Because Adam chose to be blocked. We couldn't sense him and didn't know for sure where he was. We can sense Ted, so I think this will work without a problem. But if you end up staying here, Ted, just have a seat and wait for us."

Ted grunted.

She could tell, in the few minutes they had to wait, that Ted had some doubts. He wandered the room, looking at the photographs she had of her parents and of her and Adam.

"I won't get stuck somewhere in between will I?" he asked, sitting down and then standing again.

"You'll be safe," Adam said and winked at Lexi, "as long as you watch your hands while you're holding on to Lexi."

His short laugh contained some other feeling, maybe sorrow. "I'm well aware of how you feel about each other. Remember, I've had the place bugged."

"Ah, man," Adam said and she blushed.

"Speaking of…" Ted went to the kitchen and pulled out another microphone. Adam made a face at Lexi which seemed to be some kind of question. She shook her head, still having a difficult time believing all Ted had been able to uncover about them.

Balere got a call from Sindri that New Mira was ready. They formed a circle.

"Ted, Lexi, you'll need to hug tightly to try to create one mass as much as possible," Balere said.

Adam looked at Ted with a slightly threatening expression, but she thought he was mainly teasing. She'd never seen Adam jealous and knew he had no reason to be, so she guessed it was just a guy thing.

Ted held both his hands in the air and said, "I'll only be touching her back." He smiled and winked at her. Adam didn't like that much, but let it go. They put their arms around each other and hugged tightly. She wanted to pretend it was Adam, but had to stay aware of Ted so he'd teleport with her. Adam commented, in their bonded space, that he wondered how Erik would feel if Aricia were here plastered against this Human stranger.

As the Mirans sensed each other and reached out to New Mira for assistance in teleporting, Ted's emotions mixed with theirs. It jarred her and made him slippery. When they winked out, she wasn't sure if she had him or not.

CHAPTER 11

Ted stumbled as they materialized. His legs shaky, Lexi caught him as he headed for the pavement. She straightened him up and he held on to her until he recovered his balance. Teleportation wasn't going to be one of his favorite things. Adam cleared his throat and looked pointedly at Ted's arm around Lexi's shoulder.

"Thanks," he said, stepping away. "You're stronger than you look."

"We all are," Adam said through clinched teeth. Ted held up his hands again and took a step further from her. Balere must have communicated a silent disaproval to Adam because he straightened his shoulders and mumbled, "Sorry, man."

Ted let it go and looked around. It had been full night in Pinehurst, but here, it was twilight. They stood on an empty street, next to a high fence with barbed wire wrapped around the top. "Where are we?"

"San Francisco," Erik said.

"Just that fast."

"We teleported," Erik answered as if it were an everyday occurrence.

He made a face at the Englishman, who let out a bark of laughter.

Seconds later, Sindri materialized and he forgot his annoyance.

"I brought your weapon," she said, handing him an oblong object, their fingers brushing briefly. "Are you sensing any Dabih in the area?"

"Do you?" he asked.

"This is a test of your powers, not mine." Sindri grinned.

"I've got a little buzz going," he teased as he smiled back at her.

"Then I should tell you how to use this," she said with a wink. "You simply point and push the button labeled 'block'. A Dabih should be powerless until you push the 'release' button. The wheel allows you to widen or decrease the range for one Dabih or many. Any questions?"

He examined the device. It reminded him of an old game controller or a strange computer mouse. "If I've got the range too wide, could it affect one of you guys?" he asked seriously.

"No, it's been designed specifically for Dabih brain waves."

"Then, I'm good," he answered with confidence.

She turned to the others. "I talked to the other Originals, and it was decided that I should return to New Mira to help teleport you, and hopefully those who were abducted. If you find them, you'll have to each take one in your arms as Lexi did with Ted, and we'll teleport you to Pinehurst. We'll keep teleporting until they're all returned. If the Dabih don't have them stunned, you'll need to stun them for the trip."

"Cover your tracks, right? Can't let anyone know."

She didn't seem to like that, but he couldn't help that being knocked out on a whim irritated him.

"What if they're not there?" Ted asked.

"One problem at a time," Sindri answered.

"So let's say we find them and you transport them to Pinehurst—then what? Leave them on the side of the road?"

"Do you have an idea, Human?" Balere asked.

He shrugged. "At least arrange for some transportation."

Sindri looked at Balere and nodded after a moment. He almost wished he could hear what they were thinking.

"We will have vans waiting to transport them," Sindri said.

"Just like that?"

She arched an eyebrow at him. He chuckled.

"What is it?" she asked, a small wrinkle appearing between her eyes.

"I'm just impressed."

She shook her head and teleported away. Balere took over immediately.

"I'm not sensing the Human women, but they'd be far below ground and there're many other Humans around us. And I'm only sensing one Dabih in the area of the lab where Lexi was held. Hopefully it's Terazed."

"So, he probably senses us, too?"

"No, the Dabih can't sense us until we're within a couple feet. So we can teleport in and essentially sneak up on him."

"I'm thinking I'm going to be doing the sneaking to try out Sindri's ray gun, right?"

"I don't know," Balere said, his eyes narrowing. "It could be very dangerous. If the power block doesn't work, he could kill you with his thoughts in a split second."

"I'll back him up," offered Adam. "I'll stay out in the hall connected to Terazed. If his powers don't get blocked, I'll stun him. He'll never expect it."

Balere nodded. "The rest of us will look for the women. Lexi, take Ted and we'll go."

Everyone moved into a circle and he hugged Lexi again. She squirmed and whispered in his ear, "Not so tight. It'll be over in a second." He tried to loosen up.

They materialized in a hallway with industrial lighting that smelled moldy. He grunted in pain. This time he wasn't as dizzy, but his body felt like he'd grabbed a high voltage wire.

"You okay?" Lexi asked.

"The buzzing. It'll be okay."

The group split up. He and Adam walked slowly down the hall to the left toward, what he'd been told, was the Dabih lab. The rest of them went to the right to start searching for the missing women.

The buzzing spread throughout Ted's body as they moved closer to the lab. Adam signaled that there was only one Dabih present by holding up one finger. The door was open, so he held back while Ted boldly took several steps into the room.

Terazed was bent over some equipment with his back to the doorway.

"Hey, Dabih." He used his best cop voice.

Terazed turned abruptly. Ted pointed his new weapon and closed the connection. The Dabih couldn't hide his shock.

"What did you do, Human?" He practically snarled.

Before Ted could react in any way, Terazed shot toward him and hit him square in the chest, knocking him to the floor. The Dabih's speed was amazing. Ted's head hit the concrete as the buzzing changed to real pain.

Terazed had his hands around Ted's neck before he could even defend himself. He fought back with both fists repeatedly striking the Dabih on each side of his head, but it didn't seem to faze him. He brought his legs up around the Dabih's waist to get some leverage and twist him off, but that didn't work either. Ted started to see stars.

Suddenly, Terazed was pulled off him. Adam held him by the scruff of his neck and stood him on the floor.

"This is for Lexi," he growled as he pulled his arm back and struck Terazed squarely and powerfully in the jaw.

Terazed sprawled to the floor unconscious, and Adam offered Ted a hand up.

"Thanks, man," he said as he rubbed the back of his head. "I usually hold my own pretty well, but that guy…"

"Not against a Dabih. They're too strong." He stared down at Terazed.

"You didn't seem to have any trouble with him."

"No, I didn't." He raised his eyebrows as if he was asking "Imagine what I could do to you?" Then he grinned before saying, "Let's get him on a table and tie him down before he comes to."

"I'd rather leave him on the floor and cuff him."

"Works for me."

They sat him against a wall and Ted cuffed his wrists behind his back while Adam bound his ankles with a leather strap from one of the tables. They pulled up a couple of chairs and sat down to wait for the Dabih to come around.

"You should have seen the look on his face when I hit him with that power block. I've never seen anyone so shocked. It must have stripped him of everything he had."

"I would've liked seeing that," Adam answered with a look of satisfaction. "He's still got some power left, though. He's holding his Human form. But that's really basic stuff, almost an instinct for us. It must be the same for them."

"Did you think he'd change into something else when I zapped him?" He picked up the Miran weapon from the floor where he'd dropped it when Terazed attacked.

"I had no idea," he answered shaking his head. "He used their power block device on Lexi, and she didn't change. Sindri said ours would be better, but, still, we can easily hold our Human disguise even when we sleep. I do wonder what they look like though."

"You don't know what a Dabih looks like?"

"Nope. Back when they first came to Earth, New Mira sent a group to their settlement to open some communication. We were in our natural form, but they looked Human even then."

"I'm guessing that didn't go well."

"They killed all the Mirans except one and sent him back with a message that we'd be killed on sight." Adam gave him a grim look. "That's when the war started."

"All that time, and this is the closest you've ever gotten, isn't it? That's amazing."

"It all started with Gretchen. No one else had ever escaped, so that got a couple Dabih mad and careless. They'd always hidden from us before."

"Hey. You don't have to tell me, but what did he do to Lexi?"

"Kidnapped her and backhanded her when she wouldn't tell him anything." Adam glared down at Terazed. "Split the side of her face open and cracked her cheek bone. The device he used on her had a setting to inflict pain, but they did much worse to Gretchen and other women."

"And you only hit him once?"

Balere appeared at the door. Adam stood up, and after a moment, so did Ted.

"Our new weapon seemed to have worked rather nicely," he said. "But did it also stun him?"

"No, he jumped Ted, and I had to hit him. He should come around soon." Adam answered.

The corners of Balere's mouth moved slightly, but his eyes glittered. "Interesting that you chose to hit him instead of stunning him."

Adam shrugged and looked smug.

"We have not yet found the women, but we did find another corridor. Can you come, Adam?"

"You got this?" he asked.

Ted nodded. Adam and Balere vanished a moment later. He shook his head. Instant travel—what a luxury. He imagined where he could go and what he could do, and being a cop, imagined the wrong that someone could do. He hoped the Mirans had as strong an ethical code as they seemed to have.

After a few minutes of waiting, Ted heard a dull moan signaling that the Dabih was waking up.

"About time, Dabih," he spoke coldly. "Can't take a punch very well, can you?"

Terazed glared. "How did you do this?"

"I got my hands on this little device right here that blocks all your powers," he stated as he pointed the weapon at Terazed. "As you can tell, it did a great job."

"Your restraints won't hold me," he sneered. "I'll get free and tear you apart."

"That's what this is for," Ted smiled as he pulled out his gun. "This is my weapon of choice, and it can blow your brains into the wall if you make one move toward me."

"What do you want?" Terazed's glare was cold and angry.

"I want you to understand something. You're dealing with a human cop this time, and we're not nearly as nice and forgiving as the Mirans. You've hidden from us long enough. I know about your plans for the human race, and things aren't going to be so easy. You're dealing with me, now, and I'm not afraid of you."

"The Mirans had to ask for Human help?" He had an evil chuckle.

"Are all Dabih as stupid as you? The Mirans don't need any help. They could blast every Dabih off this planet before you could blink. But for some reason, they're not comfortable with that, because they're all about living in peace and being nice to everyone.

"If it was up to me, I'd have taken you out centuries ago for what you've been doing to humans. I asked them for help because there was no way in hell I was going to let you get away with kidnapping and murder."

"They were weak enough to reveal themselves to you, then."

"Wrong again. This is all your doing. I investigated Gretchen Wagner's murder and it led me to you. You see, human cops don't like finding young, innocent girls dead on the street."

The Dabih seemed unimpressed. Balere and Adam walked in. Balere put a hand on Ted's shoulder and pulled him outside while Adam stood over Terazed with his fists clinched.

"What's up?" Ted asked.

Balere looked serious, his blue eyes flashing. "We think we found the women but are unable to get to them. We need information."

He glanced back in the room. Police interrogation techniques he knew, but he had no idea what the Mirans might do. The word *probe* came to mind.

"What are you going to do?"

"The Dabih do not respond to threats like normal people."

"Humans, you mean?"

"And Mirans. Their records indicate that they are a violent race, so violence may mean nothing."

"So are you going to threaten him with a good time, then?"

Balere seemed amused. "No, I think not. I will let you talk to him since you seem so sure of your prowess in this area."

Ted shrugged, willing to try.

Balere had been right. The normal 'make the suspect uncomfortable' routine didn't work. He couldn't tell when he lied or told the truth because he had no baseline. The Mirans, evidently, didn't have one either. They discussed the situation again in the hall.

Adam suggested putting him on the table, strapping him down, maybe trying pain. Balere contacted their headquarters for more information. Ted tried being nice to the Dabih and was ignored for his pains.

Terazed merely sneered when Adam stood him up and shook him like a dog shaking a toy.

"We will win this war," he said, and Ted could hear the hate in his voice.

"Your time is about up, Dabih. Where are the women?"

No answer, just a baleful stare.

"Forget him," Ted said, disgusted. "We'll find the women some other way." Adam dropped him and they walked out.

"Wait," Terazed called out with a little panic in his voice. "Are you going to leave me here without my power?"

Ah-ha. He turned back, not bothering to hide the grin on his face.

* * *

As they moved down the hall, Adam could sense the presence of many Humans. They were all stunned, which made their emotional signals weaker. It's no wonder they hadn't sensed them before. They came to a dead end facing a blank wall, but knew the women were on the other side. The Dabih had put them in an enclosed area where there was absolutely no chance of them walking out.

The group paused and Ted put his hand on the wall. "Are you sure they are there?"

Balere flickered out and back in a moment later.

"Are they okay?"

"Yes, they seem fine," Balere smiled. "They're all stunned, but we can bring them out of it when we get to Pinehurst. There's no doorway to the room, so you'll need to teleport with me."

"Ready or not…" Ted answered and held out his arms.

Adam couldn't resist smiling as Ted and Balere wrapped their arms around each other and teleported away. He was starting to like Ted, but why did he get so jealous of him with Lexi? Maybe because he was the first guy she'd really talked to since they'd been together.

He trusted Lexi. He really did, but Ted was a good looking guy. He knew his flirting was nothing serious, but he just didn't like seeing it. Maybe it was some heightened sense of protectiveness that came with bonding.

Adam and Erik reached out to New Mira to teleport through the thick walls that separated them from the women, and appeared in a large, dimly lit room filled with the same exam-type tables that she'd seen before in Oregon. A young woman was restrained with leather straps on each table. There were twenty-two in all, and they were unconscious. The room radiated despair.

"This is disgusting," Ted said quietly.

CHAPTER 12

The sight of those girls helplessly stretched out on those tables turned Ted's stomach. The Dabih could have groups lying stunned in other rooms right now, and there was nothing he could do about it. For all he knew, their operation might be big enough that they'd hardly notice these girls had been rescued. They'd just take other girls from a different area. Maybe he could watch missing person reports, but he didn't have access to the whole country, let alone the rest of the world.

"Are there others?" he asked Balere, letting his sense of despair show in his voice.

Balere shook his head. "We have no way of knowing. We patrol and hope."

Everyone seemed to share his gloomy thoughts about that.

Balere contacted Sindri, who appeared and called in reinforcements living nearby to help teleport the girls to Pinehurst. Balere went off to search for more data on the Dabih.

"Once all the women are out, they'll be driven around in vans. How should we proceed to avoid too many questions from Humans?" Sindri asked.

"I've been thinking about that, and I think it's best if we don't try to provide too much information. We should park them at the side of a road heading toward Boston. You should remove license plates, but the vans can still be identified by the VIN numbers. The best thing would be to change the DMV records. Can you guys do that?"

"Should be able to," she said.

He shook his head, amazed at what the Mirans could do. "We could then place an anonymous call reporting abandoned vehicles. A patrol cop will check it out, and they'll be found. Can one of you hide close and wake them up as the cops approach?"

"Yes, that will work. And it will be over, and they can go back to their families," Sindri sighed with relief.

He nodded. "Then I'll spend forever on a pretend investigation, but it'll be worth it. I can't begin to thank you guys for all this."

"We thank you, Ted," Sindri said sincerely. "This is a change in tactics that we wouldn't have known about if it wasn't for you."

"What were the Dabih going to do with them?"

"They aren't able to breed on Earth. From what Gretchen told Lexi, they're conducting experiments of some kind," she said, frowning.

He bunched his fists. "I really want to strangle that monster."

"I understand and I admire that you haven't." Her hand on his shoulder felt warm and reassuring.

Using descriptions of the girls and their clothing, Ted identified all the girls that had been reported missing, plus found three others that hadn't been reported. They either hadn't been missed yet, or were alone like Gretchen Wagner had been.

The girls were teleported out in a quick and efficient way. Balere returned and reported that he'd gathered some more data from a computer.

"What did you do with Terazed?"

"He seemed to fear being left helpless. So I left him," Balere shrugged.

A short while later, they stood in Lexi's apartment. Tired but pleased, and somewhat in shock from his experience, Ted started to say good night when his phone rang.

He looked at the caller ID. "It's the lieutenant."

"Surprise," he said with a smile as he ended the call and turned to them. "They found the missing girls."

"You're going into work?" Lexi asked.

He shrugged, "We'll be at it most of the night. So, thanks, again."

"Ted," Adam stopped him, "We're all impressed that you came to us tonight, and I'd like us to stay in touch."

He thought about that for a moment. The negative part of him said, 'they just want to keep tabs,' but his unexpected elation cancelled that thought. "Staying in touch is probably a good idea."

"Erik and Aricia are coming over to watch the basketball game tomorrow. You want to come, too?"

"Sounds good. I should be able to give you an update on those girls."

"And Lexi works tomorrow night, so she won't be here for you to flirt with," Adam grinned.

He snorted and let out an exaggerated sigh. Lexi raised her eyebrow at him.

"Yeah. I'll be here." He let himself out.

CHAPTER 13

Ted sat in his office the next afternoon feeling exhausted, but extremely satisfied. He and the other detectives had spent the rest of the previous night and all day questioning each of the twenty-two girls. None of them were injured and each had the same basic story. Two men had appeared out of nowhere, they lost consciousness, and they woke up in a van along the highway.

Doctors couldn't find any physical evidence of what someone could have used to cause them to pass out, so that would just have to remain a mystery. The Stone House case still had priority since none of the girls could identify their kidnapper, but he knew his fellow detectives would never really give up. This case would be in the back of their minds for the rest of their careers. It would live in his mind, also, but for very different reasons.

Aliens. Good aliens, bad aliens. He had moments of doubt about the whole affair. What they could do—teleportation, accessing any computer system, and stunning or killing with a thought—it seemed amazing that they weren't the rulers of the world already. Maybe they were and his fellow humans just hadn't realized it yet. That line of thought would nab him a headache.

He focused on the task at hand. He still had to get the bugs—which he thankfully found in his pocket that morning—into the suspect's car. But once that was done, he could go home. With the overnight hours he'd put in lately, his lieutenant had taken pity on him.

He had just returned from that errand, which turned out easier than he thought because the guy had dropped his car off at the Wash-o-Rama and gone to get a latte from Sean's Coffee Shop, when the officer from the front desk called. A woman wanted to see him. He mentally moaned. Those requests always happened at the end of the day when he wanted to be somewhere else.

"Any idea what she wants?"

"She won't say, but says to tell you it's Cindy. What? No, it's Sindri," the officer answered.

"Really? Send her back."

He went to meet her and watched her come down the hall. Her light brown hair fell softly around her face and her green eyes sparkled. She moved with an unconscious grace that reminded him of a dancer. As she saw him, her smile lit up her face. Dressed in cream-colored slacks, a brown and cream patterned top and a deep burnt-orange, lightweight jacket she just screamed class. She was way out of his league.

Out of his league even if she'd been human. He put that thought out of his mind.

"Hi, Ted," she said warmly and reached out to shake his hand.

"It's great to see you, Sindri," he answered as he took her hand and led her into his office, closing the door behind them and offering her a seat, "but I'm surprised."

"Really? I said I'd see you in Pinehurst."

"Yeah, but I guess I didn't think I'd see you strolling through the station."

She laughed gently, "I enjoy strolling among Humans once in a while. After all, I did live as a Human for quite some time."

"Really? When was that?'

"A very long time ago," she said obviously thinking of that time, "but that's another story for another time. I've brought you something."

"That reminds me," Ted interrupted, "I've got your, uh, device. I was going to leave it with Adam tonight, but since you're here ..."

"Oh, I intended for you to keep it. Hopefully, you'll never have an occasion to use it, but I'd like you to have it just in case."

"Okay."

"Good. That brings me to why I'm here. If you should detect any Dabih, I'd like you to be able to contact me. Here's my cell number and my email address." She handed him an embossed business card with only that information on it—no last name no actual business.

He barely knew what to say. "I figured I'd just call one of the four musketeers."

She laughed again. "I enjoy your perception of things. It's unexpected but always extremely accurate."

"Sometimes I say things without thinking." He felt his face warming.

"Keep doing that. It shows you have no hidden agenda and that's a very good quality." They looked in each other's eyes for a moment, falling silent. His mind spun slowly, going from 'she's not human' to 'man, she's gorgeous' to 'not human' followed by 'who cares?' and 'kissable.'

She blinked, breaking contact and standing. She seemed slightly embarrassed. "I'd better be going. Remember to call if you sense or suspect anything."

He jumped up. "I will. Hey, you need a ride, or anything?"

"Thank you. But I'll leave from the elevator in that office building across the street. That's how I arrived." Her smile brightened his day.

"Too bad there aren't telephone booths, anymore."

She had a confused look for a moment before she understood and blurted out, "Superman," and laughed loudly. He loved the sound of her laugh.

"Take care," she said still smiling as she left the the office and strolled back down the hallway.

"Wow." He stared down the now empty hall for a long moment after she'd gone.

* * *

Terazed awakened to darkness, stretched out on a cold metal table. He realized immediately that his powers had not returned, he was unable to move, and someone was standing next to the table, watching him.

"Please, General Dirac," he mumbled. "Let me explain."

The figure moved to his line of sight. "You have more to worry about than the traitor Dirac," the man said with toothy grin, the scar on his chin white against his olive skin.

It had been fifty years, but he recognized Nomarr immediately. Nomarr, known for his brutality, was head of the Ruling Council. The Dabih Ruling Council was composed of three members. None of them were elected, but had risen in the ranks through careful plotting and the violent conquest of the previous council. They had each fought and conspired for many centuries to gain their positions of ultimate authority and had each watched their backs carefully for the next one planning to overthrow them.

Decades ago they'd recognized each other as the ones most likely to rise to the Ruling Council and had made the decision to work together. It was widely known that they didn't trust each other. At any time another subordinate could gain enough power to overthrow one of them, and there was no guarantee of protection from the other two.

Nomarr had become the Head of Council because he was the most ruthless. Yara, the lone female to hold a council seat in five hundred years, and Faru never let themselves be fooled by their tenuous cooperation. He was certain that they watched Nomarr as carefully as he watched them. The only thing that kept them together and kept them from actively fighting each other was their common desire to hold the power. All Dabih remembered very well the attempted uprising fifty years ago that had almost cost them all their lives and resulted in schism.

The Ruling Council and the main Dabih group had disregarded Humans for a millennium. Humans were useless to them and were simply tolerated until everything was in place to destroy them. The Mirans were the enemy. They had to be destroyed first, but they couldn't be found. The present Council, like numerous Councils before them, had worked on a way to sense Mirans at a greater distance. Once that was accomplished, they would find the main Miran headquarters and destroy it.

The problem of not being able to breed on Earth was secondary, and they could address that after taking care of the Mirans. If necessary, they could use cloning. Rumor said that cloning was the method Nomarr preferred over other research. He wanted to hold his position long enough to clone himself and probably got a great deal of satisfaction when thinking of the day that he could replace Faru and Yara with clones of himself. Then he could rule forever.

The rebellion of fifty years ago was started by Dirac, who thought that breeding research should be their primary goal. He and his followers, Terazed among them, saw Mirans as an annoyance that could be dealt with when there were enough Dabih on Earth to easily overpower both Mirans and Humans. There was enough bloodshed that when they broke away under Dirac's leadership, the Ruling Council had to let them go.

The Council never believed Dirac would last for fifty years. They stated that he had few followers, antiquated equipment, and second-rate scientists. For centuries, the best Dabih scientists had worked on the problem of breeding and had determined that it would never be possible.

Dirac titled himself General and seemed to be involved in trying to breed with Humans again even though that had been tried centuries ago to no avail. Most of the offspring hadn't survived. Those that did were simply weak Humans with no Dabih characteristics, no Dabih power.

"The Council has tolerated Dirac wasting his time with experiments, but things have changed," Nomarr said with an evil grin. "You are attracting way too much attention from the Mirans. We think, rather I think, this may be the time to finally destroy Dirac and his subordinates once and for all. Which includes you, my friend."

Terazed flexed his wrists, the Human's manacles still binding him. He may not have his powers, but he still had his strength. He tried to pull them apart but Nomarr laid a hand on his arm.

"Don't bother. We've been watching Dirac's activities closely and found a weakness. Do you know what that weakness is?"

He shook his head and tried to figure out a way that he could get Nomarr's neck between his hands.

"You. You seem to have your own agenda. My spies have watched you conduct your own research. When you abducted that Miran girl, I thought about intervening but waited. You have been in contact with the Mirans and perhaps you have information that the Council can use. But first, we need to have a little discussion, Are you planning on over throwing Dirac?"

Nomarr used his mental power to send a wave of pain through Terazed body. He twisted, trying to get away from the pain but could not escape. It was everywhere. He panted his denial.

Nomarr scowled and the pain stopped. Terazed lay like a deflated sail on the table, dreading the next torture.

"When the Council got word that Mirans had invaded one of our settlements and rescued Humans that you were responsible for, I knew our chance had come. Amidst all the confusion, my minions had simply walked in, found you still stunned by the Mirans... how did that happen by the way?"

He shook his head, unable to explain.

Nomarr sighed, "No matter. I'm sure you will tell me in a moment. Dirac will think the Mirans killed you, and the Mirans won't miss you at all."

The pain started again, and it took little time for his Nomarr get all the information he needed. Tarazed gasped and mumbled his way through all that he knew - all about Dirac's plans, the location of his installations, and the failure of his latest research.

The information Nomarr really wanted most, though, was what he knew about the Mirans. It seemed there were quite a few of them in Massachusetts, and he now had the names of two of them, Lexi Collins and Adam McLane. He hated those two

Mirans with a passion for many reasons, but especially because he discovered that they'd collaborated with a Human. Nomarr even stopped torturing Terazed for a moment, appalled when he heard that.

"Obviously the Ruling Council cannot wait much longer. We have to go after the Mirans soon. But it will take careful planning. Thank you, Terazed. You've been most helpful."

Terazed hoped Nomarr would end him swiftly. He didn't.

CHAPTER 14

Ted's bugs in the suspect's car had led them to believe that not only was the Stone House a hub for drug dealing, but it was the outlet of a major smuggling operation. The DEA agent, Harris, had invited the Pinehurst detectives, especially Ted since he was familiar with Boston and the Boston PD, to join in the larger case. He jumped at the chance. The more time that passed since his experiences with Lexi and her friends, the more he felt like a bit of normal detective work would be good for him. Not that he wasn't grateful to the Mirans, but the whole alien thing and their powers disturbed him.

He and Roth and the DEA agent were in two cars tailing the Stone House suspect down near the airport. A shock went through him, like hitting his funny bone, and he dropped his phone. Roth looked over at him, but didn't say anything.

About 20 minutes later, happened again, although he didn't drop his phone, and he started to worry that he was having a heart attack or something. His hands tingled a bit, so he flexed them and tried to concentrate. They rounded a corner and the familiar buzzing feeling took over. A Dabih was nearby. He swore. Even though the signal, if he could call it that, was faint, he was glad he wasn't driving.

"You okay?"

He blamed the chili dogs they'd had for lunch. The buzzing faded, and they lost sight of the suspect shortly after that when he went into a restricted shipyard area in Jeffries Point.

"Let's hold here," Harris advised over the radio. They settled in to a parking space that gave them a good view of the gated area and waited. And waited, which gave him too much time to consider the Dabih. Maybe he'd been imagining it. Or maybe, and this made him much more uncomfortable, there were aliens everywhere—after all, both races looked just like everyone else. They could be anywhere. He glanced at Roth out of the corner of his eye. And smothered his laugh in a cough. Rudawski, he could imagine as a Dabih maybe, but not Roth. Eventually the sun went down. Harris called the surveillance off for the day. "We'll pick this up tomorrow."

Roth elected to stay in Boston, but Ted claimed he needed to get back for a different case—in fact, the kidnapping case. Roth didn't question it. As he drove home from Boston, he debated with himself about how he should handle sensing Dabih. The simplest thing would be to call Adam. He'd know what to do and who to contact. But he couldn't stop thinking about calling Sindri.

After seeing her in his office, he'd longed for the opportunity to see her again. She'd given him her number, so why not just call her directly? Because she was not just a beautiful woman, she was a powerful and ancient alien. Why would she want to see him? Puny, human male with all those male traits that had frustrated, or so he'd been told, his human girlfriends. Would an alien goddess feel any different?

Still, he couldn't have been so wrong about the way she looked at him. The way she'd held his hand just a second or two longer than she needed to.

"What do I have to lose? Just my mind I guess." He called her.

* * *

"Lexi, I had quite a surprise today," Adam said with a grin as soon as she came in the door. He'd cleaned the apartment and, from the smell of it, made dinner.

"Looks like it was a good one," she said and wrapped her arms around his waist. She could never wait to get her arms around him and her lips on his. He assured her that he felt the same.

It had been about three weeks since they'd rescued those girls. As the days had kept getting warmer, she looked forward to the summer. She thought about taking a couple of classes since they were at school, anyway. If they did each take one or two classes, their schedules would still be so much lighter than they had been, but Adam might do more than one class if he wanted to graduate a year early. If Sean hired someone to help out at the coffee shop, they might have even more time.

They'd also talked about planning a wedding. Her parents would be ecstatic, but probably still a little scared that she'd eventually decide to quit school for a family. What they didn't know was that the wedding would really be for them. Their Miran joining was most meaningful, and, because they were Miran, there would never be children.

"Yeah, it was good," he finally answered when they parted. "Professor Carpenter, the head of the astronomy department, asked me to go with him to Woods Hole in a couple of weeks."

"The oceanographic institute? Why?" What did the ocean have to do with the stars?

"NASA's been training astronauts underwater, mostly in Florida, but they're going to use some of the equipment at Woods Hole to do some research on surviving in a hostile environment. Hostile, such as on other planets." His grin was ear-to-ear. He loved the idea of traveling in space.

"Sounds like you'd be involved in survival stuff right at the beginning. That's exciting."

"So, you think I should go?"

"Why wouldn't you?"

"I'd miss classes and have a ton of stuff to catch up. I'd miss work, and I'd seriously miss you."

"I'd miss you, too, but even that far, we'd be connected. How long would you be gone?"

"Six days."

Erik and Aricia would be coming over for dinner and more basketball, college this time, since it was getting close to the final four. They'd asked Ted, but he was busy and said he'd catch them the next time.

After dinner and much discussion about Woods Hole, they settled in front of the TV to watch the game, when they sensed Sindri reaching out to then. They mentally welcomed her and she materialized. Surprisingly, she was holding Ted in a strong embrace.

"Has something happened?" Erik asked with concern.

"We're not sure, but thought you should know what Ted found," Sindri answered with a serious expression.

"I was in Boston today and sensed some Dabih," he told them.

"Did they do anything?" Erik asked.

"I don't know. I was doing surveillance with a partner and couldn't follow the feeling. I felt a strong buzzing and then nothing. I figured they'd teleported, so I called Sindri."

"So, we don't know if they took anyone," Adam said, reflecting everyone's concern.

"No, but I'll check missing person reports again tomorrow. It may be too late, but nothing will be reported until then."

"I wanted to let you know right away," Sindri said, "because we may be seeing another change in their pattern. I'm going to ask all Mirans to start patrolling again." She looked at Erik who nodded.

"We'll start tonight and get another schedule together," Erik said."

"We'll leave you to your game. I'm sorry for the bad news."

"No problem. We'd much rather patrol than take a chance."

"Come here, Ted," Sindri said quietly. They embraced and teleported away.

"Neither of them seemed to mind that hug," Lexi said, winking at Adam. He burst out laughing.

"What are you saying?" Aricia asked with a confused look.

"I was really just teasing, but Adam and I thought Ted was kind of flirting with Sindri when we rescued those girls. But I'm sure it was nothing."

Erik smiled, "I thought Sindri was enjoying it. And maybe flirting back just a little."

"Erik," Aricia exclaimed, glaring at him, "you never told me that."

"There were more important things to tell you." He shrugged. "I'm sorry, but I guess I forgot about it until I saw them again."

"He's Human." She was still surprised.

"Sindri's an Original, so she spent a couple centuries married to many different Humans. She lost her joined mate in the crash, but that doesn't mean she couldn't enjoy spending time with someone."

"Well, that's true," she said and nodded with a thoughtful expression.

"And we're probably all wrong," Adam added, trying to calm her. "They were together because he sensed Dabih. He said he called to report it to her."

"Where did he get her number?" Erik asked winking at Aricia. She made a face at him for picking on her. That caused them all to laugh.

The thought of Sindri being involved with Ted, with anyone, would take some getting used to. She was their leader, their mentor, and in some ways, their mother. But, then again, they may have been reading something into a situation where nothing existed.

* * *

They stood in the shadows by Ted's car, outside of the police station, still in an embrace. She'd seemed genuinely happy to hear from him when he called, but now she seemed distracted. Ted swallowed and stepped away gently—letting her continue the embrace or not. She didn't.

"I'm glad you called," she said. "I have to go arrange the patrols, but I'll be in touch soon." Her smile goodbye warmed him but he felt cold without her in his arms. He wanted to kiss her.

She disappeared.

He sighed. "Yeah, like that'll happen."

CHAPTER 15

Ril was filled with anger and hate as he realized that he would have to report the rescue of the Human females to General Dirac. Terazed was supposed to be guarding them, but was nowhere to be found. He knew what he'd been doing. He stole every minute to work on his useless research instead of following orders, and now, because of Terazed, he would bear the brunt of Dirac's rage.

The subtle sting of Miran brain waves filled the underground installation and irritated him like a putrid smell. They'd been hidden under the abandoned, San Francisco warehouse for decades, but now, thanks to Terazed, they'd been found.

He knew the Mirans were especially active in the holding cell and had to have teleported the females away. But they'd also spent a lot of time in the lab. In Terazed's lab.

He'd suspected for some time that Terazed had been in contact with Mirans. He'd felt their power subtly churning around him twice before, but couldn't prove anything. Had he betrayed the Dabih? He only hoped they had killed him painfully. He didn't need a partner who couldn't follow orders, who always had his own plans, and who may be a traitor.

He looked around the lab carefully, but found nothing out of place until he noticed the computer. Files were left open. Files showing the location of installations and personnel. What had Terazed been doing? Was he making plans to run to another group, or was he showing these to the Mirans? This could be a disaster.

It had been hours since the Mirans had taken the females, so he had to go to Dirac immediately. Delaying would only make his superior's rage worse. Going before Dirac in Chicago was never a pleasant experience.

As he materialized outside headquarters, he sent a mental signal inside and waited to receive another signal that he could enter. When it came, he opened the door and faced his general.

General Dirac was at his desk studying the latest research, and his plans for the new work that would be done with their new Humans. He looked up coldly as Ril approached.

"Why are you here?" he asked.

"I have dire news, General."

Dirac said nothing, but glared. He could sense his anger growing, like a wave about to crash on the shore.

"General, Terazed was guarding the females. When I returned, they were gone. Mirans teleported them out of the installation. Terazed is also missing."

Dirac stood slowly. "Where were you?"

"Checking the other installations to make sure they were ready to receive the females."

"Where is Terazed?"

"I suspect he betrayed us to the Mirans. He might have run from us, or they might have killed him."

"He is your partner. You were both responsible for the females, and I will not tolerate your stupidity and weakness."

He could feel Dirac's power surging and braced himself for the pain that would come, but he didn't dare try to use his own power to defend himself. The blow hit him, and the pain throughout his body was staggering.

He fell as the pain grew, hoping that it would be over soon. But it kept growing until he could barely breathe. He felt his heart pounding in his chest. He screamed and then lay helpless on the floor.

Dirac called for his servant. The last thing Ril heard before he expired was "Contact my advisors and captains. They're to be here in one hour for a change of plans. And toss that out."

* * *

Nomarr, Faru, and Yara formulated a simple plan to start. Watch the two Terazed had identified to wait for the opportunity to take one or both of them and concentrate on watching the east coast around Boston. It made no sense that a primary settlement would be in that small college town. The main group would most likely be in Boston, so that was where they'd watch and find what they could before completing their plans.

Having successfully risen to the Council, and holding their positions for all these decades, the three rulers had learned some very important lessons. The most vital was that they had to know when to act swiftly and when they needed to wait for the perfect time and opportunity. They would have some patience watching the Miran situation, but when the opportunity arose, they would be ready to act swiftly.

They realized that, thanks to Terazed's information about two Mirans, they could finally find the Miran settlement. If they handled things correctly, this could bring an end to the Mirans once and for all.

* * *

Erik got the patrolling schedule together, and they spent five days finding the same thing every night. The Dabih were all over the place. They sensed the Dabih, moved toward them, they teleported away. The good news was that they weren't taking anyone with them. They sensed no Human brain waves anywhere around the Dabih.

Lexi kept track of how long they seemed to be staying in one place and discovered that they teleported in and stayed in that spot for about three to five minutes before leaving again. Not at all their usual hunting technique of wandering the streets or hiding in shadows to snatch a victim. Something else was going on.

They planned a meeting with Sindri and Balere at Lexi's apartment to discuss the new pattern and what it might mean. If it wasn't for Ted being involved, they would have gone to New Mira. None of them were comfortable taking a Human there.

Erik and Aricia arrived right on time with Ted following close behind. Within moments, Sindri and Balere materialized and they were ready to start.

"It's obvious that they're not hunting," Balere started, "so what are they trying to accomplish?"

No one had any ideas.

"Maybe we should ask in a slightly different way," Adam said with a look of serious thought. "What *could* they accomplish by spending just a few minutes in many different locations?"

"Not much," Ted offered, "but they could be looking around, checking the landscape, the general environment of each area …"

"Yes," Lexi said, "that's exactly it. A Human would be looking around. The Dabih are sensing the environment."

"Very good you three," Sindri said. "Sensing is the only thing they could be accomplishing in that short time."

"And they're not looking for Humans," Adam added. "There were Humans all around most of the times we sensed them."

"So," Balere said slowly, "they're looking for us."

"We got reports from Mirans in Boston and all over this part of the east coast of the same Dabih activities," Sindri said. "They've gotten the idea we're close, and they're searching for us."

"And who knows you're in this area?" Ted asked with that slightly raised voice that said he already knew the answer.

"Terazed," Lexi stated.

"Exactly," he smiled at her. "But, you know," he hesitated, looking apologetic. "I have to feel this is pretty much my fault. I dragged you into the situation with those women, and I gave Terazed a heavy speech about not letting him get away with that stuff anymore. I'm really sorry."

"You have nothing to be sorry about," Sindri said with concern. "This was Terazed's doing. You got dragged into the middle of it. The Dabih have been looking for us for a thousand years without finding us and they won't find us now."

"But your headquarters, or whatever you call it, are they getting close? Is it in Boston?"

"Nowhere near Boston. Nowhere near the United States," she answered. "And remember that I told you most Mirans live among Humans. That's all over the world, and there are relatively few in New Mira."

"Good, I don't want to get all of you killed." He addressed that to Sindri. He seemed disturbed about something.

"Don't worry about that," Balere said, gesturing to get the detective's attention. "We really are much stronger than the Dabih. We can kill them from miles away, and they couldn't get anywhere near us without us knowing."

"So, what do we do?" Erik asked.

"The only thing we can do about this situation is watch them," Sindri said, "but we do have an advantage we haven't had before. Remember the files you downloaded from Terazed's computer? One of them contained the location of all Dabih installations. At least all in the United States. We now know where they are."

"How many are there?" Ted asked and everyone felt a spike in his anxiety level.

Sindri put her hand on his shoulder and he calmed down. Balere frowned. "That's the surprise. There are only five. Besides Oregon and San Francisco, there's Chicago, Atlanta, and New York. And it looks like only a few Dabih are assigned to each location, so there must be more around the world. There has to be a major installation somewhere else."

"How are things going on the translation of the files Lexi found?" Erik asked.

"Very slowly," Sindri shook her head. She dropped her hand from Ted's shoulder. "Most of it is full of uprisings and takeovers. It makes me wonder how they've survived this long without killing each other. We decided to skip most of the middle years to concentrate on the more recent ones."

"These guys are sounding like an organized crime syndicate," Ted scowled. "It's amazing how much these aliens are reminding me of humans."

"Then it's a good thing you're working with us," Sindri said. "Balere, I think it's time we let our young ones get some sleep. All of you please keep up the patrols and we'll see what their next move is." They reached out to New Mira and teleported away.

Lexi could tell that Ted still felt bad about something—perhaps getting them involved in the rescue of those girls, but Sindri was right, he'd just gotten stuck in the middle. She grabbed his sleeve to stop him as he walked out. "I know you feel bad about getting us involved, but, the truth is, I feel bad about getting you involved."

"Why? I came to you guys."

"I was the one that Gretchen talked to. Really, it all started with me, and it grew from there. Don't feel guilty because we're all glad you're with us now."

"Thanks."

"Are you going to patrol with us?" Adam asked.

Ted hesitated and then nodded. "If I can. Police stuff, you know." He waved good night and left.

CHAPTER 16

Business was a little off the next night at the coffee shop, so the time hadn't gone very quickly. Finally, though, the clock said 11:35 and Lexi smiled as she sensed Adam coming closer.

"Adam going to walk you home?" Lexi's boss, Betsy asked.

"I imagine he'll show up." With perfect timing, the door opened and in walked Adam and Ted.

A customer followed them in, so Lexi only smiled at them as they sat at the counter and Betsy went over to talk. The attractive lady whose order she was waiting to hear was also looking at them. She didn't blame her one bit for looking at her hot guy, but realized, as Adam went behind the counter to lift something for Betsy, that lady was looking at Ted.

After the customer got her coffee and went to take a seat, Lexi looked at Ted. He was probably about thirty, had short dark hair that wasn't really spiked, or very curly, more just loose and disheveled. He smiled and laughed lightly as he talked to Adam and Betsy, and she realized his was a warm, genuine smile that lit his face and made his blue eyes sparkle. Not like Miran eyes, but they did sparkle.

Dressed tonight in jeans, t-shirt and a light jacket instead of his usual detective sport coat, his body showed that he worked out and was in really good shape. No wonder the lady was looking, and no wonder Sindri had enjoyed the flirting. She guessed she just hadn't looked closely enough to really notice what a good-looking guy Ted was. If Adam wasn't the only one in her heart, Lexi knew she'd have given him a second look. But she also knew that Sindri had given him that second look. Lexi'd seen her gazing at him more than once.

She walked over and smiled across the counter at Adam while Ted was telling Betsy that he'd been a cop in Boston, so he'd had a lot of coffee, but her coffee was the best. Without saying a word, she slipped into that place where she and Adam could feel their love for each other as Betsy walked away to another customer.

"That's amazing," Ted almost whispered as she broke their connection and looked at him. "When you two look at each other like that, it's like you're in some other place. Like no one else exists."

She smiled and raised her eyebrows at him with a 'your point?' kind of look as Adam laughed softly.

"What do you mean?" Ted whispered, "You do go somewhere?"

"In a way," Adam whispered back. "We'll explain when we're out of here."

"There's still a lot I don't know, isn't there?" he asked.

"We'll fill you in."

They all helped Betsy lock up and walked her to her car as she joked about how she would tell Sean she'd had a police escort tonight. They headed out on patrol and explained Miran joining and their 'special place' to Ted.

"Wow," he said, "no doubts, no second guessing. You guys really know."

"Yeah," Adam said as he and Lexi smiled at each other, "and we know it's forever."

"So, like any human couple," Ted added, "you'll settle down after college, have a bunch of little Mirans and live happily ever after."

"No, Mirans can't have children. We've never been able to conceive on Earth." Lexi said.

"Wait a minute, that doesn't add up. There are only eight Originals, but now there're thousands of you, Sindri calls you 'young ones,' I hear you refer to each other as a year old and a few months old, and here you are young adult college students. How's all that add up?"

"Okay," Lexi said as they paused next to some benches. Adam sat down, so Ted did too. "I was born simply human. The Mirans crashed on Earth eons ago. They tried to breed with humans, but created simple human offspring. After centuries of trying, the Mirans gave up and hid from humans. But Miran DNA was still in the human gene pool. Periodically, those genes assert themselves and begin transforming a human into a Miran, like me." She paused to look at Adam. He blew her a kiss.

"The whole thing, while shocking, had ended up being wondrous. Scary, but mostly joyful. Once Mirans discovered what was happening, they watched carefully. Mirans can sense each other, so can easily sense a human child that will transform when they reach early adulthood."

"Crazy."

"The Miran genes stayed recessive, but many humans carry them. In some people, they become dominant and we become Miran. No one knows how it happens, or why. We've tried to discover the cause of transformation in some, but have never found any answers. There is still a lot we just didn't know."

"So you and the Dabih are both sterile and you both turned to humans to solve the problem," he said obviously doubting how much difference he saw between the two of them.

"Yeah, but the Originals had given up having their own children and they only hoped some small part of Mira would survive by mixing with the Human genome. They lived as Humans, married Humans, and became good spouses and parents. They intended to live their lives as Humans."

"I guess that is pretty different from abducting victims for their experiments," he grimaced. He looked at the ground for a moment and then looked up.

"Hey, if I had children, there's a chance they may turn Miran?"

"Not all Humans have Miran DNA," Lexi said. "You might, or might not."

"So, what about your parents? How did they take all this?"

"They don't know. I think about my parents sometimes and would like to tell them what a wonderful life their genes have given me. Sometimes I'm sorry I can't share this with them. But if you ever had Miran children, they could share their lives with you."

Whatever he was about to say was interrupted by the Dabih. She could tell there were two. They were closer this time and had just materialized. Ted seemed to feel it as well, for he jumped up and hurried in their direction. She saw the two of them standing in front of a closed restaurant.

The street was dark and deserted, but they didn't want to get close enough for them to be sensed, so they stopped and watched them, pretending to be talking about the items in a shop window. After only a couple of minutes, the Dabih walked around the corner and they felt them teleport away.

"This is irritating," Ted growled. "I doubt if they're hitting random areas each night, there's got to be a pattern of some kind. After all the centuries, why are they so intent on finding Mirans now? We need more information."

"You're right," Adam said, "but how do we get it?"

"Sindri has all of your patrol reports," Ted looked like he was thinking out loud. "I think I need to see if she'll let me study them and try to get an idea of a pattern or something. Maybe we can get a better sense of what they're after."

"That sounds like a good idea. Do you want us to contact her for you?" Lexi asked.

"No, I'll call her tomorrow. I may not find anything, but it's worth a try."

"Just good detective work, huh?" Adam smiled.

"Let's get home, guys." Lexi yawned. "It's way past my bedtime."

* * *

Ted hadn't been certain if he'd wanted to spend more time with the Mirans, especially looking for the Dabih. When Lexi called to ask if he wanted to join them, he almost didn't go—but the chance of seeing Sindri made him accept. And of course she didn't show up. Not surprising really since she was the Miran leader. She probably had many responsibilities and the group in Pinehurst was just one of many. Did she have a Mr. Sindri? He hoped not.

When they felt the Dabih, he knew joining the patrol had been the right thing, but the buzzing sensation he felt had really started to freak him out. Why did he have the feeling? Why didn't other humans feel it? Did he have Miran blood in his background, and if so, was there a way to tell? Maybe he should get a DNA test or a physical or something.

As he drove through his neighborhood, he checked things out. Everything seemed fine, quiet, just the way he liked it. Hopefully Sindri would get him those patrol reports and he could get a better idea of what the Dabih were up to. And then he'd have a chance to see her again.

After he got settled for the night, he had to laugh. Scared of aliens but crushing on their leader. What a situation.

* * *

About 3:00 a.m., Lexi suddenly woke out of a sound sleep not knowing what had wakened her, but it only took a second to realize that she sensed two Dabih. She looked over at Adam to find his eyes wide open.

"They're really close."

"Probably on the sidewalk out front," Adam answered.

"They're right outside our house, yet still not close enough to sense us. What's the point? They know they can't get close enough to us to know where we are."

"I know," he answered with frustration in his voice, "there's got to be more to this." He stared at me and I could see on his face that he was thinking. "Damn! That's it."

"What?"

"Terazed made a device to block our powers. What if they made something to sense us at a greater distance?"

"Oh, Adam, that would make it all fit. They're looking for us now because they finally have a tool to help them find us." She could feel the dread growing in her heart. This could be a disaster.

"They're gone," he said.

"Yeah, but we need to let Sindri know. Should we go to New Mira?"

"Let's just call her, it'll be faster."

Adam called, told her what had happened, and his idea about them possibly having a device to sense Mirans. Sindri said they were probably right. All their actions were logical if they could sense Mirans from a greater distance. But there were still many questions. How close did the Dabih need to be even with a sensing device? Once they found Mirans, what then? How close did they need to be to stun them, or kill them?

Sindri would talk to the rest of the Originals and get back in touch. They went back to bed and he pulled her into his arms. She rested her head on his chest.

"You getting scared?" he asked gently.

"A little," she answered. "They were right outside. If they can sense us, they could materialize right to us and …"

"Stop thinking that way, babe. We don't know they can sense us. You know, I was probably wrong."

"No, you're probably right. I'm just really glad we're here together."

"Lex, I'm going to cancel the Woods Hole trip," he said with determination.

"You can't do that."

"I'm not leaving you here alone."

"How about if I go to New Mira every night?"

"I don't know. Terazed took you while you were studying. You'll go right after work and not hang around here at all?"

"I'll only be here long enough to teleport privately. I promise."

"I don't know."

"You can't cancel because you're afraid of something we're not even sure is really happening. You'll be safe in Woods Hole and I'll be safe in New Mira. Say you'll go."

"Okay. I'll go, but my heart will be here." He hugged her tighter.

"Well that won't work," she said, her lips almost touching his. "My heart will be in Woods Hole."

CHAPTER 17

General Dirac flew into an unexpected rage at his aid, who ducked the tumbler he'd thrown at his head. It smashed against the wall of his office, splattering liquid and glass everywhere.

"What have I done, General?" his aide asked, cringing.

"Our research is a useless mess." Snatching one woman at a time from college campuses didn't work because Mirans kept catching his hunters. Besides, it was just too slow. The large group they'd taken from shopping malls seemed to go beautifully until, once again, Mirans had rescued them. How had they found those women so quickly?

He thought he'd accomplished something when they changed where they were hunting and abducted fifteen new Human women. Taken from different areas across five different cities, Dirac knew there was no way Mirans would detect them. Once they started their research, though, the results were worthless.

To avoid Mirans, they'd taken the new Human females from the worst streets of the worst neighborhoods in the largest cities. Drug addicts, prostitutes, and homeless wanderers were easy targets and rarely reported missing. He'd been sure this plan would be the answer.

Research on these women, though, had proven to be a waste of time. Their bodies were usually malnourished and unhealthy, some were diseased, and some suffered from mental illness. None of them were good subjects for helping them build a strong Dabih population.

One of the women was taken because his hunters detected that she was pregnant, just what they needed for stem cells. When they took the fetus, though, it had genetic defects. It wouldn't have survived much longer even if they'd left it in its mother's drug-damaged body.

Nothing made him boil with rage faster than having to give up, and he'd had to eventually give up on this new group of women. He'd killed them personally, every one of them, to satisfy his need for some kind of release of this consuming fury. It had barely helped.

Dirac slammed his fist into his desk as he tried to formulate another plan. His aide flinched, dropping the pieces of glass he'd been cleaning up. They had to get healthy genetic material, healthy stem cells, but the damn Mirans seemed to be everywhere and kept interfering with him.

He hadn't battled the Ruling Council and Mira all these years to simply fail. He'd come close to failure and death when he tried to take over the Council, but he'd prevailed. Letting these worthless Humans with their Miran protectors get in his way was not an option. He would come up with a better plan and find a way to produce more Dabih no matter what.

Then the Ruling Council would see that he'd been right all along. Their population would be growing, the most powerful Dabih would back him against Nomarr, and the Dabih would be ready to spread across the Earth and take control. All he needed was a new plan.

* * *

Nomarr, his feet up on his desk, considered the device in his hand. Their new technology had been tested extensively and

106

worked beautifully. They could now sense Mirans up to a mile away. Their powers had always been strong enough to stun or kill from a distance, but they were never able to distinguish Mirans from Humans until very close.

Now that weakness was eliminated. But they had to proceed carefully to use their new power most effectively. Mirans could still sense them at a greater distance than one mile, so they couldn't let them know about the new device too soon. They had to keep Mirans in the dark, make them feel they were still safe, until they were ready to strike.

They had to use the new tool carefully to continue gathering information, but the information they wanted most had to come directly from a Miran. The abduction that Yara so carefully planned would be carried out within two weeks and they'd get what they needed. They'd have a Miran and force him to tell the location of all their settlements, and their main headquarters itself.

It wouldn't be easy or fast because no Miran would give up that information without a fight. But they would have plenty of time and knew how to be patient. Pain, deprivation, and isolation always worked eventually. They'd been waiting for centuries, and they would wait for as long as necessary to break their Miran captive.

Through all the satisfaction of seeing plans working, Nomarr was still irritated, though, that their best move had been Yara's idea. When she proposed using a Human spy, he had accepted the idea assuming it wouldn't work and he'd finally have his chance to dispose of her. He knew she was plotting against him to take over as head of the Council and reasoned this insane idea would be the end of her.

But Yara put together a deceptively simple plan. She found the perfect Human subject, someone with just enough arrogance to believe he'd be the savior of his world. She had him stunned, tortured, and questioned about Human activity. Then she "rescued" him and told the stupid man that it was the Mirans that had done those horrible things to him. She'd convinced the Human that the Mirans were the ones who threatened his kind, told him lies about their intentions and purposes, and got him to work for the Dabih. Finally, Yara encouraged him to contact the only two Mirans the Council knew and convinced him these two were the most dangerous.

He knew he'd have to handle Yara very carefully from now on because she was a woman to be reckoned with. And Faru was no fool, he'd align himself to her and they'd work together to change leadership. He wouldn't let that happen. So he hatched a backup plan and set it in motion. If Yara's plan for capturing a Miran worked and the Miran captive talked, he'd get rid of Faru and Yara. If her plan didn't work, he'd still get rid of them.

He tapped his long finger against the scar on his chin. He would bring two of his subordinates onto Council and rule undisputed for years to come. Maybe even permanently.

CHAPTER 18

Adam was looking forward to a great time at Woods Hole. The only thing that would have made it better would be if Lexi'd been with him. He missed her so much and couldn't resist touching her mentally whenever possible. On the drive, Professor Carpenter had been talking about nothing important to make the time pass. Adam wished he would just be quiet so he could concentrate on Lexi.

But he also felt selfish because he knew wishing for quiet wasn't fair. Carpenter didn't have a joined mate he could concentrate on. In fact, he didn't even know if he had a wife and family. He realized he knew very little about Carpenter. He'd only been the department head since the beginning of the semester, but was supposed to be a highly published and highly regarded researcher that Pinehurst had snatched from Boston College.

When the position was announced, even Erik had mentioned that Pinehurst was really lucky to have gotten him because he would put the astronomy department on the map. He wondered what Pinehurst offered him that Boston College hadn't.

"Professor, do you mind my asking what made you want to come to Pinehurst?"

"Not at all. I just thought I'd enjoy the college town atmosphere more than Boston. It's so big and impersonal. I wanted a place small enough to get to know the students in the department and to get to know the town."

"You were looking for a smaller place, and I can't wait to get back to the big city. I was raised in New York and sometimes miss the craziness."

The professor straightened his glasses. "You gave the school Lexi Collins' name as a contact in case of emergency. What about your parents?"

"My parents died when I was little. I was in foster homes growing up, so Lexi's the person I'm closest to."

"I'm sorry, I didn't know that. You two are close, then."

"Yeah. In fact, we're engaged and we might get married this summer."

"You're pretty young for that kind of commitment, aren't you?"

"We know it's right, so there's no reason to wait."

"Did she lose her parents, also?"

"No, her parents are fine. We visited them several weeks ago. They're lawyers and live out in the middle of nowhere, but Lexi's really close to them."

"Oh, I thought maybe you were both alone."

"No, we've both got close friends and extended family we're close to."

"Like Professor Ander?"

"Yeah, Erik and I knew each other before he came to Pinehurst."

"Really? Where did you meet him?"

"It's a long story. He kind of mentored me."

"I heard he was from England, but didn't know he'd lived in New York. Is that where you met him?"

Adam felt the tone of this conversation subtly changing from where it started. Carpenter was asking questions like he was really trying to get some information, not like small talk that would pass some time on a long trip. He also sensed a deception in Carpenter. Nothing he could really put his finger on, but Carpenter was hiding something.

"Yeah, but again, it's a long story. Do you have any family?" he said to change the subject and get the conversation away from where it was going.

"No, no family. We have time for a long story though. How did you meet Ander?"

"Honestly, Professor, I'd rather not talk about it," he said letting a little irritation show in his voice. "I was going through some stuff when I was younger, and Erik helped me. That's all there is to it."

"That's fine," he said obviously trying to keep his voice light, "I just thought maybe you belonged to the same group or organization, or something."

"You mind if I take a nap while you drive?" he asked so he could end the conversation. "I've been working late and can hardly keep my eyes open."

"Sure, no problem," Carpenter answered coldly.

The deception he sensed from Carpenter was getting stronger. Now that he had refused to answer his questions about Erik, there was also a growing anger. Why would he be angry, and what was he hiding? He had the feeling there was some underlying motivation for all those questions. But what?

Could it be some professional curiosity or jealously between two professors? College professors were always in a subtle competition, so that might make sense if they were in the same department, but they really had nothing to do with each other. Erik couldn't be any kind of professional threat to him.

He kept sensing him while pretending to sleep, and Carpenter's emotions changed. There was now a sense of accomplishment, a job-well-done kind of feeling, a satisfaction. And through that satisfaction, he felt something he least expected. Hatred. A loathing, almost disgust that was directed at him.

Professor Carpenter hated him. What on earth could have caused Carpenter to hate him? Back at Pinehurst, he had sensed just the opposite. Carpenter seemed to have admired his academic work and liked him as a student. What changed?

He thought back through their conversation. Carpenter might have gotten irritated at him for refusing to answer questions about Erik, but the man's emotions were far beyond that. As he thought, he could feel Carpenter's emotions getting more intense.

Carpenter was feeling a need for vengeance. And feeling a kind of satisfaction that he would get revenge. Revenge against him? What brought that on?

He realized that these feelings from Carpenter were starting to frighten him. The professor's emotions were strong and he was almost smug with a "you'll get yours" feeling. Maybe the man was nuts. Maybe he was one of those that resented promising students who might someday outdo him. Maybe he was nuts enough to hate them and hope they'd fail. Nuts enough to make them fail?

His apprehension was growing, and he'd need to keep tabs on Carpenter and try to figure out what his problem could be. If only he could call Erik and hear what he thought, but that could wait until they were back in Pinehurst. After all, what could Carpenter do to him on a research ship with all those scientists around?

* * *

The Stone House case had run into a snag and Agent Harris had basically put the Pinehurst detectives on the shelf with a hearty, "I'll get back to you." So Ted took that opportunity to take some personal time. He had called Sindri and asked for the patrol reports and she agreed to meet him that evening.

When she walked out of the office across from the station, she looked stunning, as usual. She gave him a quick embrace and said, "It's always so good to see you." She looked like an executive just getting through with her day.

"Do you want to stop someplace for dinner?" He hadn't intended on asking that, but it popped out. His usual easy banter and joking had abandoned him. He really liked her. She was beautiful, incredibly smart, always kind and understanding, and he found that he was scared to death of being rejected by her.

"That would be nice," She said with a grin. "Where would you suggest?"

He really expected her to say something about not having time or that they really needed to get to their conversation about the Dabih. He'd just blurted it out on the spur of the moment and wasn't ready with a place in mind.

"Well, I don't know. There are an internet café and a sports bar nearby. Either of those sound good?"

"I've never been to a sports bar. Why don't we go there?"

"You sure? It can get pretty noisy."

"Sounds like it's probably a fun place. Let's go."

The thought of Sindri in Play It Sports Bar and Grill just wouldn't settle in his imagination. He started to smile and tried to control the laugh that wanted to burst out of his mouth, but only succeeded enough that he just chuckled.

"Why is that funny?" She looked like she honestly didn't understand and wanted to.

"I'm just picturing you there. I mean, you're the classiest woman I've ever known. This place is more bar than sports. You may not be very comfortable there."

"I'll be comfortable with you," she smiled and wrapped her arm through his.

His heart felt like it skipped a beat. Did she really mean that? That was more than he could have hoped for. And she actually took his arm.

Most of the women he knew would probably be offended if he took them to Play It, thinking it was beneath them. But she would be comfortable anywhere because she was a real lady, and this lady was with him.

As they walked into Play It, a deafening cheer went up from the crowd. "Yeah, baby!" "Hoo, Hoo, Hoo!" She jumped slightly, but looked around smiling.

"What's going on?"

"Basketball. Sounds like a three-pointer," he shouted over the crowd.

"I don't know what a three-pointer is, but it certainly seems exciting," she shouted back.

"Let's get a table." He put his hand on the small of her back to lead her through the crowd and to a small round table across from the bar.

"I was right," she said while she leaned over the table so he could hear her, "this place is fun."

"Good. Do you want something to drink?" Ted asked as a waitress came to them.

"I like red wine."

He ordered her wine and a beer for himself and they started looking at the menu. They decided on an appetizer platter consisting of hot wings, mozzarella sticks, jalapeño poppers, and spinach avocado dip with tortilla chips.

"You like all that stuff?"

"I don't know. I've never had any of it before."

He paused, unsure. "If you find out you don't like it, we'll order you something else."

"I'm sure it'll all be good," Sindri grinned, gazing into his eyes.

In his mind, Ted could see the deep blue of Miran eyes with the sparks of light swirling around them. All he could think was that he wanted to see them again.

They talked about the people in the bar, some of the basics of basketball, and what play-offs were. When the waitress brought their appetizers, she dug in, seeming to like everything. After a moment of eating, the conversation turned to the Dabih. He knew he'd apologized for dragging the Mirans into the kidnapping case, but he felt he had to do it again.

She assured him that there was no need to apologize again, but he couldn't help saying, "I'd like to help out—I could make it up to you by looking at the patrol statistics."

She shook her head, her disc-shaped earrings glinting red and blue from the bar's neon signs. "We have many talented statisticians working on that. It's nice of you to offer though."

"If you're sure…"

"I'm sure."

"They seemed to be searching for you in Boston. Hopefully that's not where your New Mira is."

She wiped her mouth and said, "It isn't," before taking a sip of water.

"Where is New Mira? I'm just curious."

She frowned and shook her head. "I can't tell you that. I'm sorry."

He held up his hands to indicate that it was no big deal. "I understand. I guess… I guess I just want to know everything about you."

"Peterson," someone shouted at him as two men walked toward them.

"Hey, guys," Ted greeted them with a slight cringe as they both shook his hand.

"Good to see you, man," one of them said as he looked at Sindri with some surprise and undeniable admiration.

"Sindri, this is Charlie Roth and Greg Rudawski, both detectives I work with. Guys, this is Sindri." He realized belatedly that he didn't know her last name, or in fact, if she had a last name.

"Nice to meet you," they both said, not taking their eyes off her.

"Thank you. It's very nice to meet some of Ted's friends," she answered.

"Enjoying your vacation?" Roth asked, wiggling his eyebrows.

"Yeah, it's going too fast," he answered deadpan.

"I bet it is," Rudawski said as leered at Sindri. Ted squashed the urge to punch the former linebacker.

"We'll talk next week," Roth said as he winked and started to walk away.

"Sure, guys, see ya," he answered with a subtle look of annoyance.

He looked back at Sindri anticipating that he'd have to apologize for his coworkers. They'd barely taken their eyes off her. For that, he couldn't really blame them. But did they have to check her out so obviously? To his surprise she was giggling as she sipped her wine.

"It's been a long time since young men have looked at me like that," she said. "I'd forgotten how flattering a simple look could be."

He looked into her eyes and spoke from his heart. "Haven't you noticed me looking at you like that?"

"Not lately," she said softly.

"I didn't know if you'd appreciate me showing an interest in you."

"Your friends think I would. They seem to think you've spent your vacation with me."

"Yeah, well, guys sometimes assume a lot."

"And sometimes guys are very astute."

"Are you saying you wouldn't mind being somehow involved with me?"

She looked down, her long eyelashes fluttering, and then met his eyes. "Yes, I'm saying I wouldn't mind being somehow involved with you," she repeated his words but her tone was downright sexy.

He had to remind himself to breathe. He knew he wasn't handling this well. She was actually coming on to him and he was blowing it with his bumbling questions. He figured she could sense how nervous and a little intimidated he was, but he had to say something.

"Would you like to go see a movie or something?" he asked.

"Yes."

"How about something like one of the Star Wars? Do you like science fiction?"

She leaned farther across the table to whisper more quietly, "Most people think I am science fiction."

"No. You're real," he whispered back.

Sindri stayed leaning toward him and smiling. Before realizing what he was doing, Ted closed the space between them and gently kissed her. He was amazed and thrilled that she kissed him back. She moved away slightly and gave him a smile that almost knocked him over.

"You have very nice lips," she sighed quietly.

"You're amazing," he whispered.

"No, Ted," she said wistfully sitting back in her chair and reaching for a tortilla chip, "I'm just old enough to know that when you're attracted to someone, there's no point in denying or avoiding it."

"I'm not denying it anymore," he said. "That first time I met you at Lexi's, when I was still afraid you might kill me, I was blown away by you."

"Did you really think we might kill you?"

"Oh, yeah. In fact, I thought it was pretty likely." He took a bite of a hot wing to hide his embarrassment.

"Your bravery is just one of the things that make you attractive to me."

Out of the blue, Ted suddenly realized what his breath must be like after all those appetizers he'd eaten. "Like being brave enough to kiss you with hot wings on my breath? I'm sorry."

She laughed loud enough that a couple people at the bar glanced over at them.

"It tasted good," she said through her laugh. "I've discovered I like hot wings."

"You ready to get out of here?"

"Yes. Let's go."

They held hands on the way out and up the street to his small house. He wasn't sure if he wanted the world to see or if he wanted to keep this special lady all to himself.

"Ted," Sindri said as she took his arm and walked toward his house. "Tell me more details about how the Dabih ship was different from the installation in San Francisco."

"Well, the thing I noticed the most was that the ship was really clean and all white. San Francisco was an old, abandoned warehouse. You know, dirty cement floors and gray plaster walls. I don't know what the ship was made of, but the walls and floors all looked like white marble, only not cold like you'd expect them to be.

"Did it feel different?"

"More powerful, but I just figured it was a bigger place with more Dabih. I'm still shocked that it was their whole ship with thousands of them aboard," Ted said shaking his head. "When that woman killed Carpenter and the Dabih guard, the power from it doubled me over, and I had to be at least thirty feet away, in another room."

"A killing blow is very powerful," she said nodding. "I'm glad you weren't closer. You said Adam was held in some kind of cell. How many do you think were there?"

"They lined a long, curving hallway. There had to be dozens."

"It strikes me that there would be very little reason to have prison cells aboard a space ship. It seems a waste of resources, and they have no history of taking Humans or Mirans there. Their whole purpose must be for holding Dabih prisoners."

"I see what you mean. Their aggression against each other must be a way of life for them if they planned on needing so many prison cells."

"Exactly. It's very sad that they live with such ruthlessness and hostility. I feel very sorry for them living like that."

Ted gazed into her eyes, "And it's your compassion that's just one of the things that makes you so attractive to me."

She smiled and leaned against him.

"Here we are," He presented his house with an arm wave. "Would you like to come in?"

"Yes, I would. But I also need to." Ted gave her a questioning look. "I shouldn't disappear from the street, now should I?"

Ted chuckled lightly, "Come on in."

They stood in his living room for a moment before he got the nerve to move toward her and wrap his arms around her waist. They kissed as she reached her arms around his neck. When their lips separated, they still held on to each other.

"Sindri," he whispered hesitantly, "can I see your Miran form?"

She looked surprised but then smiled and changed. He looked up into her eyes as the little lights sparkled. She had to lean down since she was now quite a bit taller than him, but she kissed him again. He realized they both kept their eyes open this time and he became lost in her eyes as more spots of light erupted and shimmered through the deep blue.

"Thank you," he whispered as they hugged.

She lifted her head from his shoulder and looked at him as if she was very touched. Through the myriad lights, he could see her eyes start to glisten as if she was about to cry.

"What's wrong?" he asked feeling like he'd done something to hurt her.

"Nothing," she gasped. "In fact, just the opposite."

"I don't know what you mean."

"I've cared about many Human men and I know they cared about me. But none of them ever knew the real me. None of them had any idea who I truly was. Only you. You know the real me, and it's okay with you that I'm not Human." She smiled sweetly as she continued. "And you kissed me like a Miran, gazing into my eyes. That's incredibly special and touching to me."

He took a deep breath. He wasn't sure if he remembered to breathe at all as she was speaking. "Everything about you is incredibly special to me."

She reached up and laid her long, lavender fingers along his cheek. "Call me," she said quietly. She stepped back from him and disappeared.

CHAPTER 19

Professor Carpenter seemed normal once they got to Woods Hole. Adam hadn't sensed any disturbing feelings from him, but they'd been incredibly busy since the moment they'd arrived.

As soon as he got his work assignments, he knew he wasn't going to learn much about the universe, but that didn't really matter. He was going to understand the equipment and learn procedures that would someday make it possible for him to study space travel. Those were the most important things, and he was excited to get going.

The first two days were amazing. Most of what he did all day was pick up data from different sensors and measurement tools to run them across the ship to the lab. He was essentially a gofer, but that didn't matter because it was the hands on, real work that he'd been longing to do. The scientists always took a little time to explain how things worked. Studying in class was never as good as getting your hands into the real world.

The third day was incredible. He almost raced from one piece of technical equipment to another gathering and compiling data and running errands for the scientists. He couldn't believe how much he was learning. They'd worked late into the evening and although he was tired, he still felt great about what was being accomplished aboard one little research ship.

Heading into his room to finally get some sleep, he thought of Lexi and had a sudden vision of her standing on the deck of a ship just like this one, with the glorious moonlight behind her. He'd be going home to her tomorrow night and he couldn't wait.

Someday, though, they should live near the ocean and get a boat. He'd love to be lost at sea with his beautiful Lexi.

He almost reached out to send her his love and feel hers in return when he noticed one more piece of data still in the printer that he hadn't yet delivered to the scientists. He grabbed it from the desk and delivered it to the now empty workroom so they'd have it first thing in the morning.

Hurrying back to his room to reach out to Lexi with no chance of being disturbed, he noticed that the whole ship was amazingly quiet. Everyone must have been tired from working hard all day, so they quickly headed toward their cabins.

He was surprised to see Carpenter standing there in the cabin and staring at him. But it wasn't his stare that bothered him. It was the feeling of cold satisfaction that he could sense in him. And the hate. His hate for him was back and mixed with an even stronger feeling of vengeance.

"What can I do for you, Professor Carpenter?" he asked, trying to keep his voice calm but knowing it sounded cold.

"I need to talk to you privately. Shut the door."

He noticed Carpenter didn't even try to hide the iciness in his voice. This was feeling very wrong, and he perceived some kind of danger. But not fear. Carpenter was small and not a young man. He could take him to the mat without even exerting himself, even without his Miran strength.

"Sure," he said without emotion as he closed the door behind him.

"I know what you really are and what your kind has done."

"I'm a little confused, Professor, have I done something wrong?"

"You *are* something wrong," Carpenter hissed, and then stood tall and cleared his throat. "I'd like to introduce you to a friend of mine who will take care of that."

What was this man talking about? Had he lost his mind somehow?

A Dabih materialized next to Carpenter. Adam's moment of shock allowed the Dabih to hit him with a powerful stunning blast, knocking him unconscious.

* * *

Spending time on New Mira was a little like going home on vacation. Everyone was as happy as they could be just to see Lexi, and it made her feel like she was the most important person in the world. Even though she still missed Adam, the Mirans made the time go much more quickly than she expected.

On the third day of her separation from Adam, she arrived at New Mira after her dinner shift at the coffee shop and Sindri was waiting to give her a tour. The leader seemed exceptionally happy which made Lexi happy as well. She met some of the scientists and engineers that had developed the device Ted used to disrupt Terazed's power.

All the labs were amazing. They were huge, modern rooms where teams worked on areas that interested them. They practiced a pure science, not science for profit. Yet most of the research only affected Humans. Mirans worked in almost every field and took their research into Human labs to help fight disease and develop new technology. She was surprised how many breakthroughs in research actually came from Mirans.

Everything, from the business offices to the kitchens, ran efficiently with a relaxed kind of joy. Everyone at New Mira was there by choice and worked in areas that motivated them. She could see herself someday choosing to live in New Mira. Not soon, but maybe someday.

She wondered how much time Adam had spent in the labs. If he had his way, she thought he'd eventually move past the confines of Human space exploration and want to do his research here. Not many Mirans were interested in going back to space, but Adam was, and they would let him investigate what he wanted without any limit of resources.

They didn't have their Miran spaceship that had crashed and been destroyed, but they still had the knowledge. Their planet, Mira, had been destroyed in a super nova, so there was simply no place Mirans longed to go.

She knew Adam would want to explore. He wanted to travel Earth's solar system, and beyond, and he would find a few others who would want to join him. His bonded mate was one of them. She'd go with him anywhere.

Suddenly she gasped, sensing a mental blast of fear, confusion, and pain from Adam. Everyone in the room sensed it. She let out a muffled shriek. Adam was gone from her mind. She put her hands over her face as she summoned all her power to sense her mate, but he wasn't there. All the most powerful Mirans in the room were trying to find his mind, also, but they didn't find him either.

"Glytha," Sindri said to the Original in charge of the labs, "get a message to our people in Boston to check Woods Hole immediately. We need a report from them within five minutes."

"Lexi," she said as she moved to take her in her in her arms, "don't despair. We lost you once, but got you back."

"I'm so empty without him," she said, her tears flowing.

"I understand, child, but we'll find him." She gave her another hug.

Nereus, the Original who was Adam's progenitor, moved to her other side, "I won't rest until Adam is back with us. We'll do whatever it takes."

CHAPTER 20

Ted, still floating on a cloud of bliss from his evening with Sindri, cheerfully drove back to Boston with his fellow detectives. The DEA agent had found a lead. The small stone house in Pinehurst, which he'd first thought was just a dealer's house, had turned out to be a major distribution point of a drug cartel who were not only smuggling drugs into the US, but stealing young women out of it. If he hadn't seen the aliens, he'd of thought that Gretchen Wagner had been a part of that.

R and R sat in the front, discussing the basketball game, which suited Ted fine. He could use the car time to think about the Dabih's appearances. From what he could tell so far, the Dabih seemed to be hanging out in and around Pinehurst, which had to mean that they were searching for the four musketeers. He smiled, remembering Sindri's enjoyment of that title.

He couldn't wait to see her again. He'd take her to Jacob's— or even Boston—for a good meal. They could even stay in Boston, or she could teleport them anywhere. He imagined having real Italian food in Rome, Sindri sitting at the table next to him, looking wonderful in a green dress that matched her eyes.

"Earth to Peterson," Rudawski said, looking back at him. Roth also looked at him using the rearview mirror.

Ted grinned.

"You in love or something?" Roth asked, "Greg asked you where Harris wanted us to be."

Was he? He blinked, thinking about that possibility.

"Ted," Roth said.

"Huh?"

"Are we meeting Harris at the airport or what?"

He pulled his mind off Sindri and got them to the right area.

* * *

Sindri materialized within just a few minutes with Aricia and Erik. Lexi could sense that she was upset, yet also felt determination and resolve.

They'd all moved to the conference room in the Original's area to gather any information that could be found.

"Sindri," Lexi pleaded, "send me to Woods Hole."

"Don't worry, Lexi. We'll be going there," she said gently, "but right now, as we speak, teams are going into every Dabih stronghold we know of. They are not just sensing for Adam, but looking for him and questioning any Dabih they find. They might find him at any moment."

"Oh, Sindri." The tears rolled down Lexi's face, but she felt a touch of relief. "Do you really think so?"

"They've taken him somewhere. Logically he's at one of their labs. But the Originals and I have made another decision. It took quite a bit of deliberation, but we think it's the only choice we have."

Lexi knew her progenitor sensed the confusion and apprehension in her heart, and those feelings obviously showed on her face.

"With these developments, we can't continue with our peaceful handling of the Dabih," Sindri continued. "For them to make so bold a move, they must think our policy of nonviolence is a weakness. So our teams are instructed to kill. They may have to kill some to get others to talk, but they'll leave no living Dabih."

"Kill them all?"

"Not all. We only know of the installations in the United States," Sindri explained. "The others around the world need to see how strong we really are. Through Gretchen Wagner, they learned of you and Adam. They've abducted both of you. It's obvious they're willing to attack any Mirans they find. We can't let that continue with no response from us."

She hated the idea of attacking and killing, but what else could they do? They'd plotted against the Mirans, developed instruments to find them, kidnapped Adam. She'd been willing to kill one Dabih to save him in Oregon, but this was so much more.

"One Dabih took you, Lexi, but this is much bigger, and must have been a detailed plot from their leaders," Sindri continued. "We have no idea if they have other plans that are being carried out or if they have spies, but this is a first strike and we can't ignore it."

"There's nothing else we can do," Nereus said as he looked at her with sadness and conviction.

Lexi nodded, but said, "We could kill all the Dabih we could find and still might not find Adam."

Sindri agreed. "The four of us and Nereus will leave for Woods Hole in a few minutes, but you have to remember that it would normally take you some time to get from Pinehurst to Boston. We'll start by sensing for past Dabih presence around the area. We may be able to follow their trail to some extent. We don't know for sure, but we'll try to get a better idea of where Adam might be."

"Sindri, what if Adam is blocked again?" Erik reasoned. "Lexi reached him before because they found their joining. Shouldn't she go to all the locations to try sensing him?"

Sindri looked at Lexi. "You should be able to sense your joining from here. Haven't you tried?"

"No. I didn't think of it."

"Try."

* * *

Ted had never been in a helicopter before. He found take-off to be noisy and somewhat frantic, but once in the air, when he got a view out of window down at Boston Harbor and the ocean, he immediately thought of showing it to Sindri.

Once they made it to Cape Code, Harris handed him a set of powerful binoculars and he had to remind himself that he was working. Fantasy had to come later.

They flew out to sea, looking up and down the coast for a small freighter. On the water, he could see a Coast Guard ship cruising the traffic lanes, looking, Harris assured him, for the same small vessel.

After half an hour or so of circling, they spotted a suspicious ship. Ted almost immediately lost his lunch when the helicopter turned downward. Harris shook his head and handed him a bag, but that wasn't the reason he wanted to vomit. A terrible, painful buzzing filled his body.

Dabih. There were Dabih on that ship.

But as they got closer, the feeling went away. Did that mean the Dabih were in the water somewhere? How could that be?

The pilot radioed the Coast Guard to give them the coordinates of the small ship below them. The Coast Guard would board and search, so once they were alongside the suspect vessel, the helicoptor soomed off to keep searching.

He had to call Sindri but couldn't do that from the coptor. Ted gazed over the pilot's shoulder at the control panel. It took a few moments, but he finally spotted the coordinates that revealed exactly where they were over the featureless stretch of the Atlantic.

* * *

How could she not have reached out to find their love? Lexi'd been so upset over the pain she'd felt from him, and so afraid, she hadn't even thought of it. Sindri must have assumed she'd tried and not felt him. Not felt him because he was dead.

She closed her eyes again and reached out to that special bonded space that only she and Adam shared. In the background, she heard Erik and Aricia talking to Nereus, and Sindri using her cell phone to call Ted. Ted, with his connections in the police force, could probably help them. She felt nothing at first, but then a flicker—as if Adam were unconscious—then nothing.

Lexi opened her eyes to find Sindri frowning at her phone. Ted's phone had gone directly to voice mail.

"He's there!" Tears ran down her cheeks again, but everyone else smiled with relief. "He's still there. I don't know if he's sensing me, but Adam's alive."

"Is he blocked?" Aricia asked.

"It feels different from the wall he hid behind before. The Dabih may be blocking his powers like they did mine. When Terazed used his device on me, it took all my strength to reach out. I didn't sense Adam. He physically touched me before I knew he was there."

Sindri called Balere to communicate this to the teams searching for Adam. Erik and Aricia hugged her with relief.

"I'm ready to go," Lexi said with determination.

"Then let's go," Sindri said simply.

Nereus joined them as they changed to their Human forms and started to move into a circle before teleporting to Woods Hole, but Sindri's phone rang. They all hoped it was Balere saying that one of the teams had found Adam, but the caller ID said it was Ted.

"Yes, Ted," Sindri said sweetly. Lexi could hear Ted's voice faintly but couldn't tell what he was saying.

"You're in Boston? On the water? That strong? I don't know, I'll have to talk to Balere. Yes, I agree. No, I'd prefer you stayed away to be safe. I can't answer that, Ted, we'll have to make that decision. Thank you. Stay where you are and we'll be in touch."

Sindri stared at the disconnected phone and for a moment before she dialed quickly and said, "Balere, we need to talk immediately."

They could sense her anxiety and confusion as she teleported away.

CHAPTER 21

Balere materialized in front of Lexi and her friends a few minutes later. Sindri sat on the edge of the conference room table, visibly upset.

"I need to tell all of you about the call I just got from Ted," she said. "He said he's investigating a case in Boston, and was several miles out to sea on a Coast Guard helicopter looking for a suspected drug smuggling ship, when he sensed the Dabih. He said the feeling was stronger than ever. In fact, he was in great pain and doubled over, and it was coming from below. From the water. He wanted us to come immediately and take him back out on a boat, but I said we'd have to make a decision here, and I'd get back to him."

Lexi almost asked a question but Sindri held up a hand to stop her.

"You, Aricia, and Erik know Ted Peterson, and the rest of you know about him. Several days ago, Ted asked me to meet with him to discuss some ideas he had about the Dabih. He wanted access to our patrol records so he could try to establish a pattern.

"When I hesitated, he became rather insistent. He said he still felt guilty about endangering us by asking us to rescue the abducted females, which I sensed was probably sincere, and he was trained and experienced in this kind of investigation.

"I convinced him that Miran statisticians were busy compiling the data and we dropped the subject. Before, when he helped us rescue those girls, he'd raised the subject of the location of New Mira. At the time, he'd been concerned that it was in Boston, where Dabih were looking for us, and I'd assured him that it was far away. This time when he asked for the location, I got the feeling my answer wasn't enough. He wants to know where we are."

"Sindri," Lexi said, "I hate to interrupt, but Ted probably listened to Adam and me talk about New Mira when he bugged our home. Do you think he might have heard something more?"

"I don't know. It probably doesn't make any difference – what's done is done. For some reason, though," she continued, sounding uncomfortable, "it bothered me that he was asking again for such vital information. I sensed that he wasn't being completely honest emotionally, but his guilt might have caused that. Human motives can be difficult to interpret sometimes.

"After that, I started to think again about why Ted could sense Dabih. I needed to know if he carries any Miran genes that give him this ability we've never seen before in Humans. But I didn't want him to know about my investigation.

"So ..." Sindri hesitated and was obviously embarrassed. "Ibon," she gestured to the geneticist and Original in charge of new Mirans, "and I materialized into his home that night and stunned him. We took a DNA sample, released him, and left. I'm not proud of taking these actions against a Human, but felt we had no other way to get what we needed."

Everyone in the room was shocked by Sindri's revelation and knew that she sensed it too. She really didn't harm him, but Lexi knew she felt regret that she didn't trust the first Human that trusted them. Surprisingly, she was also a little scared.

"Ibon's tests revealed that Ted has no Miran DNA," she continued, "but something else was present that shocked me and made me fearful for the first time in a millennium. Ted carries Dabih DNA."

The shock was so great that the emotions in the room were blank for a moment. Lexi needed time to digest that information enough to even have an emotional response. Ted had been trusted with knowledge of Mirans, with working with them on patrol, and even with strategizing with them. So many questions dashed through her mind, she couldn't even sort them out.

"Before we address any questions," Sindri said without letting her emotions show in her voice, "I'd like to continue with some implications that Balere and I have already discussed. The fact that Ted has Dabih DNA makes it obvious that the Dabih have at some time attempted to breed with Humans, but we have no way of knowing how successful they were. We could say that Ted is a kind of hybrid. He has stayed Human, but has the ability to sense those who share his DNA. Some Humans may become completely Dabih, like our Miran children, but we have no evidence of that happening.

"It is possible that the Dabih have no knowledge of Ted and his genetic inheritance. This could all be a strange coincidence. Ted, who just happens to have recessive Dabih DNA, just happened to be investigating a case that lead him to us.

"But I don't think we can trust coincidence when dealing with the Dabih, because it is also possible that they know Ted, and other Humans, carry their DNA. When sensed, Ted appears to be completely Human. He would be the perfect plant for the Dabih, the perfect spy. He could get close to us, as he has, and relay information to the Dabih that they've never been able to collect before.

"The fact that significant changes in Dabih activities coincide with the appearance of Ted in our lives could also be considered coincident. But I don't think so. I think we have to consider the possibility that Ted is a Dabih spy and treat him with the utmost care."

"Should we continue to act like we trust him?" Erik asked.

"I think that's our best choice," Balere answered. "If he's a spy, we would be better off stringing him along until we find out what his ultimate goal is."

The silence in the room grew heavy. Lexi considered everything she and Adam had talked about when around Ted and the fact that he'd bugged their apartment. Adam had been upset by that, and now she grew even more upset. Maybe he hadn't taken all the bugs. It'd been a set up—the whole thing.

"Ted did this to Adam," Lexi said, the fear and anger she felt made her voice rough. "He trusted Ted, and Ted led the Dabih to him. That's been the plan all along, hasn't it? To abduct him. Now Adam's alone, without any other Mirans."

Erik and Aricia had joined Sindri and Nereus, forming a circle around Lexi. They sent her calming thoughts to try to ease her pain, but her heart wouldn't stop aching. Without Adam, she didn't think it ever would.

"Lexi," Erik said gently and she remembered how much his calming tone had helped in the past. "We can't jump to any conclusions, yet. Ted might have been involved, but he might not have been."

"Erik, we have to go there," Lexi said with all the strength she could find.

"When you were taken, Adam wanted to move immediately, but we had to wait for more information. It turned out to be the right thing to do. We need to get the reports from Boston."

She sobbed. "I don't know if I can wait."

"Is he trying to lure us into a trap?" Balere asked, pacing the space between the table and the white board. "Or are we wrong about him, and he's honestly reporting new findings?"

"I couldn't sense his feeling so far away." Sindri sat calmly although her hands were knotted together.

"I think we need to follow our original plan and pretend to trust him," Balere said. "If it's a trap, it may be a trap that leads us to Adam."

"We'll delay him for a time while we continue our search," Sindri stated matter-of-factly. "If we can't find Adam quickly, then we'll walk into the trap. It might lead us to Adam, or it might lead us to a battle that will be an end to this war."

Balere looked her in the eye. "I'll stay connected to you for a signal. If I feel fear from you, I'll send a hundred Mirans to your side."

"Thank you, Balere," she spoke softly. At times like this, it was easy to see how much they cared about each other after all the centuries they'd worked to build a life on Earth.

Ibon came back in the room, and everyone sensed his sadness.

"Sindri," he said quietly.

"You might as well tell all of us," she answered.

"None of them have sensed Adam," Ibon began, "but there was a disturbance at the docks. There were police and Coast Guard boats heading out. People were saying that a student researcher fell overboard and might have drowned. They are searching for him."

"He drowned?" Lexi asked with disbelief.

"No," Sindri said emphatically. "He could not have drowned. If he fell overboard and was in trouble, he would have reached out to us, and we would have teleported him out of the water immediately."

Lexi's cell phone rang. She only had it with her in case Adam sent a text, and that is what she was praying for as she took the phone in her hand. But it was a call from a number she didn't know.

She glanced at Sindri, who nodded. She put the call on speaker.

"Miss Collins," the male voice said. "This is Professor Carpenter and I'm sorry, but I've got some bad news."

"Bad news?" She tried to keep her voice calm, but her hands shook.

"Adam fell overboard. They're looking for him. I'm sure they'll find him, but I thought I should let you know."

"Oh, God … how did it happen?"

"Right now, no one's really sure. We were heading for the dock, and no one saw him fall in. He's not on the ship, so that's all that could have happened."

She sniffled. "Are the police there?"

"Police, Coast Guard, Woods Hole officials. Everyone's looking."

"I'll come down right away."

"No, no, let the professionals do their jobs." Aricia made a face and Erik shook his head at her. Lexi concentrated on the call.

"Will you call back to let me know how the search is going?"

"Certainly. I'll keep you informed."

"Thank you, Professor Carpenter. I'll wait to hear from you."

"I'm very sorry," he said with no emotion in his voice. She ended the call.

Everyone just looked at each other for a moment before Erik spoke, "I guess we're all thinking the same thing. The Dabih must have teleported onto the ship to take him and left his disappearance to be a mystery to the police."

"The Dabih have him," Sindri said coldly. "And it was well planned."

Lexi couldn't think anymore, she just sat and cried. Eventually, Erik and Aricia walked her back to her room and waited with her for the cell phone to ring and for Sindri to let her go to Woods Hole.

* * *

General Dirac's plans had always involved high population areas where more abductions could occur in a shorter time. His problem was that Mirans chose the same places. He had to find areas that were less likely to contain Mirans. Why hadn't he seen that before?

All he needed to do was find more isolated areas and send his troops hunting. It would take longer, but his research would be completed without interference. Searching for population maps on the internet, Dirac was interrupted by his first lieutenant, Gelar.

"General," Gelar said, not waiting for permission to start, "Our installation in Chicago has been infiltrated by Mirans. A subordinate was able to escape."

"Have you sent in other troops?" Dirac asked.

"Yes, General, but there's been no word from them."

"Bring in the one that escaped."

The Dabih from Chicago was obviously terrified. He reported that Mirans had teleported into the installation and had used a weapon that disabled Dabih powers. He'd only escaped because he happened to be near the corner of the room and hadn't been affected by the weapon. He had teleported immediately, so had no idea what the Mirans wanted, or what they did to the other helpless Dabih.

Dirac tried to contact Chicago, but got no response. Then he tried to contact his other installations and again got nothing. The Mirans had attacked before to rescue Humans, but he had no Humans in any of his installations. Was this a blatant attack or were they looking for something else? He trusted no one to judge the situation except himself.

Leaving Gelar to send him any other information that came in, Dirac teleported to Chicago with three of his guards.

Chicago seemed at first to be deserted, but he soon sensed the weak brain wave of one Dabih. Dirac found him unconscious in the hallway and used his power to wake him.

"The Mirans stole all our powers and questioned us about a Miran named Adam, the Dabih said weakly."

"Who's Adam?"

The survivor shook his head. None of the Dabih knew anything about someone taking a Miran, so each of them had been killed.

For the first time in his very long life on Earth, Dirac wanted to contact the Mirans and get to the bottom of this. Why were they attacking now? And how had they found his installations?

"Why were you not killed?" asked Dirac suspiciously.

"They wanted me to tell my superiors that they know about our spy and they'll continue searching and killing Dabih until Adam is returned. They said that Adam is the second Miran we've kidnapped and they now consider it an act of war."

"We have no spy. We have no Miran!" Dirac shouted. "Wait," he said more quietly, "what did they mean that they'd keep searching and killing?"

"I don't know General. That's just what they said."

"What happened to the troops sent in by Gelar?"

"They were killed, General."

"Get yourself back to my headquarters. Be prepared for more questions."

With a look of growing rage, Dirac turned to his guards and said, "San Francisco."

Dirac searched each of his installations and found nothing but dead Dabih. The Mirans were on a rampage and wanted one thing. Another Miran named Adam who had supposedly been abducted. Why did they think he had him?

He went back to his headquarters. Catching sight of Gelar who stood patiently waiting for instructions, Dirac had an idea that might work.

"Gelar," Dirac said, "only one Dabih has ever been suspected of having dealings with Mira, and that was Terazed. You worked with Terazed while questioning that Human who escaped from Oregon. Did he ever tell you how he contacted them?"

"No sir, but we have his computer files. I could search them, maybe he left something there."

"You have always been my most logical advisor," Dirac stated. "Can you think of anything that may be behind these Miran attacks?"

"I think we have to assume that they wouldn't leave a message that was a lie because that would accomplish nothing. So they obviously believe that we are holding a Miran. But I have no idea what might have made them think that."

"They think we used a spy to abduct a Miran," repeated Dirac. "We don't have spies, and we have no interest in the Mirans. No. We don't, but the Ruling Council does. This Miran was taken by the Council."

"That sounds like the most logical conclusion, sir."

"See if you can get anything from Terazed's files. Maybe it's time Mira realized there are two Dabih factions on this planet."

* * *

Gelar returned to the small desk in his quarters, but didn't need to search Terazed's files. He'd made that search long ago and knew there was no contact information. But, most importantly, there also was nothing on that server that could implicate him.

He had talked to Mirans three different times after Terazed killed that Human. He thought leaving her body would be a message that would get them to back off, but it had simply made things worse. He'd decided to never contact a Miran again, but kept the numbers for those named Lexi and Balere just in case.

His own stupid curiosity about the situation in the Oregon cavern had sparked the first call, which gave that Miran named Balere the nerve to call him back. But it was Terazed's stupidity in abducting Lexi that had made him have to call them that last time. Terazed could have started an all-out war if she hadn't been rescued.

Now, the Ruling Council had put him in a similar position. This time, though, it would be Dirac who made contact. Gelar would tell him he found the phone numbers in Terazed's files and he would be finally free of this.

Complications always surrounded him, but he knew it would be like that when he agreed to join Dirac as a Ruling Council spy. Nomarr had been looking for a good reason to do away with Dirac for years. Now, once they got his report that Dirac himself had betrayed them to Mira, Dirac and his pitiful little subordinates would be history. Then he would be back where he belonged, working directly for Nomarr. Hopefully, if things went as he planned, someday replacing Nomarr.

CHAPTER 22

Adam woke up groggily on the floor of a ten-by-ten, empty room. There was nothing around him but white walls, floor, ceiling, and one door. He reached out with his power to sense Mirans, Dabih, anyone, but found nothing. He felt fine, like his powers should be working, but there was just nothing.

He knew he was being blocked somehow, but didn't feel anything unusual. His powers didn't feel dimmed or pushed aside, they were simply gone. Almost as if he were Human again. As his anxiety grew, he found himself talking aloud just to hear a voice.

"Keep it together champ," he said to the wall. Isolation had never been something he enjoyed. He knew the Dabih had abducted him; he knew he was being held in an unknown location; he knew Mirans, especially Lexi, would have sensed that he was gone, and would be looking for him. He couldn't sense Lexi, but could she sense him?

He had enough power left to still hold his Human shape, so maybe Lexi could sense him. He tried to find their private place, tried to find Lexi, but he felt nothing. Maybe she could feel him. Maybe she knew he was alive and trying.

The door started to open and he stood up to lean against the opposite wall. It was strange not being able to sense who was on the other side. It would have to be Dabih. No Miran or Human would or could do this to him. But he had no idea how many would walk in or what their emotions might be.

Three Dabih, two men and one woman, stood barely inside the door staring at him

"So, Miran," she said with grim satisfaction in her voice, "feeling a little peculiar? Tell me, can you sense us? How do we feel to you?"

"The words vile and disgusting come to mind," he answered, trying to keep his emotions as blank as possible.

"So judgmental." Her falsely sweet voice made him want to slug her, woman or not.

"If you still had your Miran powers," she continued, "you'd know we're feeling delighted to see you, and eager to get to know you better."

"What do you want, Dabih?" he asked, still holding on to his emotions.

"We want you to be our friend," the taller man answered. The word friend sounded evil when he said it.

"You make friends by abducting them and incapacitating them. Very interesting," he said and studied each of them. The woman's sinister grin detracted from her gold blonde hair and expressive blue eyes. The men were both brown haired. The taller one had a small scar on his chin and was obviously the leader. He stood a little ahead of the other two, stood a little straighter, and had the most confident, arrogant look. The woman and the other man didn't really look subordinate to him, though. They had a lot of power themselves, maybe a second-in-command-type relationship.

"We simply had to get you here safely and protect ourselves from you," the same man said nonchalantly.

"Well, that explains everything, then." Adam answered with the same nonchalance. "So you can just send me back, I'll let all the Mirans know how sweet you were, and we'll all live happily ever after."

"I had no idea Mirans could be so humorous," the female said still sporting that evil smile.

The other man hadn't said a word and looked like he had no intentions of joining this conversation. Adam figured he was the third in command and would defer to whatever the other two wanted.

"Why don't you forget the games and tell me what you want?"

"It's really very simple. All we want is the location of all your Miran installations."

"So you could pay a friendly visit, I'm sure. Why would I tell you that?"

"Because you won't be leaving here until you do," she answered. "And your stay with us won't be pleasant."

"Now we're getting to the truth," he said staring into her eyes. "But you forgot one thing. You know, the part where you kill me. Or I kill you."

"Such arrogance," she said dismissing his comment and letting her smile fade.

"You don't think I could kill you with my bare hands?" He let his anger show. "Step on over here and I'll give your two friends a demonstration."

She stared coldly at him. "We'll be back to continue our conversation later," the tall one said.

The three of them left and he heard a locking mechanism engage as the door closed. He sat on the floor, leaning against the wall wondering what would come next. A nagging pain began to grow behind his eyes. It didn't stay nagging for long. It grew, causing him to close his eyes and wince.

Then it grew some more. He furrowed his brows and massaged his forehead and temples as the intensity increased. He understood the game, now. No beatings, no quick torture. They would leave him here in severe pain until he couldn't take it anymore. Until he broke down.

This wasn't the usual snatch-and-grab, strike-and-run maneuver the Dabih had always used. This was much more sophisticated. They had no visible devices to block his powers and inflict this pain. Thinking about it, he realized the Dabih had barely come through the door. Maybe the whole room was blocking him somehow. Maybe some mechanism in a wall or the ceiling was causing the pain.

He tried to think through some kind of plan, some way he could get in touch with his people, some way he could get back to Lexi. As he struggled to come up with a plan, the pain level increased again. He leaned sideway until he was lying on the floor with his arms covering his head. He didn't know how long he could take this pain, or how much worse it would get.

* * *

Lexi, Erik and Aricia materialized with Sindri to an isolated area outside of Boston where a car had been left for them. Nereus stayed in New Mira to help transport people—hopefully Adam. She begrudged the time spent driving, but understood it was the only way. They would be dealing with many different Humans and had to arrive in the traditional Human way.

But the real task would be sensing for Adam and any Dabih. If they could find even one Dabih, they could try to get information from him. So they drove along the coast sensing for anything that would give them any hint of where Adam might be.

About an hour later with no sign of Adam or anything else, they finally parked at Woods Hole and looked for someone to question about the search efforts. Erik spotted Professor Carpenter talking to a Coast Guard officer.

"Professor Carpenter," Erik called to him. "Do we know anything, yet?"

After a few introductions, Professor Carpenter explained that they still had no sign of Adam, but were not giving up, yet. The Coast Guard officer was polite, and promised they would do everything in their power, but Lexi knew it was completely out of his power to find Adam. She only hoped it was within theirs.

"This situation is so terrible. I feel so helpless," Carpenter repeated himself. He reached for Lexi but didn't actually touch her. "There's still hope, you know."

Carpenter was distracting. His emotions were all over the place and seemed very different from his words. Mirans could so easily read Human emotions, but not what was behind what they were feeling. She sensed accomplishment in him. He was proud of himself. He felt like someone who had worked hard on a project and had finally finished it successfully. Had they made some breakthrough in their research, something he'd been looking for?

Even if that was the case, was he so uncaring about one of his students that his work would overshadow the expected feelings of grief or at least concern? He also seemed so shallow and uncaring until he turned to talk directly to Lexi and Erik. Then he seemed suspicious, like he didn't trust them and almost hated them. What was with this guy? Did he think they did something to Adam? That was impossible.

They made an excuse of leaving to get something to eat, and Lexi asked Professor Carpenter to please call if there were any developments, even though she knew there wouldn't be.

"Erik," Sindri asked once they walked away, "is there something between you and Carpenter?"

"Not that I know of." He shook his head.

"Odd. Well, we don't have time to wonder about him," Sindri said.

The only thing they could think to do was drive the streets as close to the coast as possible. Ted had sensed the Dabih several miles out in the Atlantic—if he was being honest. They could only hope that the Dabih were close enough to be sensed.

While driving a deserted street, Sindri's phone rang again. She looked at the caller ID to make sure it wasn't Ted. It was Balere. She put it on speaker.

"I got a caller on the other line that you need to hear," Balere said when she answered. "Can you come back?"

"Is it about Adam?"

"Not directly. It's something new. Something we never considered."

Sindri gestured for Erik to park the car and looked at Lexi without saying anything.

"Okay," she told Balere. She hung up. Lexi felt her reach out to the other Mirans and they were teleported to New Mira before they could even react.

CHAPTER 23

Ted had been anxiously waiting for over an hour for the chance to call Sindri. When he'd finally gotten through to her, she had practically blown him off. He'd never heard her voice so cold or impersonal and she wouldn't give him any kind of answer to what he or the Mirans should do. Maybe Lexi or Adam would know what Sindri's problem was.

When he grabbed his phone, he remembered that Adam wasn't home, but at Woods Hole. Since he was on Cape Cod anyway—and the bad guys were now in federal custody—he decided he'd just drive out there and see if he could find him. Maybe they'd go out for something to eat.

He was surprised to see all the emergency and Coast Guard activity as he got to the dock. Something not good must have happened. He showed his badge to an officer and asked about what was going on. A college kid had gone overboard. A kid named Adam McLane.

Shocked, he thanked the officer and dialed Sindri again. How could Adam let that happen? If it had, couldn't he have teleported to safety? He got a strong sense of foreboding as he remembered all the Dabih he'd detected earlier. The call went to voicemail.

He started going into detective mode, thinking about what he could do about Adam without the Mirans. If he could find a Dabih, he could use his stunning weapon and question him, but, even if he got some answers, he couldn't get to Adam without a Miran to hold onto.

Maybe he should talk to the people on the research ship that Adam had been on. A researcher referred him to a Professor Carpenter, who was evidently Adam's mentor. Maybe he saw or heard something that would give him a clue. He had to do something, so Carpenter would be some place to start.

The research vessel was docked at the end of the marina. He had to show his badge several more times before he got on the ship, but was finally on the deck heading for Carpenter's cabin. Then he felt a Dabih.

The sensation was coming from in front of him, so he crept closer as quietly as possible and could finally hear two voices. He peeked carefully around a stairway that blocked his view down the deck and saw two men talking. The older, scholarly one had to be Carpenter, which meant the other was Dabih.

His first instinct was to use his weapon to save Carpenter, but the conversation seemed to be mutually friendly. Carpenter would have no way to know he was talking to a Dabih, but the friendliness was unusual, and anything unusual to his detective's mind was suspicious. He wanted to hear what they were discussing.

Looking ahead, he noticed crates of some kind of equipment stacked on the deck, partially obscuring his view of Carpenter. The Dabih had his back to the crates, and neither of them was directly facing him. If he could get there without being seen, he might be able to listen to them.

He got on the floor and did a belly crawl around the staircase and stayed close to the wall as he approached the stack of crates. He hadn't realized how close he would be as the voices carried through the night air, right to him.

"Yara is very proud of you and wants to thank you in person," the Dabih was saying, "but she is in the middle of something and asked me to wait for a message before transporting you."

"I understand," said Carpenter, "I'm just anxious to see her."

"It won't be much longer, I'm sure."

"Do you think she'll let me see what she's doing with the Miran?" Carpenters voice was almost excited.

"I don't know."

"After what they did to me, I'd love to see a Miran suffer."

What the Mirans did? His stomach let out a large gurgle of protest and he froze. The conversation didn't stop though.

"We'll just need to wait, but it shouldn't be long," the Dabih answered.

They had a Miran and Carpenter was working with them, therefore Carpenter probably had something to do with Adam's abduction. His mind was completely blank when he tried to consider what he could do about it.

The Mirans had to know that the Dabih had Adam, but he hadn't heard back from Sindri and he sure couldn't call her again now. They would have checked all the Dabih locations they knew of, and he knew that if they'd found Adam there, this conversation wouldn't be happening.

The Dabih must have Adam somewhere else, and the Mirans probably had no idea where. Sindri said there had to be more locations than the five they'd discovered in Terazed's computer files. That's probably why she'd been so short with him on the phone and hadn't called him back. They were too busy searching.

He needed his own plan. He still felt somewhat responsible for the escalation of this war, and couldn't abandon the chance to help the Mirans and especially Sindri. He liked the kid and no one should be tortured—male or female—by sicko Dabih aliens.

Then he had an idea that he really didn't like at all. The Dabih teleported on their own and they could take Humans just by touching them. If he could touch the Dabih at the last moment, he should teleport with them to Adam's location. He'd thought before that going to the Mirans could have had dire consequences, but the Dabih? Purposefully heading into an alien torture pit. Great plan. He pulled out the Miran power blocker device, moved the wheel to the widest range, and placed his finger over the button.

He couldn't go into a Dabih stronghold with half a plan, but what choice did he have? He glanced at his phone, wishing for Sindri to call. The buzzing he felt then wasn't the vibration of his cellphone but his Dabih sense intensifying.

"They're ready for us," the Dabih said as he reached to place his hand on Carpenter's shoulder.

It was now or never, and he would figure out the rest when he got there. He leapt forward and grabbed the Dabih's arm.

* * *

They appeared just outside of the conference room. Lexi had many questions, but Sindri held up a hand for silence. She led them into the room where Balere had someone on the speaker phone.

"Sorry for the delay. Please go ahead," he said.

"Miran, I know Terazed the traitor was working with you and that you killed him."

Balere looked at Sindri who shrugged. "We were not working with Terazed."

"But you did kill him."

"He was a live when we left him. Stunned, not dead."

The voice on the phone laughed.

"Oh Miran, I'm not angry. I'd have done the same."

Everyone at the conference table exchanged worried glances. The laughter continued for a few moments and then trailed off.

"What angered me is that you raided my installations and killed my men without provocation."

"Who is he talking to?" Lexi whispered to Erik. Erik shrugged. Balere ignored them but Sindri wrote a name on the white board, General Dirac.

"General, we know the Dabih have a Human spy. You used him to abduct a Miran."

The General laughed again. "You know so little. You don't even know who you're fighting."

"He seems to think this is all pretty funny," Aricia whispered to Lexi. Sindri motioned for her to be quiet.

"You blame me for what the main Dabih organization has done. I and several followers broke away from the Ruling Council many years ago. We have our own research. I think it's hilarious that you've been protecting Humans from me all these years, while the Ruling Council has been plotting against Mira. And you didn't even know."

Sindri and Balere exchanged a concerned, questioning look.

"I have no spies and would never trust a Human. I am not holding your Miran. Look for the Ruling Council."

Before Balere could respond, the General continued. "You will never find their stronghold. The next time you go to war, Mirans, try to be smart enough to find out who you're really fighting."

The call ended. They sat in silence for a moment, absorbing.

"How much of that do you think is true?" Erik asked.

"I have no idea," Balere answered. "It could have all been true, or all lies."

"It could explain some things," Sindri added. "Their research is years behind, the installations are almost primitive, and they often seem disorganized. It all makes more sense if they're a small faction broken away from the main Dabih group."

"So," Lexi said, "if what he says is true, this Ruling Council has Adam and we are actually fighting two wars."

"And if it's lies?" Nereus asked.

"Then he's trying to confuse us and get us looking for something that doesn't exist," Balere answered, "which might mean we're getting close to destroying them and he's getting desperate."

"There's no definitive answer," Sindri said, "so we need to continue looking for Adam, and mainly stay aware that we may be encountering a more sophisticated Dabih than we're used to.

"One more thing. I got a voicemail from Ted saying he had just heard about Adam. He sounded genuinely upset and asked me to call him. Since then, his phone's been off. I still don't know how I feel about the situation with Ted, but he may be at Woods Hole. Just be careful if you see him."

CHAPTER 24

As they materialized, Ted used the Miran device and the Dabih got the same shocked look on his face that he'd seen on Terazed's. This time, though, he was ready. He reached back and hit the Dabih as hard as he could and watched him fall backwards to the floor. But he wasn't unconscious. He drew out his gun and, just as the Dabih was trying to get up, hit him with it, finally knocking him unconscious.

Carpenter gave him a frightened look and tried to bolt through the only door.

"Freeze! Police." Carpenter, well trained by modern culture, froze. Ted flashed his badge at him.

"What did you do with Adam McLane?"

"Officer, I have no idea what you're talking about. McLane fell overboard. Please, I must go."

He pointed his gun at the professor who started screaming "Help, help, a Human invader!"

Ted decked him.

"Sorry, professor," he told the unconscious man, "You chose the wrong side." He checked his pockets and those of the Dabih and found nothing useful.

The buzzing radiating through his body told him he had made it to an unknown Dabih installation, and the pain level indicated there was a bunch of them around. Thankfully, none seemed to be very close. He'd played football and baseball through pain, so he'd just have to do the same thing here. He checked his cellphone but there was no signal.

The room felt like some kind of a cell. Was Adam in a different cell? Or maybe it wasn't a cell and he was in a closet? The windowless room's white walls told him nothing.

He knew the Dabih had to be within feet of Mirans to sense them, but was it the same with humans? Would they sense him if he kept his distance? He knew that was the only chance he had.

He tried the door and was a little surprised to find it unlocked. He looked out cautiously. A long curved hallway went in both directions. Many doors, just like the one to the room he was leaving, were lined up along the wall as far as he could see. This was a much bigger place than San Francisco.

He moved carefully down the hall to his left. There was nothing to indicate which direction he should go - it was simply a fifty-fifty chance. He'd only taken a few steps when he felt a couple Dabih getting closer. Glancing around for a place to hide, he noticed the next door was slightly open. He stepped in, found a room identical to the one he'd just left, flattened himself against the wall behind the door, and waited.

Ted couldn't see who was approaching, but could hear every word as they got closer.

"After I 'thank' Carpenter for his help in abducting the Miran, I want you to dispose of the body for me."

"Yes, Council member Yara."

"I'm going to enjoy doing away with that stupid, gullible Human myself. He was so proud of himself and really thought I'd be grateful and reward him." Her laugh grated like bad brakes. "So gullible. I can't wait to laugh in his face as he realizes."

"Yes, Council member."

"What is this?" The sound of a door hitting the wall echoed through the hallway.

Ted figured they'd found Carpenter and the Dabih.

"I don't know, Council member," the subordinate said.

"Shut up, I wasn't asking you."

A sharp pain jabbed Ted behind his right eye. He pressed his hand to his eye and tried to remain silent.

"What happened here?" Yara asked.

"Someone teleported with us, Council member," a different Dabih answered with obvious fear. She must have awakened the guy he slugged. "He did something that took my powers, then hit me over the head with something."

"A Miran followed you here? You let a Miran follow you? How did he do that?"

"I don't know. I barely got a chance to sense him, but he felt Human."

"That's impossible," she shouted. "No Human could do this."

Someone moaned.

"Yara," Carpenter's groggy voice said. "Thank goodness you've come. Someone attacked us."

"Shut up, you brainless Human fool."

Wave after wave of pain washed over Ted as he slid to the floor and went into fetal position. He hardly registered when it stopped.

"Take care of them," Yara said. "Wait. That won't do."

Another sickening wave washed over him and he had to fight back the bile that rose in his throat. Someone screamed in agony and Ted bit his lip to keep from joining in.

He may have blacked out for a moment.

The sound of someone dragging something down the hall made him realize the pain had passed. Still woozy, he peeked out the crack of the door.

The woman dragged two bodies at once with her down the hall. One of those bodies was Carpenter's.

Ted knew this woman was someone he needed to be afraid of. Regrettably, she was also the one who could lead him to Adam. He heard her return, her clomping shoes echoing in the hallway. When she left again, dragging the last body, he hesitated. If she didn't return, he would have to select right or left and take his chances. If he did follow her, she'd probably go to the place where she dumped the bodies and maybe that'd be an exit route. Of course, if she found him, he'd have a more permanent exit route, and Adam would be stuck.

He followed her to the left. The curve of the hallway gave him some cover, but he still kept his distance. At least he now had the answer to one of his most important questions. Like a Miran, he obviously had to be pretty close for the Dabih to sense him.

He followed her to an alcove that had a large chute. She opened it up and manhandled the body—which now didn't look anything like a human—into it. She pressed a panel once she got it fully loaded and a grinding sound started. It lasted for a minute and then silence fell. She waved her hand over the wall to her right, and the wall became transparent. His gasp of shock made her look around quickly. He ducked back and waited, fingering the Dabih power-blocking device.

A moment later, she walked past him, neither looking right nor left.

He let out his breath. The transparent wall had revealed his true location. Not just underwater, but deep under. A few strange fish, some things Ted didn't recognize as anything he'd ever seen before, and the bloody, shredded body parts of Carpenter and the two Dabih. She'd put them in something that functioned as a garbage disposal which dumped them into the ocean water. The sea life was enjoying a feast. He wouldn't be exiting that direction.

"You're in deep now, buddy," he muttered. His chances of survival seemed to be slipping away. He could be killed by a Dabih, ground up and dumped, and he could never find Adam. He started out wanting to save Adam, but Adam was now his only hope for getting out alive.

He hurried to catch up with the psycho alien women.

He wondered where she was going, but soon realized there could be only one place. She said it was only a Miran that could have followed her guard. She'd have to make sure her captive was still there and then look for the Miran she thought was wandering around.

About ten doors away she stopped. He had to back up several steps to keep from being seen as she stepped through the door. He was close enough to hear her voice, but not close enough to understand what she was saying. Within a few minutes, her voice was louder and he assumed she was back in the hall, leaving. Her last comment, he heard very clearly.

"Be stubborn, Miran. It will accomplish nothing. You'll only be able to stand the pain so long. You will beg us to listen to you. We have waited centuries to find you Mirans, and we can wait that long again. Can you bear the pain that long?" She chuckled as she went down the hall away from Ted.

After a few moments of silence, he went toward Adam's room. He had no idea how he was going to get in, or what he would do once he was there, but he had to try. If nothing else, he wanted to at least let Adam know he was there and was working on getting him out. If Adam knew that, maybe he could hold on a little longer.

He looked at the lock to see if there was any way he could pick it, but it was not a normal key lock. It was some kind of electronic mechanism. Ted thought for a minute and remembered his Taser. He imagined an alarm going off and twenty Dabih running down the hall.

He looked around, trying to formulate an escape plan. All the doors were identical. If he had to run to hide in one of the empty cells, he wasn't sure he could find Adam's door again. He took out his gun and used it to scrape a mark on the door near the floor.

As the Taser zapped, he heard a pop from the lock, and it was open. So far, no alarm - no audible alarm at least.

He found Adam on the floor. He was on his side facing the wall, with his arms holding his head and his knees pulled up to his chest, rocking himself back and forth and moaning.

He knelt on the floor behind him and quietly said, "Adam."

Adam jerked slightly and turned to look up. He smiled, but his eyes still showed how much pain he was in.

"Ted?" Adam asked as if he didn't believe it.

"Yeah, man, I'm here." At least Adam was still with it enough to talk.

"How ..."

"Doesn't matter how I got in. We need to come up with a way to get us out. Are your powers blocked? Is there some device?"

"My powers are gone, but I haven't seen them use anything," he said obviously straining. "Seems like the whole room does it. And the pain ..."

"Then I'll drag you out, and once in the hallway, your powers should come back."

"I can crawl."

Ted stepped into the hall and concentrated to sense any Dabih, but there were none close. He turned back to tell Adam the coast was clear and saw him struggling as he crawled across the floor. He looked up and tried to smile, but his smile turned to a strangled scream of pain when he got to the doorway. He fell to the floor cradling his head in his hands, scooting back toward the wall as he gasped trying to breathe.

"What happened?"

He gasped. "My brain is going to explode. They must have another pain device there."

"Shit. Probably to keep you from attacking any Dabih in the doorway."

"Yeah," he said. He continued crawling back into the room and his breathing became steadier. "They always stand in the doorway when they're here. You don't feel any of it?"

"No, I'm sure it's designed for Mirans. Okay, let me look around."

He moved slowly around the room inspecting every inch of it. He hoped he would find some kind of a panel or anything that looked like it was electronic and could be blocking Adam's powers. There was nothing on any of the walls or ceiling except an overhead light.

He tried to jump to get a better look at the light, but couldn't really see if there was more to it than there should be to light the room. Adam crawled over next to him and stopped under the light.

"Stand on my back," he grunted.

"I can't stand on your back."

"It can't hurt more than I'm already hurting. Just do it."

They didn't have any other option. He stepped onto Adam's back carefully placing one foot over his hips and the other over his shoulders. Adam didn't even budge. Miran strength. He inspected the light and found a small panel that looked similar to the locking mechanism on the door.

"Ah-ha. I don't see any switch to turn it on from here, so it's probably hooked to a central control. They'll know immediately that it's off. As soon as your powers are back, get us out of here fast."

"Right."

He pulled out his Taser and heard the same 'pop' that he'd heard from the door lock. The room immediately went dark and a loud beeping sound came from the hallway. Adam jerked, knocking Ted off his back. He tumbled and landed flat on his face, sprawling onto the floor. He felt Adam land on his back and wrap him in a bear hug, and his world spun.

CHAPTER 25

When Lexi and the others teleported back to the car in Boston, they decided to go back to Woods Hole and try to talk to Carpenter again. It irritated her that he hadn't called back after Adam had been missing for almost thirty hours. And Erik and she were both curious about his attitude and wanted to see if his emotions were really directed at them.

They had a hard time getting close to the research ship until Lexi made it clear that she was Adam's next of kin. The Coast Guard officer they found this time was much nicer once he learned that. He apologized for not having found him yet and explained gently that things were not looking good.

Lexi sniffled back more tears when she heard that. They had no idea even where to look anymore, but none of the Mirans could bring themselves to say it. She didn't even know for certain if Adam were anywhere close to where they were searching.

They got on the ship and asked someone for Carpenter, but they didn't know where he was. He hadn't been seen for many hours, but that didn't seem to surprise anyone. The research was done, his assistant gone, they all assumed he'd just gone home.

If he'd just given up on Adam and gone back to Pinehurst without even calling her, she was going to find him and give him a serious piece of her mind. Erik was even more irate than she was. He was going to report this to the university and ask that Carpenter not to be allowed to take students on research projects again. That was a big deal to a serious researcher since students usually did the grunt work.

They left the ship and were almost back to the car when Lexi felt that change she'd been longing for.

"Adam!"

Erik grabbed her around the shoulders and kept walking toward the car. She wanted to teleport immediately to wherever he was, which Erik knew, but there were many Humans around.

They got back to the car as fast as possible and drove quickly to the first spot that would conceal them. Lexi reached out to New Mira even before Erik stopped the car and materialized to find Adam holding out his arms.

* * *

Nomarr heard the alarms go off in the holding cell area and looked in question at Yara. She didn't seem as shocked as she should have been. Nomarr tapped his fingers on his desk and summoned a guard to go see what the alarms meant.

"Is that your Miran escaping?" Faru asked. An astute question. Perhaps Faru and Yara were not yet in league.

She fluttered her eyelashes. "I have no idea." She walked around his office, looking at his books and his collection of art. Faru sat back, tapping a finger to his lips, watching her. Nomarr watched them both.

Within a few minutes, one of the guards reported that the Miran captive was gone. The door lock and the power block panel both had been shorted out.

"Then he had help to escape," he said as soon as the guard left.

"Are you suggesting we have a traitor?" Yara asked.

"Possibly, or someone from outside. Could even have been another Miran." He looked at Yara and grinned.

She smoothed her slacks and glared at Nomarr's unspoken accusation. "Did Dirac have any way of knowing we captured a Miran?"

"Dirac?" It would make much more sense for this escape to be with the help of a Dabih. Mirans had never found them. It was too much of a coincidence to believe that they discovered the location of their primary installation at the same time that a Miran was kidnapped. Dirac had been getting so much bolder as the years passed. Could his arrogance have grown so much that he would again plot against the Ruling Council itself? Faru raised an eyebrow in response to Yara's question.

"It will take some careful thought to come to any conclusions," he finally said. "Leave me for a while."

They left together.

Nomarr contacted Gelar and arranged a meeting at a Human office right in the middle of Manhattan. He'd had many such private places over the centuries that had been useful in ensuring that his conversations were never overheard.

"Tell me what Dirac's been up to." He requested when Gelar came in. He still had that ridiculous looking hair color. He pretended to be Irish in the Human world. Nomarr much preferred the look of the nomadic peoples of the African continent.

"He's been up to a great deal, and very proud of himself about it. That's why I had trouble getting away from him."

"Start at the beginning."

"About thirty-six hours ago Mirans attacked all five of Dirac's installations, killing everyone except one guard that they left with a message. The Mirans felt we'd used a Human spy to abduct a Miran, and they wanted him back. Dirac was as mad as

I've ever seen him and he reasoned that it must have been you that took the Miran."

"And I'm only hearing about this now?"

Gelar shrugged. "I had no excuse to get away from Dirac. Cocky, that's what the Humans called that attitude, Nomarr thought.

"What did he do about it?"

"He had me search Terazed's files hoping I'd be able to find the phone number he once used to contact a Miran. I found it."

"Did Dirac contact the Mirans?" Hard to believe.

"Yes." Gelar smiled. "He told them about breaking away from the main Dabih organization, and that he suspected the Ruling Council had taken the Miran."

Nomarr stared at Gelar and didn't even try to hide his seething anger. He knew Dirac would someday do something to get himself killed, but this was beyond anything he imagined. How could he have been so stupid as to reveal the Ruling Council to the Mirans?

"Did you hear the entire conversation?"

"No. I actually heard none of it. He sent me out of the room, but later told me what he said because he is arrogant enough to think he was being very clever."

Nomarr slapped his hands down on his desk as he rose. His anger felt like a physical presence inside him.

"Gelar, your time with Dirac is over. Don't even report back to him. I have a new assignment for you."

"Thank you, Council member."

CHAPTER 26

Sindri hurried to the Original's common area to welcome Adam. She didn't know how he had escaped, but was overwhelmingly relieved that he was home. Then she saw Ted on the floor under Adam, and acted out of the need for haste and a little rising panic. She stunned Ted.

Sindri couldn't take the chance of Ted seeing their home. She still didn't know if he was a Dabih spy or the friendly Human he seemed to be. She didn't know how this came about that he was with Adam. Had Adam captured him somehow? Was he with the Dabih when Adam got his opportunity to escape?

She had so many questions that still needed to be answered, and the first questions had to be about Ted. They had to come to some conclusions before he could see anything or know where he had materialized. No matter what had happened with Adam, they had to reconcile the fact that Ted was genetically Dabih.

"Adam, welcome home!" she said.

"Sindri!" he answered, standing up with a huge smile as he sensed the joy, relief and welcome of all the Mirans gathered around him.

Expecting Ted to start getting to his own feet, Adam realized Ted wasn't moving. He'd been stunned.

"Why did you stun him?" he asked Sindri with disbelief.

"As a precaution. We'll keep him safe, but there are things we need to discuss."

Sindri asked two Mirans to take Ted away to a private room. She'd keep him there stunned until they had a chance to sort through everything that had happened in the last couple of days.

"Where's Lexi?" Adam asked, all thoughts of Ted pushed aside. Adam felt Lexi reaching out to be welcomed to New Mira and she immediately became the most important thing on his mind. Anything else could be dealt with later.

Adam thought his emotions in that second before she materialized would overcome him. He wanted to cry. He wanted to jump for joy. He wanted to fall to his knees with relief. All he did was smile and hold out his arms for her.

Lexi ran into his arms the moment she materialized. Nereus, Erik and Aricia materialized a moment later. All three of them felt they couldn't have seen anything that could have made them happier. Adam was home and reunited with Lexi.

Sindri had to finally break the spell of Adam's homecoming. She'd been struggling to keep her anger at Ted in check. If he had been instrumental in spying against the Mirans and had plotted to abduct Ted, she couldn't do anything except execute him.

They'd never killed a human, but was Ted really human? He had Dabih DNA, but was it a meaningless, inconsequential part of him, or was he closely involved with the Dabih and their plans? How had she grown to trust him so quickly, so blindly?

She knew how that had happened. She was falling in love with him. Eons old and she'd been acting like a teenager. She needed answers, and needed them quickly.

"Adam, Lexi," she said gently, "we need to discuss some things. Let's go to the conference room so we can all hear how you were taken and how you escaped."

"Where'd they take Ted?" Adam asked Sindri as he raised his head and moved only slightly from Lexi. "He needs to be part of this. I don't know how he got in to save me but, man, I need to thank him."

"He saved you?" Sindri asked seeming more than a little surprised.

"Yeah," Adam smiled. "Are you surprised by that? Is something else going on?" Adam sensed that Sindri was suspicious and puzzled about something with Ted. He could also sense an anger she was almost able to hide.

"Several things have happened," Sindri answered as she led them to the conference room. "We need to all hear everything before we can decide on our next action."

They settled around the conference room table and Sindri asked Adam to begin with his capture. He started by telling them about the trip to Woods Hole and his sensing of Carpenter's anger and hate.

"We sensed similar feelings from him," Erik said.

"He must know you're Miran, too," Adam said with worry showing on his face. "I wonder how much he knows about us."

"Where's Carpenter now?" Sindri asked.

"I have no idea," Adam answered. He continued his story, explaining everything that happened and Ted's involvement. "I'm still amazed he found me, and haven't had a chance to thank him or find out how he did it. Can't we bring him in on this?"

"Adam," Sindri said gently, "we're not sure how much we can trust Ted. Since you've been gone, we did a DNA test on him. He's got Dabih DNA."

"He's Dabih?" Adam asked shocked. "How can that be? He rescued me."

"It could be just recessive genes and could have nothing to do with his actions. But it could have *everything* to do with his actions. We've been told the Dabih have been using a Human spy. We conjectured Ted might be that spy and might have been deceiving us from the beginning."

"I think it's obvious that Carpenter's the spy. He's the one that handed me over to the Dabih," Adam argued.

"I agree. Carpenter's most definitely working with the Dabih, but we didn't know that until you just told us. We'll need to find Carpenter, but we need to hear Ted's story first. I'm still torn, though, on how much we want to reveal to him." Sindri looked toward Balere, "Should we meet him as Humans or Mirans?"

"I think we should all be in Miran form," Balere answered. "He needs to see the reality of what he's dealing with. We should bring him here still stunned. His emotions when he wakes up and sees us might give us a hint to his true motives."

* * *

They carried Ted to the conference room and sat him in a chair between Lexi and Erik. They all looked at the Human that knew so much about them and wondered what would happen when he woke. They all wanted to be able to trust him, but didn't know if they could.

Before Sindri awakened him, she said, "I think we need to hear Ted's story without many comments from us. Balere and I will question him."

Ted awoke as if he'd been in a deep, peaceful sleep. Opening his eyes to see himself surrounded by the tall, lavender creatures he'd only glimpsed through Lexi's window startled him and he jerked as adrenaline started to flow through him. He knew his Human fight-or-flight response was kicking in, but he wasn't going to do either of those.

He looked around with his eyes wide and his mouth slightly open and easily recognized those he knew in their Human form. Their eyes captivated him, and he couldn't stop staring from one to the other. All the twinkling lights against the deep blue background of their irises held him as the wonder of these creatures mesmerized him.

Once his initial shock started to subside, he smiled. All he could see was their beauty. He had no memory of how glorious they were when he'd peeked at them that night. He was just too shocked and scared then. The Mirans didn't scare him now, they fascinated him. He didn't think he'd ever seen anything so beautiful, and knew he was the only Human who'd ever seen it. They were magic come to reality. This sight he'd remember forever.

"You're all so incredible," Ted said quietly with obvious awe.

Sindri gazed back at him. "Thank you, Ted. Welcome to New Mira."

"Wow! What a welcome," he said looking around the table again. His smile broadened. "Hey, Adam," he said with excitement, "we made it, buddy! I'll bet that psycho-bitch had a cow when those alarms went off. She's probably still ranting and raving."

Adam laughed as he and the rest of the Mirans felt Ted's honest relief and sense of accomplishment. He was incredibly happy and excited because he'd saved Adam and because he was seeing their natural forms. They all knew his excitement and joy were real. He wasn't faking a thing. And he wasn't scared of them or intimidated. He was thrilled.

His reaction told them more clearly than any words could have that he was *not* working with the Dabih. There was no anger, fear, or disgust, no hint of scheming or pretense. Just honest happiness that Adam was back with Lexi, relief that neither of them had been injured, and self-respect for accomplishing something that could have had deadly consequences.

Sindri joined the laughter with the greatest relief of all of them. She had trusted Ted and had revealed to him so much that they'd hidden from Humans for thousands of years. If her trust had been misplaced, it could have meant the end of New Mira. It could have meant that her poor judgement had failed all Mirans.

"Ted," Sindri said as the laughter subsided, "I'd like to thank you on behalf of New Mira. When one of us is lost, we all feel that loss as an emptiness in our hearts. You've done what we weren't able to do. Please tell us what happened and how you were able to rescue Adam."

"Sure," Ted started as he continued looking around the table. He obviously couldn't get enough of the sight of all those Mirans around him.

"When I heard Adam fell overboard, I knew something just wasn't right 'cause I figured he could teleport from the water. Then I remembered all the Dabih I'd sensed from the helicopter. Did you get my message, Sindri?"

"Yes, I did, Ted. But I wasn't able to call back."

"Yeah, I figured you were searching for Adam. Anyway, I wanted to get some more information for you if I could, so I decided to question Professor Carpenter."

"Do you know Professor Carpenter?" Sindri asked.

"Nah, but I knew that was who Adam was supposed to be with. When I got close to Carpenter's cabin, I noticed him talking to someone on the deck, and sensed it was a Dabih." Ted continued his story explaining how he got close to them and heard what they said.

"How did you plan to find Adam?" Balere asked.

"I really didn't have a plan. The opportunity came up to teleport, and I took it. I knocked out both of them and started to look around but sensed Dabih coming". He continued until he got to the part about the woman killing Carpenter.

"Carpenter's dead?" Sindri asked with surprise.

"Oh, yeah," Ted answered, nodding. "I don't think she had any intentions of letting him live much longer, anyway." They all cringed when he got to the part about what he called a giant carbage disposal. Then became fascinated when he told them about being in the deep ocean.

"After that, I followed her and she led me to Adam. I used my taser to short out the lock on the door, Adam tried to leave the room with me, but they had a pain device on the doorway. So, we found the power block device on the ceiling, and here we are."

Ted smiled again at everyone around the table, but especially Adam. They could all feel his sense of accomplishment.

"I said once before, Ted, that you are a very resourceful man, but this is amazing," Sindri said. "You risked your life for Adam. I don't know how we'd ever re-pay that."

"I'm a cop, Sindri," Ted shrugged. "I was doing what I was trained to do."

"Nevertheless, we owe you a great deal."

"Did you hear anything that might have indicated where you were? What ocean?" Balere asked.

"I didn't hear a thing, but it was really different there. Not like the installation in San Francisco at all. This place was all white and seemed modern, yet really old somehow. It's hard to sort out how it felt because there were so many Dabih around. The place in San Francisco felt like any old Human warehouse, but where that Dabih teleported me, felt not quite human. I don't want to offend any of you, but New Mira feels kind of the same to me. Like it's not really part of the Earth."

"We're not offended," Balere answered. "In fact, one of the reasons we're so comfortable here is that it feels more like Mira than Earth to us. And the way you felt while with the Dabih makes sense with some information we recently became aware of.

"While Adam was being held, we got a call from a Dabih named Dirac who said that he didn't take Adam. He claimed to be the leader of a splinter group that separated from the Dabih about fifty years ago and said the main Dabih contingent had been responsible for the abduction. It sounds like he might have been telling the truth. I think you and Adam were in the main Dabih settlement and that's why it felt so alien."

"So you've been fighting two different groups of Dabih?"

"It seems so," Balere answered. "If we can believe what he said, it was Dirac's group that was abducting the Human females. The leaders of the main group, ones he called the Ruling Council, had been plotting against us and took Adam."

"I heard one of the guards call the woman Council member Yara," he said. "Maybe she was part of this Ruling Council."

"Maybe," Sindri said, taking over from Balere. She knew this part was something she needed to tell him. "We'll need to discuss the implications of all that when we have more time. We need to get Adam officially rescued soon. But, Ted, there's still one more thing that you need to know. And you won't be happy with this news."

"Does this have to do with why you stunned me when we arrived?" He looked with suspicion around the table. "I may not be able to feel emotions like you guys, but I can see that there's something going on that's not good news at all."

"Right before Adam's abduction, I became suspicious of you." Ted could hear the sadness and apology in her voice.

"What? Did I do something?"

"I couldn't understand how you could sense Dabih, so Ibon and I did something that neither of us was very proud of at the time. Now I'm horribly ashamed of it. We teleported to you while you were asleep, stunned you, and took a DNA sample."

Speechless, he put his hands on his hips and leaned back in his chair. He couldn't sort through how he fel. Hurt or mad as hell. Sindri, the woman he thought he was falling in love with, didn't trust him.

"We apologize for that," she added, "and swear nothing like it will ever happen again, but we did find something that we weren't expecting."

"Am I part Miran?" Ted wanted to be part Miran and almost smiled as he asked.

"No, Ted. You have no Miran DNA." Sindri paused as if she didn't want to say what he had. "Ted you carry some Dabih DNA."

"What?" he shouted. He couldn't help it. "You're telling me that I'm Dabih?"

"No," Sindri said emphatically, leaning toward him across the table. "You're no more Dabih than the thousands of Humans with Miran DNA are Miran. You just have some recessive genes from the Dabih."

"Can you fix it?"

"There's nothing we can do."

They all felt his devastation, how much he hated this part of him that he never knew was there. It was Lexi, though, who reached her long, lavender arm around his shoulders and held him in a nurturing embrace.

"How can you guys trust me knowing I'm part Dabih?" Ted asked while leaning against Lexi. He seemed to need that support.

"Part of your DNA probably gave you the ability to sense Dabih, but that doesn't make you who you are. We trust the man you have shown yourself to be, not a few genes that you carry around. We know you're worthy of our trust and you'll always be our friend."

"Thank you" he mumbled. "I want you as friends."

Ted had nothing else he could think of to say in response to all this. He didn't even know what to think. What if he someday turned into a Dabih?

He'd have to give this genetic revelation serious thought, so he forced himself to tuck it away. It was easier to think about a believable rescue of Adam.

CHAPTER 27

"I'm having a hard time with all this," Ted murmured quietly, moving away from Lexi and shaking his head. "I need to go home."

"Ted," Sindri started.

"No, Sindri. I just can't take anymore. When you make plans about Adam, remember that those drug smugglers were out there. They would have held him so they weren't caught." Ted finally looked up at Sindri. "I need to go home."

"You don't have to leave," she said as quietly as he'd spoken.

"Yeah, I do. I'd walk out, but I can't really do that, can I? Are you going to force me to stay?"

"No," Sindri shook her head. "Would you take him home, Balere?"

After Ted had walked out on the conference and Balere returned to New Mira, they had carefully made up all the details of Adam's rescue. They kept the story as simple as possible. They teleported Adam to an isolated spot on the coast of Cape Cod. He waded into the freezing water, completely soaking himself before he climbed up a sandy bank covered with sea grasses and walked barefoot about a mile down the road to a gas station. The clerk didn't want to let him use the phone until he explained that he'd fallen off a research ship. She had heard the reports on TV and seemed impressed that he'd walked through his door.

He wanted to make the story believable, so he called Lexi before he called the police. It was easy to show the appropriate emotions on the phone with her because he only had to tell her the truth. He was safe, he'd missed her desperately, and he couldn't wait to see her.

He wasn't sure the local police believed him when he called. He had to tell them details about the research ship and what they were studying. He reasoned that they had a patrol car on the way and were intentionally keeping him on the phone. Would anyone fake such a call to the police? He wondered if they'd gotten false reports of people seeing him. Who knew what some people would do to feel involved with an exciting news story?

When the Boston police showed up, Adam told them the whole story. Luckily Ted wasn't in the Woods Hole precinct because he wasn't sure he could tell his made up story in the face of a man who'd rescued him and then walked out on them. He kind of understood his anger, but it bothered him. Sindri had only been doing the logical, if sneaky, thing. Just as Ted had only done the logical, if sneaky, thing by bugging their home.

"Tell us again how you fell off the ship? And tell us where Professor Richard Carpenter was."

"What do you mean?" Why were they asking about Carpenter?

"Just tell us the story."

Adam repeated his story. "I'd taken that last piece of data to the workroom and was heading back to my cabin when I slipped on the wet deck. Just as I slipped and reached for the deck railing, the ship lurched in a swell. I lost my balance and went over the rail into the water.

"I watched the research ship move away. I guess no one had seen me fall. It was really cold and I started to swim after the ship. Luckily, within a few minutes though, I heard another ship.

They must have been pretty close. I don't know how they spotted me, but they rescued me."

"And Richard Carpenter wasn't around and you didn't have a fight?"

"Huh? No, he'd gone to bed I think. We got along fine. Why?"

"Mr. Carpenter is missing."

"What? Really?"

The detective nodded. "So who rescued you?"

"I have no idea. The guy who pulled me out had a hood pulled halfway over his face. He blindfolded me—which was scary. He and some other man I didn't see asked how I'd gotten into the water and why I'd been on a research ship. They told me him they'd put me ashore, but not until they made some other stops along the coast. They put me in the hold with a cot, brought me water, and left me there until about three hours ago."

"And you never saw or spoke with anyone else? Do you know what they were doing?"

"Nope."

"Could you identify the ship or the men again?"

"Maybe, but it was dark and I was freezing."

"You should go to the hospital, kid."

Adam refused. He told them he just wanted to get home and put this whole incident behind him. Lexi, Erik and Aricia showed up and eventually the police were satisfied they'd heard everything Adam knew. They drove to an isolated spot, left the car to be picked up by other Mirans, and teleported back to New Mira.

* * *

"No trace of who released the Miran has been found," Nomarr commented, which Yara and Faru both knew. They'd been arguing for hours and were all sick of Nomarr trying to blame them for the escape.

The Mirans had always been able to ruin any plan they'd made, or action they'd taken. Now, the Mirans likely knew the location of the main Dabih installation and may be making plans for an attack at any time. Yara hoped that a Miran had simply followed a guard and didn't really know where the teleport had taken him.

No matter what the Mirans were planning, they all agreed that the best way to defend themselves would be to attack first, but they still didn't know where the Mirans were.

"I've ordered our technicians to develop a new weapon," He told his co-rulers. "One that will prevent the Mirans from detecting us as Dabih."

"That will only be effective if we can find them," Yara argued. "And we need to find a weakness we can exploit." He found her voice to be particularly grating that evening.

"And I repeat," he said, blowing out his breath, "their weakness is their concern for Humans. Our new device will enable us to appear Human and we can get one of us close enough to gather information."

"They're not going to reveal anything to a Human friend," Yara said dismissively. "Your plan will get us nowhere."

"Like your plan to use a Human spy to capture a Miran?" He was privately thrilled that Yara had failed, but couldn't tie the escape to anything Yara had done. He hadn't completely given up though. If he could turn the escape around to being her fault, he could justifiably get rid of her once and for all.

"My plan worked," she answered sharply. "We had him. It was your guards that didn't detect the escape attempt."

"You go too far, Yara." He didn't try to hide the threat from his voice. "My plan won't work quickly, but after a time, my agent will get information that will lead us to the Miran settlement."

"What if the Mirans detect him?"

"We'll get a new agent and refine the technology until it does work. I'm finished with the argument. Gelar is already in place and he'll know soon if the new device works."

Faru rose, forcing Yara to stand as well. Physical positioning of the others amused him momentarily. Yara knew she'd never physically be as imposing as the two males, and she glared at them both.

"I'm concerned about Dirac," Faru said calmly to interrupt their silent stares. "He betrayed us when he revealed our existence to the Mirans, yet he is now happily carrying on with his own plots."

"You don't need to concern yourself with him"

"But I am concerned," Faru said. "If he continues his activities, he could interfere with your spy. If we get rid of him, the only Dabih in Pinehurst would be working for us."

"You make a good point, Faru," said Yara. "We need to be rid of Dirac."

"You two underestimate me, again," Nomarr said with a grin of satisfaction. He liked to catch them unaware. "Dirac's subordinates are dead, and he is in one of our holding cells. He'll endure the pain until I get bored with hearing him beg me to kill him. That may take a little time. I don't bore of such things easily."

CHAPTER 28

Adam and Lexi were relieved to get home. They'd missed classes and work but with the media coverage of Adam's supposed fall overboard, everyone knew where they'd been. She'd talked to her parents as well as Sean and Betsy several times during the whole ordeal, but they still needed to call to assure them they were home and well.

Sean told her he'd finally hired a new person after they'd been talking about it for months. The original purpose of getting someone new was for Sean and Betsy to have more time off together, but with Adam and Lexi gone, they'd realized how much they needed an extra employee.

Adam was scheduled to work the next day, but she threatened to stun him if he tried to go. He was exhausted physically and emotionally and needed to get some rest. Besides, after all the extra hours he'd put in when she was recovering from Terazed's rough treatment, she owed him.

Sean was still training the new guy on Lexi's first night back.

"Lexi Collins," Sean said, "this is Gelar Davis."

As she shook his hand, Gelar looked at her really funny, like he was analyzing something. He was about Adam's height, not as muscular, but still seemed to be in good shape. His hair was a reddish blond, and his eyes were green making him look like he might be Irish.

"Are you a student, too?" she asked.

"No, but I might enroll next semester. I haven't decided yet."

"Gelar's a local. Actually born here," Sean added with a grin. Pinehurst would have been a really small town without the college, so most of the people Lexi met had come from somewhere else.

It was obvious that Gelar was a man of few words. He also never smiled. Her first impression was that he was a quiet, serious person, which would not help him fit in at Sean's very social Coffee House. The rest of the staff were always talking and laughing. Gelar might find that a little awkward, but she was certain that he'd eventually get more comfortable.

As the night went on, though, she found out that he was a very good worker. He was polite and pleasant with customers, kept up with cleaning tables, and made sure all the supplies were filled. Sean was pleased enough with him that he went home for a couple hours before coming in again to help close.

The time went quickly, Sean came back about 11:30 p.m., and Adam walked in about 11:45. After all Adam went through, she hadn't even thought about him walking her home, but there he was, smiling at her. Sean introduced him to Gelar who asked about his ordeal.

"You're the guy that fell overboard and was in all the papers?" With all the media coverage, everyone knew about Adam.

"That was me." Adam was embarrassed. Sean seemed to recognize that Adam was getting a little uncomfortable about answering all the questions, but Lexi sensed that he was getting aggravated. He'd told his story so many times to the police, her parents, and college friends. Everyone wanted to know what happened. But it could have been much worse if he'd answered any of the questions the news media kept calling to ask.

She also knew that he felt a little guilty about lying to everyone about the whole episode, but he certainly could never tell anyone what he'd really gone through. She understood that feeling very well as she remembered her lie about tripping in the street and hitting her face on the curb. Adam's situation was so much bigger, though.

"It's time to go home guys. You three get out of here, and I'll lock up," Sean said.

They said good night and nice-to-meet-you to each other and headed out. Gelar walked the same way as Adam and Lexi, and she was afraid for a few minutes that they'd miss their usual stroll home, but he turned toward campus when they got to the corner.

"We work together in a couple days," Adam said, "so see you then."

"Yeah," Gelar answered, "see ya."

As Adam and Lexi put their arms around each other, he said, "Is that guy a little strange, or did I just get a bad first impression?"

"He's different, but a hard worker. Maybe he just doesn't do well with new people."

"Probably, but he was starting to irritate me with all his questions."

"I sensed that." She chuckled. "What did you do tonight?"

"Erik and I patrolled for a while, but didn't find any sign of the Dabih."

"You were supposed to be resting," she said, raising her eyebrows at him.

"That was resting," he smiled while leaning down to kiss her temple.

* * *

Ted sat on his couch staring at the TV with no idea what was happening on the screen. His first day back to work had been tiring and irritating. There had been a metric ton of paperwork and just as many questions about the drug smuggling operation that had sent him to Boston and about the kid who'd fallen overboard. He'd just wanted to get on with work and forget about the whole thing, but it seemed no one would let him.

All day, two thoughts tormented him. Sindri's statement, "You have some Dabih DNA," repeated itself over and over like a song he couldn't get out of his head and the fact that she'd stolen his DNA in the first place. She could have just asked.

He felt like he was the enemy. What if he became Dabih? Would he wake up one morning and look in the mirror and discover that he had bizarre eyes and some funky, green smears across his face? He'd never gotten a clear look at that crazy woman, but the little he'd seen made him cringe.

If he changed into a full Dabih like the Mirans changed, would his beliefs and attitudes change too? Would he suddenly think killing Humans and Mirans was the right thing to do? Would he find more Dabih, go to the Ruling Council, and tell them everything he knew about the Mirans? That seemed to be what Sindri thought he would do.

"You're letting this make you nuts," he said aloud as he dropped his head into his hands and rubbed his forehead.

He made himself get off the couch, go to the kitchen, and look for something for dinner. He opened the freezer and stood there staring at the little boxes of frozen stuff, but he couldn't stomach any of it. He closed the freezer and opened the refrigerator for a beer.

He screwed off the cap. "Just drink it all away. Yeah, that's a great plan."

He plopped down on the couch again reaching for the remote as he heard someone knock on his door. The last thing he wanted was company, and if it was another neighborhood Girl Scout selling cookies…

Balere stood on his porch. For a split second, he'd hoped it was Sindri, but no, she wouldn't come. Why would she?

"You seem in a pretty dark mood," Balere said.

He moved to shut the door in Balere's face. He didn't want to talk to any of them, but Balere held the door firmly open.

"What's got you so upset?" Balere asked gently.

"Oh, no big deal," he said sarcastically, motioning the Miran in. He sat on the couch and Balere joined him as companionable as could be. He took a pull on his beer. "I'm part Dabih. I could change anytime like you Mirans do and be all Dabih. The whole thing has me jumping for joy."

"Ted, we don't see how that could happen."

"Why not?" Ted practically shouted. Mirans change when they're around twenty. Maybe Dabih change around thirty? The thing is, you don't know."

"Then we'll watch you. We sense Mirans when they're still small children, long before they start to change. I think we'd easily sense that you would change to Dabih."

"But you don't know." He stared at the floor. "I have to ask you a favor, Balere, 'cause I think you're the only one I know who could do it for me."

"What?"

"If I change, if there's any hint that I'm starting to change, I want you to promise that you'll kill me."

"Come on, Ted. You're not going to change."

"It's the possibility that's making me nuts. The idea that I may turn on you guys, that I may want to kill you. I can't get it out of my mind. If I can't control it myself, then I need to know that you'll take care of it."

Balere looked at him with great sadness in his eyes. "I understand. The thought of someday turning against every one that trusted you would be hard to face. I won't let you turn Dabih. I promise you I'll take care of it."

"Great." He got up and held the door open, but Balere didn't move from the couch. "You know what my mood's about, so you can go."

"I didn't come because I sensed your dark mood. We don't do that because it feels like an intrusion to get in your head when you don't know it. I came to ask you for a favor."

"A favor? And what have you done for me recently but ruin my life?"

"We didn't do anything to you."

"Stole my DNA, didn't you? Lied to me. Made me think you trusted me."

"Sindri was against that decision. I am sorry, but I am the one who talked her in to it. You must understand, sometimes we have to protect ourselves in order to protect you."

He grunted and walked to the kitchen for another beer. After a second of staring at the two bottles left, he brought the other one to Balere, who accepted it with a nod.

"We'd like you to work with us on finding the Dabih installation where they had Adam. We think it must have been their installation you sensed from the helicopter. Do you think you could get us back to the general area where you sensed them?"

"Sure," he said as his mood finally lifted a little. "I looked at the coordinates from the chopper, but not until the buzzing started to go away."

"You know the latitude and longitude?"

"Like I said, we were past it, but I could get you close. I just don't know how close."

"Could you take some time off work and head out to that area with us?"

He chuckled softly, shaking his head. "You have no idea how good that sounds. When do you want me?"

"It'll be a few days before we're ready to go."

"I'll tell them at work tomorrow that I'm taking vacation. Hell, I've got three weeks coming."

"Good, I'll call you with our final plans." Balere got up to leave.

"Hey, Balere, thanks again."

"No. I need to thank you. I didn't ask just to be nice. We really do need your help on this." He shut the door softly.

Ted sat back on his couch. They needed him, with all of their technological magic and instant transportation. He marveled at his own excitement at the idea of working with the Mirans, again. His anger at them seemed to melt away now that he didn't have to worry about turning Dabih. Balere would take care of it.

Besides, searching for their ship certainly seemed more stimulating that filling out endless reports on cases that had to go to court. And then going to court. And then fillng out more paperwork. Besides, the Mirans had been protecting Humans since before recorded history. They were asking him to help, so how could he not want to help them?

* * *

Gelar teleported directly to Nomarr's quarters exactly as he was ordered to do. He'd been working at the coffee shop for three days and had very little information to show for it, but, after all, this was designed as a long-term operation.

"Have you met them?" Nomarr asked without any preliminary remark or greeting.

"Yes, I worked with Lexi tonight and met Adam when he came into the coffee shop to walk home with her."

"Did you get any indication that they could sense you?"

"None whatsoever. They talked to me like a Human."

"None of us has ever talked to a Miran. What did you find to talk to them about?"

"Lexi and I just talked about what we needed to for work, nothing special. I questioned Adam about his abduction."

"You questioned him?" Nomarr couldn't hide his surprise and a little admiration.

"According to the Human newspapers, he told the police he fell overboard and was picked up by a boat of people that kept him isolated and wouldn't let him contact anyone. I asked who these people were, and he said the police think they were drug smugglers."

"Interesting," Nomarr said slowly with the hint of a grin on his face. "They are so tied to Humans that they had to make up a story the Humans would accept. I hadn't even thought of that possibility."

"I found it interesting that I sensed him feeling uncomfortable and somewhat guilty about discussing his made-up story."

Nomarr laughed. "He lied to the Humans because they wouldn't be able to handle the truth, and then he felt guilty about lying to them. I'll never understand Mirans."

"After work, I followed them home."

"Really, what did they do?"

"They held each other the whole way and talked too quietly for me to hear. Several times they laughed. I think their relationship is genuine and they live in the same place."

"Are you sure they stayed in that place?"

"I didn't wait around. I can do that if you'd like."

"Yes," Nomarr said thoughtfully, "I'd like to know if they really live among Humans or just appear to."

"I'll watch them at my next opportunity."

"Good. When will you see them again?"

"I work with Adam the day after tomorrow."

"Report to me after that."

"Yes, Council member."

Gelar left Nomarr and headed for his personal quarters. As soon as he got there, he contacted Faru, who immediately teleported to him. They stood in his cooking/eating area. He made the wall transparent so they could watch the ocean's creatures swim past. Per their agreement, he told Faru everything he'd told Nomarr and the orders he'd received.

Faru thought carefully about this information. "Nomarr is thinking too small. His ideas could take you forever because he knows almost nothing about Mirans or Humans. You'll need to become their friend and see them outside of work. Maybe even get an invitation to their home. But keep giving Nomarr only the information he asks for."

"By becoming friends with them, I may also get the chance to observe the other two, Erik and Aricia. Then we'll have answers to questions Nomarr hasn't even thought to ask." He smiled and offered Faru a chocolate chip cookie.

"Exactly," Faru said, accepting it and taking a bite. "What is this? This may be our opportunity to finally get the upper hand on the Mirans, not to mention Nomarr and Yara."

"It is a Human treat from my workplace." He took a bite of his own treat. "Nomarr wasted so much of my time all these years having me work with Dirac. He should have just killed him when he first broke away from us."

"Nomarr likes to play games with his subordinates. The whole situation with Dirac and his followers was a game that he's still playing. He hasn't killed Dirac, yet. He leaves him in a holding cell. That accomplishes nothing."

"If Dirac is still alive when we take over the council, I will kill him personally." Gelar liked that idea.

"Our opportunity will come. Keep me informed when you report back to Nomarr." Faru picked up another cookie before disappearing.

As soon as Faru left, he settled down to rest for the night. He felt very satisfied that he was finally doing something that would help him move ahead to the Ruling Council. It wouldn't be easy to oust Nomarr and Yara, but he and Faru had been making plans for years.

He knew that Nomarr thought Faru was weak and simply followed Yara. Neither of them had any idea of Faru's real strength. He had gathered more information about Mirans than Nomarr and Yara ever had.

It was Faru's idea that he call Lexi about not killing the Dabih that attacked her, and Faru who decided they should tell the Mirans where Terazed held Lexi. The best decision he ever made was to align himself with Faru, and he felt certain the two of them would go far together.

CHAPTER 29

Gelar teleported from his quarters to an isolated, dark alley a couple of blocks from the coffee shop for his 6:00 p.m. to midnight shift with Adam. He'd been thinking all day about how he'd go about getting to be friends with Adam and decided he'd have to find some things they had in common. Whether they were true or not didn't matter.

He planned to question him carefully and feign interest in anything Adam brought up. It was a simple plan, but Gelar knew he'd have to be more casual with the questions than he'd been when they met. He'd sensed that Adam was uncomfortable and probably thought he'd been prying.

The most important thing was to get Adam to like him. If Adam liked him, the others would too, and he'd eventually be in position to get some useful information.

The coffee shop was busy for the first couple of hours, but finally slowed down. Adam and Gelar hadn't said a thing to each other except what was needed to be said to get the work done, so, once the opportunity arose, Gelar plunged into his plan.

"Adam," Gelar said casually, "I've been thinking about taking some classes in the fall, but I'm not sure about a major. Are there general classes someone could start with?"

"Sure. There's stuff like English, history and math that everyone takes. You can start with them and decide on a major later."

"Good. What are you and Lexi majoring in?"

"Lexi's in business and I'm in astronomy."

"Astronomy? I've thought about astronomy, but didn't know if I could handle the math. Is it tough?"

"Well, I started with calculus, but math's kind of my thing. They've got others you can start with if you didn't take calc in high school."

"I took it in high school, but it's been a few years now. I'd probably need some help getting back in the swing of it, you know?"

"They have tutors if you need them. I could probably help you some, but I'll be busy. I'm taking extra classes next year."

"How are you going to find time for extra classes with your work schedule?"

"Actually, next year will be easier since I quit the wrestling team."

"You were on the wrestling team? I wrestled in high school, but wasn't nearly good enough for a college team. How come you quit?"

"Mainly it was the time, but I started wrestling in seventh grade and just had enough of it. College teams demand a lot."

"You must be good. Pinehurst is known for their wrestling team."

"Well, you only stay good if you're willing to work hard at it. I wasn't willing to do that anymore."

"I bet you're looking forward to time off from classes this summer." Gelar smiled. "Are you going on a vacation or anything?"

"Nothing definite. We're just going to visit Lexi's parents for a couple of days when the semester's over."

"Neither of you are from here, are you?"

"No, but Lexi's parents just live a couple of hours away."

"I'm not doing anything either. I'll just spend the summer working."

"Us, too. Not very exciting, are we?" Adam laughed.

"I guess not," Gelar laughed with him.

Their conversation had been interrupted several times by customers, but Gelar felt like he'd made some real progress. Maybe he should really enroll in this college. He'd already had to make up his last name and arrange for legal identification to get this job, it shouldn't be too hard to manufacture the school records he'd need. He might look into it.

At closing time, their goodbyes were much friendlier than they'd been the other night. Gelar went in the opposite direction from Adam, but soon turned back to follow him. He wasn't really following because he knew where Adam and Lexi lived, but he needed to find out if they stayed in the apartment or teleported somewhere else.

When he got to the apartment, Gelar could sense the two Mirans inside. He hid in the shadows of the alley behind their parking space. After all, he didn't need to see the place. With the new technology, he was not only hidden from their sensing, he could sense them from almost a mile away. Developing that stuff was the one good idea Nomarr had ever had.

After only an hour of waiting, Gelar had his answers. He'd sensed the depth of their love when they greeted each other, their passion for each other as they made love, and their profound contentment as they fell asleep. He'd been right. Their relationship was real, and they did actually live among the Humans.

Gelar teleported directly to his own quarters. He wanted to think before he reported to Nomarr and Faru. Now that he was sure they really lived among the Humans, a million questions swam through his head.

Did they have a choice, or were certain Mirans placed in the Human world as he'd been? What benefit did it really have for them? Adam and Lexi both seemed so comfortable in their lives, and they interacted with Humans so easily.

It surprised Gelar that he'd sensed no lie, no deception when Adam talked about college and wrestling. He said he'd wrestled since seventh grade and Gelar not only sensed honesty, he sensed a fleeting impression of fond memories. How did Adam do that?

Gelar felt constantly on guard when he was among the Humans. He concentrated on not giving away anything that would point toward his otherworldliness. Adam and Lexi seemed to just be themselves.

Maybe the Mirans had some kind of training program. If they did, it was a good one. Except for the constant mental hum that signaled a Miran, he would never know Adam and Lexi were any different from the Humans that came into the coffee shop.

The big surprise, though, was when Adam mentioned Lexi's parents. That proved that Mirans were breeding, unless Adam just made it up, which was certainly possible. Since Adam thought he was talking to a Human, he might have simply thrown in a common Human element such as parents. He'd sensed no deception, but Gelar was getting the idea that Adam was a very good liar. Maybe all the Mirans were.

Nomarr wouldn't be interested in any of this, but Gelar was eager to talk to Faru about these questions. He and Faru shared an interest in Humans and their relationship with Mirans, and they both felt the Dabih had wasted centuries by not gathering this kind of information. Nomarr, like all the leaders of the Ruling Council before him, was only interested in killing and conquering.

After reporting to Nomarr only the information he'd asked for, Gelar called Faru to his quarters. He told Faru everything Adam had said and all his questions and concerns.

"You know," Faru offered, "none of us has ever really talked to a Miran except you. It's possible that we can't sense their deception. Maybe there are other things we can't sense in them."

"I hadn't thought of that," Gelar answered. "We've never really learned anything but the basic details about them."

"You'll have to watch for another opportunity when you're sure he's lying and see if you can sense it. Maybe it'll be the same with all their emotions."

"I never sensed a thing when he was telling me about the ship that supposedly picked him up in the Atlantic, and we're sure he was lying about that."

"Yes," Faru said thoughtfully. "That's why the work you're doing is so important."

"This is going to take longer than I originally thought. I may have to actually get a place there if I can get to be a friend."

"We'll see what happens," Faru said thoughtfully. "Maybe I could help by coming in the coffee shop as a customer."

"That might be a good idea. You could listen and sense them when I'm doing something else or when I'm with a customer."

"I'll have to wait for the opportunity to get the new devices without Nomarr's knowledge. If I show up, you just act like you don't know me."

"Good plan. By the way, Nomarr didn't give me any orders or a time to report in. I got the feeling that he's lost interest in my mission. Does he have another plot he's working on?"

Faru shook his head considering what Nomarr might be doing. "Nomarr often has more than one plan, and it wouldn't be unusual for him to keep things from Yara and me. I'll keep my eyes and ears open."

"Things will be different when we can finally get rid of Nomarr and Yara."

"Not just different. Better." With that, Faru teleported away.

* * *

Ted finished packing while he waited for Balere to call. It almost felt like he was really going on a vacation because he was only packing casual clothes appropriate for days aboard a small ship. The last time he went anywhere, he was on duty and had to figure out how to fold dress shirts, sport coats, and trousers so they wouldn't wrinkle too horribly. This was much easier.

Sometimes it worried him a little that he was starting to like Mirans more than most of the Humans he knew. That's why he'd been so certain he had Miran DNA in him somewhere. How could he be part Dabih?

No matter what his genes said, he'd do whatever he could to support the Mirans and fight against the Dabih. He just didn't see the Dabih ever giving up their fight. The hatred in Terazed's voice still rolled around in his mind. That guy had wanted to wipe out all Mirans and Humans. And the woman, Council member Yara, who held Adam. He could still hear her voice, too, and his body remembered the pain he'd felt when she'd killed Carpenter and the two Dabih. If their leaders were that ruthless, the rest of the Dabih must be the same.

Balere materialized in Ted's living room right on time.

"You ready to go?" Balere asked.

Ted picked up his duffel and paused. "How do we take my duffel bag?"

"Just hold on to it. It'll go with us just like your clothes."

"Is it okay to take my gun? I've also got my Dabih power blocker and my Taser."

"We'll all have power blockers. I hope you don't need the gun, but I was going to suggest you bring it along. If it comes down to it, we're prepared to kill Dabih, and your gun is the only weapon you have to accomplish that."

"That's what I was thinking, too."

Balere held out his arms.

Ted put his duffel bag on like a backpack and wrapped his arms around Balere. Together, they teleported directly to a cabin on a small ship already just off the coast. Even though he had teleported several times now, it still made him a little queazy.

He left his duffel in the cabin and followed Balere up to the bridge.

The narrow deck and steep ladder to the bridge illustrated to him just how small the ship really was. Two men and one woman stood in the bridge watching dials and other displays. Balere introduced them. "I think you know Ibon. This is Cascadia, she owns this ship."

He paused when he shook Ibon's hand. "You helped Sindri test my DNA."

Ibon, who reminded him of a 1940s movie star–clean cut with dark hair parted to the side–gave him a flat smile.

"I want to ask you about that later," Ted added.

"I am certain you do," the geneticist said. Ted expected his voice to be deep and resonant, but the Miran seemed to have an unusual accent. Of course, he was an original. Who knew what his native language was like.

"I've heard a great deal about you, Ted," Cascadia, a petite woman with short, ink black hair, shook his hand with a strong grip. "It's nice to meet you."

"All the Mirans talking about the Human, huh?" He smiled back.

"We all felt Adam's absence," she said, "and we all owe you our thanks."

Ted looked out across the bow and saw fancy, million-dollar homes along the coast.

"Where are we?" He asked, enjoying the view of the extravagant backyards passing by.

"We're heading straight to the coordinates you gave Balere. It'll take several hours," she explained. She turned the wheel slightly and the boat changed course toward open water. "Then we'll start a circular search pattern away from that spot. Since we're not sure how far your helicopter traveled after you sensed the Dabih, we don't know how long we'll have to search. So you can all go get settled in while I get us where we need to be."

After he unpacked his clothes in his cabin, he found Ibon out on the rear sundeck. The scientist sat with his feet up, a book in his hand.

He gestured for Ted to join him and didn't wait for the inevitable question.

"No, I didn't make a mistake. I tested your DNA thoroughly against other Dabih DNA we have gathered. You have genetic markers for that race."

He digested that for a moment. He always thought he was mostly English and a little Italian on his mother's side.

"Balere says I will not change into a Dabih."

"It doesn't seem likely."

"How do you know?"

"Conjecture, I admit. If their offspring mutated as our offspring do we'd be hock deep in Human-turned-Dabih twenty-year-olds. I think we'd have noticed by this point."

Although not a scientific confirmation, it did make him feel a bit better. He sat back and stared out at the water. The Dabih were out there somewhere. He was sure about what he'd sensed. But how? An underwater jail, maybe a submarine? Except that he hadn't heard any engines and had felt no sense of movement. The transparent wall indicated that the Dabih had more technology than what the Mirans had been expecting. If the jail, or whatever it was, moved, they might not find anything. And then what would they do?

CHAPTER 30

Nomarr called Faru and Yara to meet with him in his meeting room. His latest endeavor was ready and he said it was "The one they'd all been waiting for," which Faru doubted.

"Welcome," Nomarr said with a satisfied grin. "I have some news that signals the beginning of the end for Mirans." Faru was surprised at this grand proclamation and he could tell that Yara was, too. It was gratifying to notice that Yara had also been left out of Nomarr's plans.

"What has happened?" He asked feigning excitement.

"We finally have the resources to destroy Mirans and it is only a matter of time before their elimination begins."

"Have you found their stronghold?" Yara asked, obviously doubting that he had.

"No, I have been working in another direction," Nomarr grinned. "I sent Gelar out to test our new technology to see if Mirans could sense him. Not only has he proven that the blocking device works, he has discovered that they do actually live among the Humans."

"That's remarkable." Faru suppressed a smile, thinking of how much more Gelar had discovered.

"It seems there are just a few Mirans in Pinehurst, so a larger area would logically contain more of them. So, I've put together a first team of hunters to target Mirans among Humans. They will be based in Chicago and simply hunt the streets day and night until they find Mirans."

"Are they ordered to kill them on sight?" Yara wanted to know. She had always been bloodthirsty and anxious to start killing Mirans.

"No, they will report to me. I'd like to get an indication of how concentrated they are in an area and wipe them out in one stroke."

"The Mirans will retaliate," she stated, and he thought for a moment he might have sensed fear from her.

"They will try, but they can no longer sense us. They'll have no idea what is happening, and Chicago will just be our test area. Once we're successful there, we'll send dozens of teams into other cities and destroy all Mirans we find. They'll have no way to stop us."

"Won't they all just retreat to their stronghold?" Faru asked. "Don't we need to find that stronghold before we chase them all away?"

"That's why I'm leaving Gelar in place in Pinehurst. I'll have him watch them constantly until they teleport. I'm hoping he'll be able to follow them without being detected."

"Do you really think that will be possible?" He was shocked by this plan that put Gelar in so much danger. "If he succeeds, he'll end up in a nest of Mirans. He'll be killed instantly."

"Not if they can't sense him." Nomarr dismissed Faru's concerns. "He'll immediately teleport here and we'll then know where the Mirans are. I don't see any real danger for him."

"You must trust Gelar a great deal since so much depends on him succeeding," Yara said.

"I do. He's been of use to me for many years."

"When will your team begin hunting in Chicago?"

"They'll be in place and hunting within a couple of weeks. I'll let you two know when we're ready to proceed," Nomarr said, obviously dismissing them.

"This could be a very perilous plan, Nomarr," Yara said. "Should we not be working on it together?"

"I'm handling it, Yara," Nomarr glared at her. "Are you saying I'm not capable of accomplishing this without help?"

"I'm only saying that we might be of use." Yara's words were submissive, but she returned Nomarr's threatening glare.

"Leave," Nomarr said coldly.

They turned and walked from the meeting room without another word. Once out of Nomarr's sight, Yara looked at Faru, touched his shoulder, and teleported both of them to her quarters.

"He's left us completely out of this," she said, pacing across the floor, too irate to sit down.

"What can we do about it?" Faru remained standing in the middle of her quarters, his hands folded behind his back.

"I don't know, but we'll have to come up with something. The Mirans have always been stronger than us and everything indicates that they greatly outnumber us. This kind of blatant attack will be our destruction, not theirs. They will attack in force as soon as Nomarr starts his killing."

"I agree Nomarr is putting us in danger, but you seem awfully certain the Mirans will be able to attack us. They've never found us. How could they find us now?"

"Faru," she answered as she stared at him with a look of resignation on her face, "you and I have worked together for a long time, but we both know we've hidden things from each other and have never been completely trusting in our relationship."

"Yara, I …"

"Don't try to deny it. The time has come for honesty. I have to tell you something that will be my death if you use it against me. But it could be our salvation if we truly work together against Nomarr."

He looked at her for a moment without responding. He sensed no deception in her, but knew how good she was at hiding her true feelings. "Tell me."

"When the Miran escaped from our holding cell, I convinced Nomarr that Dirac was responsible. The truth is that another Miran followed my guard as he brought the Human spy aboard. That Miran rescued the captive."

"Then the Mirans know where we are?" He didn't try to hide the shock from his voice.

"Yes," she answered. "At least one, besides the one we captured, has been here. He blocked the guard's powers and I couldn't sense him. I don't know how he accomplished that."

"They obviously have blocking technology like we do. Did the guard give you any information?"

"He was useless. In fact, he thought it was a Human that teleported by touching him. No Human could have been involved. The guard just didn't recognize the Miran because he had somehow blocked his signal."

"This is disastrous." He considered his next words very carefully. "But there is one part of Nomarr's plan that is out of his control. Gelar is working with me."

"Since when?"

"For a very long time."

"Are you saying that Gelar is not Nomarr's puppet?"

"Far from it," Faru smiled. "He is an accomplished strategist."

"In other words, he has plans to join the Ruling Council?"

"Yes, and we've watched for the opportunity to work with you, Yara. He feels the three of us could be very powerful for a very long time." A convenient, easy lie. Once they overthrew Nomarr, then he and Gelar would deal with Yara.

"How far is he willing to go with Nomarr's plan?"

"He may not be as willing to put himself in danger as Nomarr thinks he is, but we'll need to talk to him and get an idea of what he's thinking. The news that the Mirans know where we are could change things a great deal."

"Excellent," she answered. "We need to have our own plan before Nomarr starts the killing."

"He'll contact me as soon as he returns from Pinehurst, and I'll contact you. I think he'll be pleased that the three of us are now working together."

Faru left Yara to her own thoughts and teleported to his quarters. He suddenly had two partners against Nomarr. He could use Yara's information against her, but she now had information against him and Gelar. He would have to be very careful.

* * *

Gelar delivered coffee to the cute redhead at the table by the front window. They exchanged a few words as she smiled up at him and played with one of the curls falling onto her shoulder. She flirted and seemed to enjoy the light conversation.

"So, have you asked her out yet?" Adam asked when he got back to the counter.

"What?"

"Emily," he tilted his head toward where the girl sat. "She's been in here flirting with you for three days in a row."

"That girl at the window table? You know her?" Was she another Miran? She hadn't seemed Miran. No. Gelar felt no mental signal from her.

"She has some classes with me, but I think she's more interested in you than Sean's coffee."

He shook his head. "That's ridiculous."

"Trust me. Did you see the way she smiled at you? Why don't you ask her out?"

"No, I couldn't do that."

"Look, I know you're not Mr. Social. You're a quiet guy, but I'm sure she'd say yes."

"Where would I take her?"

The Miran laughed. "Okay, we'll make this easy. We both get off at 6:00 p.m., and Lexi and I are going to try that new Chinese buffet that opened down the street. Why don't you ask her if she wants to come along? It'll be the four of us, and she already knows me and Lexi. No big deal."

"I don't know …"

"It's up to you, man, but I think she'd love to go."

"Let me think about it."

Shocked, he couldn't believe that Adam suggested he date a Human woman. He hadn't been interested in any relationship since his mate was killed in the uprising fifty years ago. He felt his anger and hatred of Nomarr and Dirac surge back to the surface. Their battle for control had caused her death.

It was after she died that he'd started plotting to destroy Dirac and overthrow Nomarr to take control of the Ruling Council. He wanted them dead to avenge his wife's death, but over the years he realized he wanted more. He'd seen too many innocent Dabih die because some would-be tyrant wanted power. Gelar wanted more than power. He hoped to make some serious changes to the Ruling Council.

The most shocking thing, though, was that he had to admit that he was attracted to this Human. She was beautiful. She had the sweetest smile he'd ever seen and deep blue eyes that he couldn't resist staring into. He'd definitely noticed her. But she was Human.

Maybe spending this much time pretending to be Human was influencing him more than he'd realized. He'd been enjoying her flirting as if he was a Human male. He'd even flirted back a little. When Adam suggested a date, he'd actually been thinking of a real date. That was ridiculous. He had to get control of his feelings and remember that he was here for a purpose.

Nothing could ever come of any relationship with a Human, but Adam had finally suggested a social activity outside of work. After all, the whole point of his mission was to make friends with the Mirans. Whether he thought Emily was beautiful or not didn't matter. He could use her to get closer to Adam and Lexi, so that's what he would do.

He walked over to refill the girl's coffee. "Your name's Emily isn't it?" he said as he poured.

"Yes. Emily Thomason."

"I'm Gelar Davis."

"Nice to finally meet you, Gelar."

"Nice to meet you, too. Uh, Adam just asked me to go to the new Chinese Buffet with him and Lexi. You know Lexi, don't you?" He was practically stammering and had to find a way to control his voice.

"Sure, I know her."

"Well, we're off work in a half hour, and I wondered if you'd like to go with us? If you don't have any other plans or anything."

"No, I don't have any plans. Chinese food sounds great."

"Okay. Lexi should be here soon. I'd better get back to work until then."

"I'll talk to you in a while."

He felt like an idiot as he headed back to the counter. He'd planned on acting confidant and ended up being awkward and hesitant. As he approached her, he'd started feeling like he was really asking her out. He had to remember that this was part of his mission. This was not a date with a beautiful woman. This was a game he was playing with the Mirans to get information. So why did he feel so distracted when she smiled at him?

"Is she going?" Adam asked with a grin.

"Yeah."

He laughed. "Don't look so serious, man. It'll be fun."

He forced a smile. "Yeah, it'll be great."

"Here comes Lexi. I'll fill her in." Adam he walked over to hug Lexi.

He watched them talking as he started a new pot of coffee. Lexi smiled and headed over to sit with Emily to wait for them. He thought about how pleased Faru would be that he was finally getting friendlier with the Mirans, but then found himself watching Emily.

He saw her eyes sparkling as she smiled at Lexi. He watched her lips move as she talked and suddenly realized he'd been thinking about how nice it would be to kiss those lips.

He mentally shouted at himself. Human. Not a female he could be interested in.

A short time later, the four of them walked to the restaurant, talking about the beautiful evening and the possibility of a storm coming overnight. After a few minutes, he noticed that they moved to walking by two's. Adam and Lexi ahead with their arms around each other, Emily and him rather awkwardly following behind. He tried to think of something to say to her.

"Where does your family live?" he finally asked.

"My parents and little brother live in Colorado right now, but we've lived almost everywhere."

"Why so many places?"

"My dad's a pilot, so he's been based out of a lot of different cities."

"Colorado's pretty far away."

"When I started school, they lived here in Pinehurst. I moved into the dorms second semester when they had to relocate again." Her laughter reminded him of wind chimes. "By the time I graduate, they'll probably have lived in three different places. You learn to be pretty independent growing up all over the place."

"I guess so."

"How about you? Where are you from?"

"Pinehurst. I grew up here." For some reason, he felt awkward lying to her.

"Really? It's hard for me to imagine living in one place that long."

"Pretty different from your life." He smiled. If she only knew where he was really from, she'd run away screaming.

The buffet was pretty busy, but they got a table without waiting long and proceeded to sample all the different foods.

"I figure we have to try almost everything the first time we're here," Adam laughed as he came back to the table with a huge pile on his plate.

They all laughed as Lexi said, "But you do know you can make more than one trip?"

"The second trip's for the things I decide I like," he said with a cheesy grin.

They all settled into tasting and talking about the different things they were eating. After a moment of everyone quietly chewing, Emily broke the silence.

"Adam, are you taking Vector Analysis first semester next year?" she asked.

"Yeah, I want to get it done before I take Galactic Astronomy second semester."

"Good, I was thinking the same thing."

"Are you in astronomy, too?" Gelar asked to keep in the conversation.

Adam answered for her as she nodded her head with her mouth full, "She's not just in astronomy, she's the star of the program. No pun intended. Gelar wants to start in astronomy in the fall, too," he added to Emily.

"Really?" She seemed pleased.

"You mean I'm the only one of this group that's not got my head in the stars?" Lexi asked. "None of you want to be lawyers?"

"Sorry, Lexi," Emily answered. "Adam and I are in a race to see which one of us discovers life out there first. How about you, Gelar?"

He almost choked when she said they were looking for life. Little did she know she was having dinner with three aliens.

"Do you really believe in other races out there?" he asked.

"Don't you? It just doesn't make any sense that we'd be alone in the universe."

"Yeah I do, but I don't know how many people would agree with us," he answered hesitantly.

"I think a lot of people believe there's other life in space, but some just don't want to admit it."

"What about aliens visiting Earth?" he asked.

"I'm not so sure about that. You know, the whole Roswell thing, alien abductions and UFOs. I think that stuff's overactive imaginations. But, hey, wouldn't it be a hoot if it was like that Men in Black movie? Aliens living right here and us stupid earthlings never noticing a thing? That could be interesting."

"Interesting, but bizarre," Adam added. "But I did love that movie. It was hysterical."

"I never saw it," Gelar said. Movies were part of the human world and he hadn't had time for such things while keeping tabs on Dirac. "Was it a comedy then?"

"Yeah. And you've gotta see it. We may have to rent it some night."

"I'll bet Erik and Aricia haven't seen it either," Lexi added. "They're not much into space movies, but I know they'd love it."

"Well, that's a tentative plan, then. These nights when none of us are working don't come along very often, but we'll get one, eventually." Adam seemed sure about another social gathering.

"Speaking of working, it's almost 8:00," said Emily. "I've got a final project I have to work on yet tonight."

"Then I'll walk you home if that's okay," he said, and wanted to clamp his mouth shut. Why had he said that?

"That'd be nice," Emily smiled. His mind went blank as he stared at those smiling lips.

"I have to have one more won-ton," Adam said. "You guys go ahead."

"Good night, you two," Lexi added. "This was fun."

"Yeah, it was," Emily said. "Good night."

"Are you really going to eat more?" He heard Lexi ask as soon as they started to walk away.

"God, no. I'm stuffed," Adam answered. "I just wanted them to have the chance to leave alone."

Gelar thought that lie had been interesting. He gathered Humans encouraged other Humans to find mates. Did Mirans do the same? He had gotten the impression that Mirans had only one mate forever and that the selection process seemed predestined.

Emily smiled at him when he held the door for her, and he stopped worrying about what the Mirans did or didn't do.

Three hours later, Gelar sat in his quarters staring at the floor, considering the conversation he'd just had with Faru. He'd told him everything because he'd known that if he even mentioned Emily, Faru would sense how attracted to her he really was.

If he hadn't mentioned her and just pretended he'd gone to dinner with Adam and Lexi, then Faru would have sensed his lie. But Emily was still a huge problem and he was still reliving their time together in his mind.

They were headed to the dorms talking about the universe, she took his hand, and they walked close with their shoulders touching. Before he knew what was happening, he'd put his arm around her shoulders and she had leaned into him. It had all felt so right. He tried reminding himself that she was Human, but he couldn't make that matter.

As they stood talking at her door, he suddenly knew he was going to kiss her. And he knew she wanted to kiss him. Her lips were wonderful, their arms around each other felt perfect and he had to make himself move away from her.

As she smiled up at him, he heard himself saying, "I'll be out of town a couple days, can I call you when I get back?"

"I'd like that," she'd answered.

They'd both said good night as he gazed into her eyes and lightly squeezed her hand. Then he'd walked away in a daze. He'd almost teleported away from the middle of campus in front of Humans, he was so distracted by her.

Faru thought it was great that he had a Human woman interested in him. She was already friends with Adam and Lexi and could help him get important information. Besides, she was their first Human connection. She could be very valuable to them.

"I can sense your attraction to her," Faru had said, "so have sex with her. We've mated with Humans before. Your mission will be over in a matter of weeks, and you'll be gone."

"Yeah. I guess."

But he didn't want to just use her for sex. She meant more to him than that. She was beautiful and sexy, but she was also funny, intelligent, and independent. She made him laugh and she made him think. He liked her for all of that, and he respected her.

Faru didn't really get it. He felt like he was falling in love with Emily. It seemed insane after one date, one kiss, but that's what he felt. He would have to take things really slow with her.

Maybe he thought he was falling in love because he hadn't been interested in any woman since his mate died. Surly he was old enough to know the difference between love and lust. He should forget Emily and look around at some of the available Dabih women. Flirting with Emily had simply reminded him how long it had been since any woman had smiled at him with interest.

Yeah, he needed to find a Dabih woman. There were plenty who lost their mates over the years and, once he was on the Ruling Council, they'd be more than interested in starting a relationship with him.

He couldn't think about Humans and Mirans anymore. He had to get some sleep because Faru wanted to meet with him and Yara in the morning. Faru wouldn't say anything more than that there was news the three of them needed to discuss, but he was too tired to be worried. Besides, he trusted Faru. His curiosity would wait until the meeting.

CHAPTER 31

Ted ate a quick lunch of cold meat sandwiches and salads on the fifth day of the search for the Dabih. When he'd first arrived, he thought this was going to be a boring, nothing-to-do-all-day trip, but that had changed quickly.

Cascadia had called them to the bridge the first afternoon and began to explain the high tech equipment that would hopefully aid them in their search. Ted had spent his days learning the basics of devices he hadn't even known existed. There were underwater cameras, active and passive sonar and satellite links to computers back on New Mira. He was immediately fascinated by the technology, but was really surprised by how much he understood. Cascadia was a good teacher.

Since the trip started, they'd been using active sonar to search the sea floor. The equipment sent sound waves through the water and received those sound waves as they bounced back. The computer would analyze each 'ping,' as the returning sound waves were called, to map the sea floor. The contours were then compared to established sea floor maps of the area. They looked for discrepancies between what was currently on the sea floor and what should be there. His job was to monitor the computer display. He'd been taught to recognize anomalies that were meaningless to their search and was surprised at how many there were.

Whales, schools of fish, floating vegetation, and debris from shipwrecks all showed up in the sonar echoes and were identified on the computer monitor. He watched for anything that couldn't be identified by the database. So far everything was easily identified, but that didn't dim his fascination. Not only was he captivated with the equipment, he was also impressed with the depth of scientific knowledge of the Mirans. Sindri told him that Mirans were in most Human careers, but he hadn't really thought about them having experts like Cascadia. She was a serious scientist, and he felt a little foolish that he'd originally thought she just knew how to run the ship.

A few hours after lunch, he sat at the computer noticing one more school of fish swimming along under them, when he started to get a headache. As he stood to stretch and give his eyes a break from the monitor, he felt the buzzing and the pain intensified.

"Cascadia," he almost whispered, "do you feel that?"

"I sure do," she said as she inclined her head trying to find the direction of the signal. "We've got them." She grinned.

"You guys sensing them?" Balere asked as he and Ibon came quickly onto the bridge.

"It seems to be coming from dead ahead and below," she said.

Ted winced. "Man, that hurts. We must be right on top of them."

"No. They're not very close," Balere shook his head. "I think your pain is caused by the number of them, not their closeness. There're thousands of them out there."

"Thousands?"

"And they're definitely underwater just like you thought."

"You've got a good Dabih sensor there," Cascadia smiled at Ted as she gently rubbed his shoulder. "Is the pain subsiding, yet?" He felt the warmth of her hand and it reminded him of Sindri. He stopped that thought immediately.

"Actually, it is." He smiled back and patted her hand. "I must be getting desensitized to them a little." She squeezed his shoulder and let go.

"We'll stay on the same course to zero in on them." Cascadia turned the boat slightly to the south.

Ted watched sensors and stared intently at the displays.

"Look at this." The computerized sonar was indicating that it had found an anomaly that couldn't be identified in the database. This was no whale or school of fish.

"Let me in there." Cascadia took the chair in front of the monitor. She started on the keyboard asking for analysis of shape, size, material and depth. Data started scrolling across the monitor as the computer did its work. Her face showed her concentration. After a few minutes of silence, she leaned back in the chair still staring at the screen.

"It seems we've found the edge of a huge object. Very deep, but the sonar signal is pretty weak. It looks to be just off the continental shelf along the continental rise."

"Any determination of what it is?" Ibon asked.

"It's still analyzing," she answered. "Damn. It's metallic, unknown composition." She spun her chair around to face them with a slight grin. "The database can't find a match to any known metal."

They all stared at her until Ted broke the silence. "Are you saying that it's some metal that doesn't belong on Earth?"

"It looks that way right now, but we need more information," she answered.

"So, what do we do?" His thoughts were swarming through his brain and he had trouble concentrating on anything coherent. Part of that was the Dabih signal buzzing through his head.

"Let's follow the contour to get a better idea of its size and shape," Balere said. "Is it too deep for the cameras?"

"We may not get anything but a shadowy image, but it's worth a try," she answered as she reached again for the keyboard. "I'm asking for a computer generated image based on the sonar findings. It won't be complete until we've finished our path around it. Meanwhile, I'll go launch the underwater camera."

"I'll come help you," said Ibon.

"Good. Ted, watch the monitor and call me back immediately if you get a signal that it's found anything new."

"I'll go to New Mira to make sure they're getting all this," Balere said. "I think we should also have some backup ready in case the Dabih detect us."

Ted looked at Balere's apprehensive expression. They could be in huge trouble if the Dabih figured out they were right above them.

"All of you," Balere said looking around the room, "if there's any response from the Dabih, abandon ship and teleport immediately to New Mira. Ted, do nothing but grab Ibon. Don't be brave."

"Don't worry, I'll grab him like I was his new girlfriend."

Cascadia made a face and then laughed. Even Ibon laughed. They went to deploy the camera and Balere teleported to New Mira.

Cascadia and Ibon returned in about fifteen minutes, turned on another monitor, and began to boot up the video software. They were soon viewing and recording images from deep below them, but there was nothing they could see except dark grey emptiness. He voiced his disappointment, but she seemed almost pleased with the images they were getting.

"It's actually clearer down there then I thought it would be, so don't worry about the live images. Once we're done and get this back to the labs on New Mira, we'll do some computer enhancement and might be able to see something."

"Can we see anything, yet, from the sonar generated image of the shape?" Ibon asked.

"Not much. We're still just following a curved edge line, but this thing must be huge."

"Guys," Ted asked, "how could they build something this big without using Earth materials? How much could they have brought with them?"

"Good questions." She watched both monitors. "We just don't know, yet. Once we get a better idea of what it is, we may be able to figure out how they constructed it."

They continued slowly collecting data for several hours. Balere got back from New Mira after being gone for only about a half hour. He'd assured that all their findings were being received by their main computer system and had arranged for fifty Mirans to be on standby to either teleport all of them at a moment's notice, or to send in a force to do battle if necessary.

Although Ted kept asking, Cascadia wouldn't commit to any firm analysis of the data until it was all in. He knew she was being a good scientist, but the logical detective in him was hungry for answers. It didn't help any that she would occasionally exhale noisily and grin at some new bit of data that only she understood. A couple of times Ibon commented that they were making a fairly sharp turn to follow the outline of the object. Each time she commented that they should keep going. Finally, she sat back in the chair and looked up at them.

"This is amazing," she said with a shake of her head. "I haven't wanted to say anything until I was pretty sure, so I messaged the lab in New Mira and we agree on what we think this object is."

"What?" Ted blurted out. He thought he was going to explode if he had to wait any longer.

"It seems the Dabih haven't built a settlement. They're living on the ship that brought them to Earth."

"No shit. That's their spaceship down there?"

"Seems to be," she answered. "It's roughly football shaped, made of materials not of Earth and is resting near the bottom of the continental rise, the slope that goes from the relatively shallow shelf off the coast to the Atlantic rift."

"How can a spaceship be at the bottom of the ocean?"

"A ship designed to keep out the vacuum of space could easily withstand the underwater pressure. You know the team that's been working on the translation of those files Lexi found in Oregon? Part of the oldest text seemed to refer to them looking for a water planet and landing in water. This seems to be where they landed."

"What would it be like to be on a ship like that at the bottom of the ocean?" Ted pondered, shaking his head.

"I was going to ask you that, Ted," Balere answered.

"What do you mean?"

"Remember Dirac? He said the main group, the Ruling Council, had abducted Adam. I think the Ruling Council is on that ship. That's where they most likely held Adam, so that's where you teleported to rescue him."

"Good God in Heaven." He whispered staring across the room. "I was on a spaceship."

"I think you were," Balere nodded, his lips pressed together.

"Congratulations, Ted." Ibon's excitement brought out his accent more. "You found what we've spent centuries looking for."

Ted could only shake his head in astonishment.

"Should we head for port?" Ibon asked Cascadia.

"Not quite, yet," she answered. "Let's use the passive sonar to see if we can get some more information on their power source and maybe their systems."

"What do you mean? Haven't we been using the sonar?" Ibon asked.

"We've been using active sonar. It sends out a signal and waits for it to bounce back. The passive sonar doesn't send out any signal, it just listens. If there's any life on that ship there'll be sound waves we should be able to pick up. It could be generated power, mechanical power, or possibly even the activity of the Dabih. Living creatures are very noisy."

Ted had been staring numbly during most of the conversation, but his brain finally registered what Cascadia was saying. "That sounds like one of those old World War II movies where the submarines had to run silently so the Nazi's couldn't find them."

"That's pretty much what it is," she answered. "If the Dabih are living down there, they're not going to be running silently. We should be able to hear them and analyze the data to get an idea of how they're generating power."

"Give me the coordinates of the center of that ship and I'll move us right over it," Ibon said as he went back to the ship's controls.

After about an hour of "listening" Cascadia had the data they needed and took over the wheel. She turned the ship toward the coast. Ted, Balere and Ibon went back to their cabins to start getting their stuff together.

"Ted?" Balere said as he knocked on the cabin door.

"Come on in," Ted answered.

"Sindri wants Ibon and me to teleport to New Mira right away instead of waiting until we reach port tomorrow. Do you want me to drop you at home, or do you want to stay aboard until Cascadia docks the ship?"

"I don't know. I guess I might as well go on home. Someone would just have to teleport me from Boston, anyway."

"You sure? Cascadia would take you home."

His wonder at the spaceship dimmed at the possibility of seeing Sindri again. "Yeah, I'm sure."

"Kind of a shock, isn't it?" Balere asked looking at him intently.

"But amazing, too. Hard to imagine Adam and I were on that ship."

"You fill Adam and the others at Pinehurst in. I imagine Sindri will be calling a meeting soon, and will probably want all of you there. Can you be ready to go in about five minutes?"

"Sure thing. I'll come to your cabin when I've got my stuff together."

* * *

The meeting with Faru and Yara had been a shocker for Gelar. He'd had no idea how Adam had escaped and figured it was Dirac. Hearing that a Miran had rescued him and that Yara was involved meant he had to seriously re-think his plans.

Faru had acted like the three of them were now colleagues working against Nomarr. Gelar had seen Yara's involvement in too many plots and double-dealings over the years to ever trust her. If Faru was now in league with her, than his partnership with Faru couldn't continue. He couldn't trust Faru if he was in league with Yara.

Faru would be coming to Gelar's quarters any minute and he knew he'd be having one of the most important conversations of his life. He was either stringing Yara along or he was changing his alliance. Gelar would have to read things very carefully to determine which.

Faru contacted him seconds before teleporting in. Gelar said nothing. He wanted the chance to judge Faru's first words to him and to hear Faru's opinions without influencing him.

"Did you enjoy hearing Yara hang herself?" Faru said, smiling and taking a seat at the table.

"She certainly did hand us the ammunition we've been waiting for," he answered slowly. "Why didn't you tell me beforehand?"

"She asked me not to so she could see your reaction. I honored her wishes so she would trust me."

"Does she trust you?"

"Probably not any more than we trust her."

"Why did she tell us?"

"Fear," Faru's grin became sinister as he continued. "She's terrified that Nomarr's plan will bring the Mirans here in force, but I don't think that's their style. She knows so little about them. But she's right that Nomarr's plan is ill advised. We can't move against the Mirans until we're ready to wipe them out."

"What do you propose we do?"

He shrugged. "We kill her."

"No," he stated and stood up. Faru squinted at him. "She's too strong and has too many followers among the various factions. Only Nomarr has the support to kill her."

"But if I tell Nomarr, he'll think that I was involved and take the opportunity to kill me, also. He's always felt I follow Yara blindly. He won't believe I turned against her to support him."

"You're right. Let me think." He paced across the room. "What if I tell him I overheard a conversation between the Mirans?"

"Could you pull that off?"

"He wants me to watch for an opportunity to teleport with them. I'll tell him I was doing just that, waiting outside their apartment, and they started talking about Adam's escape. I'll say they were expressing gratitude to the one who rescued him. I'll name Balere, the one Dirac talked to. I'll tell Nomarr he said they couldn't have done it if Yara hadn't been so easy to intimidate."

"Excellent. He will think she not only betrayed him, but showed weakness to the Mirans."

Gelar sat again, confident. "It will work."

"Will you go to him tonight?"

"No. He knows I've been here all day and would have brought him something this important right away. I'll wait until I return after work tomorrow night and act as if I was coming to him directly from the Mirans."

"That's good," Faru conceded. "I would like to see his face when you tell him."

"And, while I'm there, I'll ask him to appoint me to the Ruling Council as Yara's replacement."

"Do you think he will?"

"If I convince him that I'll be there to help him get rid of you."

"That will work as long as you remember that everything you have against me, I also have against you."

"That's what makes ours such a good alliance," Gelar smiled. "Besides, if he doesn't appoint me, then he will have to appoint one of his followers, and we'll have the two of them against us. We could have more problems than we had with Yara."

"But remember," Faru added. "Yara's smart. She knows we may decide to use this against her, and she can be very dangerous."

"What can she do without telling Nomarr she caused the Mirans to find us?"

"Kill us herself, or arrange for us to just disappear."

"Not this soon," he shook his head. "She'll wait to see what we come up with to stop Nomarr's plans."

"True. That's most important to her right now."

"But she won't be planning on letting us live very long with this information. If Nomarr doesn't kill her, we'll have to take care of her ourselves. She'll have to be the one that disappears."

"Either way, within twenty-four hours, Yara will no longer be a problem."

Faru left and Gelar spent the next few hours thinking about all the ramifications of their plans. He was confident that Faru had not turned his allegiance to Yara, but was not as comfortable with asking Nomarr for a position on the Ruling Council as he'd pretended to be.

Nomarr had always seen him as his spy, not as a co-conspirator. Nomarr would have to believe that he had never aspired to the Ruling Council, but was offering his help against Faru. He would have to convince Nomarr that their relationship wouldn't change. Nomarr would have to see it as having his best spy right on the council with him.

On top of all this, he had to go to work tomorrow and be friendly with the Mirans who could attack at any time. He'd actually been starting to like them, but needed to remember just who he was dealing with.

Thinking of Adam and Lexi, though, led him to thinking about Emily. Thinking of Emily led him to remembering their kiss. He couldn't help but sigh, as he thought about how much he wanted to kiss her again and hold her in his arms.

Of all the problems he was facing, his relationship with Emily was the one that bothered him the most. It was easy to deceive the Mirans and easy to lie to Nomarr, but he didn't want to deceive or lie to Emily.

And there was no truth that he could tell her. She might have laughed about it being fun to discover aliens on Earth, but she wouldn't think it was so funny if he told her aliens really were here and he was one of them. And, by the way, his kind is planning on taking over the planet.

The only thing he could do was end it. He'd told her he'd call tomorrow, but he couldn't let himself do that. She'd be mad and probably hurt, but it wouldn't be the first time a guy didn't call after he said he would. She'd be hurt more if she found out what he was.

And she'd be hurt a lot more if he continued the relationship, convinced her to have sex with him, and then disappeared. There was no way he could do that to her.

He'd been foolish to even ask her to go to dinner with them, foolish to say he'd call her, and incredibly foolish to hold her and kiss her. But the most ridiculous thing was sitting around feeling like he was falling in love with her.

No, this wasn't love. This was just a beautiful woman showing an interest in him after fifty years of being alone. The first woman he'd kissed since his mate died, and he thought he was in love. What an idiot. If he was tired of being alone, then he'd find a Dabih woman, not a Human.

CHAPTER 32

Once back at his apartment, Ted decided he wanted to talk to Adam. He couldn't share with anyone else his thrill/fear of being on an alien spaceship. Adam might understand. He called, but it went to voicemail, so he called Lexi and she suggested meeting at Sean's Coffee Shop when Adam got off work.

He met Lexi on the street outside and she didn't say anything, just patted his arm. They walked in and he noticed that there were absolutely no customers, which seemed like a rare occurrence even after 10:00 p.m.

"Why'd you chase all the customers away?" he asked Adam, who had his back to them as he cleaned a coffee pot. Adam spun around, ready to object and laughed when he saw them.

"When did you get back, man?"

"About a half hour ago," he answered and winced slightly, his forehead responding to a buzzing radiating through his brain.

"What's the matter?" Adam looked confused as he quickly walked toward them.

"Ted?" Lexi said at the same time.

"I can feel a Dabih's been here."

"In the coffee shop? Are you sure?" Adam looked around, his hands held out as if he were about to wrestle someone.

"Here comes Sean," Lexi warned. "We'd better talk about this on the way home."

They kept their conversation light as Adam finished his shift.

"A Dabih was really in the coffee shop?" Adam asked as soon as they got outside and started walking.

"The buzzing hit me hard, but faded quickly, so yeah, I think so."

"One of them could have been in when we weren't working. We can't sense them once they're gone," Lexi said.

"What about Erik and Aricia? Are they around?"

"No, we've hardly seen them," Adam answered. "Aricia's been sent to Boston and New York for work a lot lately, and Erik's been teleporting there after classes most days."

"But they can't sense where Dabih have been either," Lexi said. "Except for you, Ted, only the Originals can do that."

"Then we may have to get one of them in there to see if my sensing is accurate."

"Do you think they were looking for you?" Lexi asked Adam.

"I don't know, but we'd better tell New Mira."

"Balere was on his way to a meeting with Sindri when he dropped me off."

"I hate to interrupt them," Adam said. "It's not really an emergency. Maybe we should just email and let Sindri get back to us when she has time."

"Good idea," Ted agreed. He really didn't want to come to Sindri's attention at all. He scuffed at a stone on the sidewalk and tucked his hands in his pockets. "Balere thinks Sindri will want a meeting with all of us soon about what we found, so you can tell her about the coffee shop then."

"What'd you find?" Adam asked.

Adam's excitement reminded him of his own, so he teased them, saying "Not 'till we get to your place." He could tell Adam and then maybe Adam could tell Sindri. In fact, if Erik and Aricia and Lexi knew, then maybe he wouldn't have to go to that meeting at all.

Adam called Erik and Aricia and they agreed to teleport to the apartment. Ted walked the rest of the way in near silence because he wouldn't talk about what was on his mind, and couldn't think of anything else. When they got to the apartment, he found Erik and Aricia already there.

"You guys sure didn't waste any time," Ted said as they all greeted each other.

"We can't wait to hear this," Aricia said.

"Okay, guys," he said as they all sat in the living room, "I've gotta tell you the important part first and we'll get to the details of the search later."

"Just tell us," Aricia said.

"Out there, on the bottom of the ocean, we found the Dabih ship. The one they flew to Earth. They're still living on it. Balere said he sensed thousands of Dabih."

Adam jumped up and let out a yell while Lexi gasped. "Their spaceship?"

"Their ship is there intact?" Erik asked at the same time. "Did you see it?"

"Not yet, but they got video. They're going to computer enhance it, but the ship might have been too deep to get good pictures."

"How did you find it?" Adam asked, obviously fascinated.

"Cascadia, she's a scientist and owns the ship we were on, had all kinds of high tech equipment. Sonar, cameras, uplinks to New Mira. It was amazing."

Lexi beamed a smile at him. "It sounds like you had fun."

"I did," he admitted, smiling back. "But the not fun part was what Balere figured out. He says they must have been holding Adam on that ship. So that's where I teleported with that Dabih and Carpenter."

"What?" Adam's huge smile fell off his face. "They had me on their spaceship at the bottom of the Atlantic? I thought I was somewhere like Oregon or San Francisco."

"That's scary guys. There were thousands of Dabih there?" Lexi reached over to take both of Adam's hands.

"That goes along with what Dirac told Balere, and it must be where the Ruling Council is," Erik said.

"It all starts to fit together, doesn't it?" Aricia added.

"We talked to Sindri a couple of days ago," Erik said. "There've been no reports of Dabih anywhere. No hunters at all. It looks like all we've been fighting was the group that broke off. We killed all we found, but that couldn't have been all of them. I wonder why they've stopped."

Erik's casual mention of killing Dabih made Ted shudder and remember the Dabih lady who killed Carpenter and two of her own kind. What an ugly way to die.

"Hey, Ted thinks there's been a Dabih in the coffee shop," Adam said.

"Does New Mira know?" Erik asked.

"We decided to email Sindri," Lexi answered. "She's in a meeting with the Originals and we didn't want to interrupt. I'd better do that now. Hand me your laptop, will you Adam?"

"Do you think Sindri will want us to meet tonight?" Aricia asked him.

He hoped not. "No, the ship won't be in port until morning, and I think she'll wait for Cascadia. Unless she wants to talk to us about the coffee shop."

"Balere may want to come see what he senses," Erik said.

Ted left Balere a voicemail, adding that he didn't think Sindri needed to be bothered with this development. After disconnecting, he caught Lexi giving him a perplexed look.

* * *

Lexi finished her first final exam and headed for work. Finals made her think about the end of the previous semester, and she couldn't believe that everything had changed so much in just a few months. The unexplained changes she went through seemed a lifetime ago. Now, she felt like she'd always been Miran and always loved Adam.

She worked with Sean that afternoon, which was always fun. He knew everyone in town, both the college people and the locals, and joked and teased all of them. She could spend a whole shift laughing when she worked with him.

She wondered what was going on between Ted and her progenitor. Sindri hadn't emailed back yet. She hoped Ted at least got in touch with Balere so the two of them could come in to check whether or not a Dabih had been in the coffee shop. Whether they were looking for Adam or not, a Dabih being in Sean's wasn't a coincidence. They had to be up to something.

The afternoon went quickly with all the students in the shop, studying for their finals. She hardly had a chance to see if she felt any Dabih and Ted and Balere hadn't shown up. She was glad for the assistance when Gelar came in about 4:30. She hadn't seen him since they'd had dinner with him and Emily, and she wanted the chance to talk to him.

"So, Gelar," she asked when they got a quiet moment, "what did you think of Emily?"

"She seems like a really sweet girl," he answered without any emotion.

"Yeah, she is." He acted like he didn't want to talk about Emily, but she couldn't resist asking him about her. Maybe he was just being shy. "Are you going to see each other again?"

"I don't think so," he said looking away.

"Oh, I thought you seemed to be hitting it off."

"Look, Lexi, I'd rather not talk about it, okay?"

"Sure. I didn't mean to pry." She went over to clear some tables. He seemed so upset. This was more than him being shy about a girl he liked. She'd seen Emily on campus that morning and she acted like they'd gotten along great and said he had asked if he could call her. She wondered what had happened.

Ted and Balere finally came in. Lexi smiled at them and immediately noticed the pain on Ted's face.

"Are you sensing someone?" She whispered to him.

"Yeah, and it's stronger," he answered. "Balere, you got anything?"

Balere concentrated for a moment. "Nothing," he finally said shaking his head.

"Why don't the two of you have a seat? Adam should be here any time."

She watched Balere and Ted talk while she got an order ready and it was obvious that Ted was still uncomfortable. Why would he be feeling a Dabih so strongly when the rest of them, even Balere, felt nothing?

Gelar had been working in the storeroom and finally came out to the counter. She took Ted and Balere refills, but then a bunch of fraternity brothers came in, loudly talking about their English final. When they cleared, the shop seemed quiet. Wanting to get Gelar out of his shell a little more, she walked him over and introduced him to Ted and Balere. They greeted each other and shook hands. As Ted took Gelar's hand, he cringed.

"Are you okay?" Gelar asked.

"I think I'm getting a migraine," he answered.

"Those can be rough." Gelar looked thoughtful but didn't say why. He excused himself and went back to work.

"Ted, what's wrong?" She whispered to him.

"My brain is telling me he's a Dabih," Ted whispered back.

Lexi looked at Balere and he shook his head. The two of them felt nothing. Adam came in and knew right away that something was wrong.

"What's going on?" Adam asked.

"We shouldn't talk here," Balere said.

"I'm done in about five minutes," Lexi told them.

"I think I need to wait outside. I'm having a hard time around that guy," Ted answered as he glanced over at Gelar. Lexi could see the pain and confusion on his face.

"Adam and I will come outside with you," Balere said.

The three of them left and Lexi went back to help the next customer. She could hardly wait for Sean to get there and thought about leaving at 6:00 p.m. even if he hadn't come in yet. But Sean showed up a few seconds later and she quickly left. Adam, Balere, and Ted were waiting around the corner.

"I called Sindri," Balere said. "She's going to meet us at your apartment."

They walked home as quickly as possible. Lexi could easily sense the worry and confusion in Adam and Balere, but purposely reached out to sense Ted. He was scared. She didn't understand what, but something was really scaring him. He was so miserable, she couldn't resist taking his hand to offer him some kind of comfort. Adam raised an eyebrow at her but didn't make any comment.

Sindri opened the door for them. She hadn't seen Sindri since Adam's rescue, so it was good to find her waiting in the living room.

"Hello, everyone," Sindri said calmly. "It's good to see you again." Ted tried to hang back in the doorway, but Lexi pulled him in. He stood in the corner and didn't say anything. Everyone else sat and she offered them beverages. No one wanted anything because we were too anxious to hear what Ted was feeling.

"Ted," Sindri said looking at him with care and concern in her eyes, "Balere said you felt a Dabih in the coffee shop. Was it different from what you've sensed before?"

He cleared his throat and straightened his shoulders. "No. The same as what I've always sensed."

Sindri tilted her head and gestured to the chair next to her. He sat but didn't relax. "But no one else can feel it," he added a moment later.

"So, there's something different about this guy."

"Or something different about me," Ted said avoiding Sindri's eyes. His upset made them all twitch.

"What could be different about you? What's scaring you like this?"

He looked at her for a moment and then dropped his head into his hands. "What if this isn't really sensing a Dabih? What if it's the beginning of me changing into a Dabih?" He was so incredibly miserable, Lexi's heart ached for him.

"Ted, look at me," Sindri said gently. When he didn't move, she took his chin in her hand and raised his face toward her. "I sense nothing in you that indicates you're Dabih or changing into one."

"Then what else explains this? That guy's not Dabih. Adam and Lexi have been working with him for weeks. Balere sensed nothing. No Dabih has ever been in there."

"I've been thinking about that since I received Lexi's email and Balere's report," Sindri said as she let go of his face and sat back in her chair. "I think he might be like you. He might have Dabih DNA and you're sensing that."

"Wouldn't you guys sense that, too?"

"Ted," Sindri smiled warmly, "we didn't sense you."

"You really think that's it?"

"Yes, I do. Balere, can you think of any other explanation?"

"No, that's got to be it," Balere said. "I wonder if Gelar can sense Dabih, but doesn't know that he can. He told Ted migraines can be rough. Maybe he gets a buzzing headache, too."

"There's no way we can find out except by revealing ourselves and the Dabih to him. We can't very well do that," Sindri said.

"But maybe Adam and I can at least find out if he gets headaches," Lexi offered.

"That may give us some indication." Balere nodded. "But it's likely he's never encountered a Dabih."

"I wish we could find out for sure," Ted said, rubbing his face.

"Are you already tired of being the only Human that knows about us?" Sindri teased.

He looked at her and finally relaxed. Everyone relaxed as well.

"Not really." He finally smiled back. "In fact, I like you guys a lot. I don't think I want to share you with other Humans."

Sindri laughed. "We like you, as well. And we aren't about to share you with the Dabih. Which reminds me, we have some information about the Dabih settlement but we can't all get together until late tomorrow. Would 9:00 p.m. work for everyone here? I've already checked with Erik and Aricia."

They all agreed to the time. Adam would have to ask Sean if he could leave work early, but that shouldn't be a problem. Gelar would probably appreciate the extra hours.

"Ted, I have a few questions to ask you before the meeting," Sindri said. "How about if I escort you home so we can talk?"

"Alright," he answered, but stopped smiling.

Sindri rose and they said their farewells. "We'll see the rest of you tomorrow."

Lexi sensed the relief Ted felt at the explanation, but he still seemed tense. She wished he would trust Sindri. Mirans all trusted their leader implicitly. If Sindri wasn't worried, Lexi couldn't see any reason Ted should be.

Ted and Sindri left, Balere stayed only long enough to say good night before teleporting back to New Mira and Adam and Lexi were finally alone.

"Do you think Ted has his arm around Sindri, yet?" Adam asked after he ordered pizza.

"I don't know if he's worked up enough nerve." She laughed. "Maybe she'll make the first move. On second thought, maybe inviting herself to his place was the first move."

"You think he'll tell us," he asked with a grin, "or will they keep it to themselves for a while?"

"I don't know, but I hope they do get together. They seem to be a good match."

Uprising

CHAPTER 33

Ted and Sindri walked silently for several minutes. Finally, he found the words he needed to say.

"Sindri, I don't know you enough to assume what you're feeling–I mean, you have the advantage over me in that area–but I thought we were starting something."

She paused under a streetlamp, its yellow light made her look tired.

"What do you mean? Nothing has changed between us."

He grunted. "At least you think that I'm not going to turn into a Dabih. That's something I guess." He put his hands in his pockets and they continued to walk.

She put her hand on his arm gently and said, "I only told you the truth. We would know if you were becoming Dabih."

"You'd tell me if you start to sense it?" He could feel a little of that apprehension coming back.

"Of course I would. I couldn't hide anything from you."

"Only DNA testing."

She sighed. "I wish you would forgive me for that."

He gave her an exasperated look. "I understand it, I guess. I…" He blew out his breath.

"Ted," she said as she took his arm and walked toward his house. "It's going to be okay. I should have asked you for a DNA sample. I felt in my heart that I could trust you, but had to act to protect all the Miran people. I'm sorry I hurt you."

The warmth of her arm entwined with his made him relax a little. Maybe she did trust him. They reached his door and paused, unsure if she wanted him to invite her in or keep their relationship–whatever it was–casual. He opened the door and waited.

She gave him a small shake of her head, grinned, and sauntered in.

And he thought human women were complex.

* * *

Gelar left work thinking of how he would approach Nomarr. He had to convince him that he'd overheard the Mirans talking about Yara's treason and be persuasive enough to get an appointment to the Ruling Council. That would be the more difficult part and Nomarr would have to believe that he hadn't been planning a position on the Ruling Council all along.

He walked over a mile away from campus before teleporting to give himself time to think things through, but also because he chose a different dark spot each night. If a Human accidentally saw him teleport, he didn't want to take the chance of that same Human ever seeing him again.

He'd gotten into an area with several restaurants and bars. There were way too many people around to teleport, so he kept walking. Turning a corner onto a side street that he hoped would be more isolated, he felt the presence of a Miran.

He knew immediately that this was a very strong Miran, like that guy that had come into the coffee shop with the Human named Ted. Ted was another issue Gelar needed to think through and talk to Faru about.

He had no doubt that Ted was Human. Nothing about him was similar to Mirans, but he sensed something extra that was not Human or Miran, something that he hadn't noticed until they shook hands. Something he had never encountered before.

Ted had flinched when their hands touched, and he had felt a subtle power pass between them. For a second, he had been afraid Ted had sensed that he was Dabih, but that was impossible. Humans couldn't sense Dabih or Mirans.

He had been with a Miran that was incredibly more powerful than Adam or Lexi, and now he sensed another Miran with that same level of power. Why were there two such powerful Mirans in Pinehurst tonight? He followed at a distance, just close enough to continue sensing the Miran. From a block away, he saw them stop in front of a house. It was Ted and a powerful, female Miran. They went inside and a few moments later he felt a surge of Miran power. The Miran was gone and Ted was still there.

The Miran had teleported, presumably in front of the Human. Had Mirans revealed themselves to Humans? Is this how Mirans were reproducing? Did they actually have relationships with Humans, reveal their true identities and produce children? Had they done something to this Human? Is that why he felt different? He would have to watch Ted very carefully.

But not just then. He slipped in the shadows between two houses and teleported to his quarters. In a split second he knew he wasn't alone. Someone was sitting in the dark waiting for him. Yara.

"Good to see you Gelar," she said as she turned on the light next to her. "I'm afraid I have some bad news."

He saw her satisfied, almost sinister smile as his eyes adjusted to the light. "Bad news?" he asked.

"Yes, it seems our good friend Faru has disappeared."

He'd had years of experience hiding his reactions, but this time it took every ounce of his practiced control. He knew instantly that Faru hadn't just disappeared. Yara had killed him.

"No one knows what happened to him?" he asked with no emotion.

"Nomarr seems to think you killed him." Her feigned innocent look didn't fool him for a moment. She had put that thought in Nomarr's mind.

"Why would he think that?"

"How would I know? But I do know he wants to see you immediately."

"Then I should go." He gathered his powers to teleport to Nomarr.

"Not quite yet," she said as she tilted her head with a calculating expression on her face. "You should know that I recommended you as Faru's replacement on the Ruling Council."

"Was that before or after you told Nomarr I killed him?"

She feigned surprise and innocence. "I have no reason to betray you. It was after Nomarr told me his suspicions. I don't know why he suspects you, but I told him you would have had a very good reason to kill Faru. If you did it. I told him that if he found your reasons valid, you could be a valuable asset to the Council."

"And why would you want me on the council?"

"Because Nomarr believes you are his puppet, but I know you have already plotted with Faru against him. What better position could we be in to overthrow him?"

He squashed any thought of choking her and said, "I shouldn't keep Nomarr waiting. I'll contact you after I've talked to Nomarr."

She gave him a look that Gelar knew was supposed to be questioning, but ended up evil. "So confident that he will believe any story you come up with?"

"Yes." He teleported away before he did something rash.

He settled in the outer office for a moment and tried to center himself before asking for Nomarr's permission to enter. There would be no point in denying that he'd killed Faru, even though he hadn't. Nomarr hated nothing more than for someone to prove him wrong, so he was willing to let him think he was right. The only acceptable reason for Faru to be instantly killed was treason. He would have to accuse him of betraying the Council, but the details of the betrayal would have to wait until Nomarr gave him some clues. Thinking quickly had saved him many times before, and he'd have to rely on his quick reasoning and believable lies. Otherwise, Nomarr would kill him.

He asked for permission to enter and approached Nomarr with the same submission that he'd always shown.

"Why did you kill Faru?" Nomarr asked before Gelar had a chance to even greet him.

He forced a look of surprise and admiration to his face as he said, "You amaze me, Council member. How could you already know what I was coming here to tell you?"

"He teleported to Pinehurst and disappeared. Who else should I suspect?"

"No one, sir. I did kill him." He was often amazed at how simple it was to manipulate Nomarr. All it took was a little flattery and he spilled vital information. The mention of Pinehurst was all the hint he needed. His mind easily formulated the lie that would convince the Council member that Faru had to die immediately.

"I knew I was right," Nomarr grinned arrogantly, "but why?"

"Faru came to the coffee shop on the pretense that he wanted to help me study the Mirans. As I moved closer to him to quietly tell him his help wasn't necessary, Faru grabbed the power blocker that I wear on my belt and turned it off."

"He revealed you to the Mirans?" Nomarr's shock was genuine.

"He tried. He failed because he was stupid. I was working with the owner, Sean, and the Mirans weren't there. Naturally, Sean noticed nothing."

"How did you kill him without the owner knowing?"

"Many of the Humans that come in are visitors to the college and often ask for directions. I simply told Sean he was asking for directions and I was stepping outside with him to show him the building he needed. I had lightly stunned Faru so he couldn't teleport away from me, forced him outside to an isolated area between the buildings, questioned him, and killed him."

"What did he tell you?"

"That your policies are insane. That my study of the Mirans is useless. And that he would welcome me in an alliance against you."

"Who else would be in this alliance?" Nomarr obviously hoped he'd named Yara.

"He named no one else, Council member."

Nomarr stroked his scarred chin and paced for a moment, obviously thinking. Gelar stood at attention and kept his mouth shut. Nomarr sat at his desk and punched some buttons into his console.

"Congratulations, Gelar, you have just earned yourself a position on the Ruling Council."

"Sir, that was never my intention," he said with faked astonishment.

"I am aware of that. You have the skills of one that serves well, not one that leads. But I need you to now serve me on the Council."

"Whatever you wish me to do, Council member."

"Then it's settled. I will announce that Faru was found guilty of treason and Council member Gelar will take his place. I am sure that Yara will be furious when she hears this news. She has plotted with Faru for years, so you'll have to be careful of her."

"Do you want me to continue in Pinehurst?"

"Yes, and I want you to watch them every night as they go to their home. Eventually they will teleport to their headquarters, and I want you to follow them there."

"Are we ready for that?" This time his surprise was real and he let it show.

"Yes. They won't sense you. Find their location and immediately teleport back here to report to me. Then we can proceed with the rest of my plan."

He made himself smile as if he liked the plan. "Should I assume the rest of the plan involves attacking their headquarters?"

"As a Council member you will learn never to assume, but in this instance, you're right. We will attack them as soon as we know their location."

"That will be enjoyable."

"You can leave me now," Nomarr said, waving his hand while looking at his console.

"Thank you, sir."

CHAPTER 34

Ted sat for several minutes after Sindri left, feeling her in his arms. The brief kiss she gave him still tingled on his lips. His whole brain buzzed with her. Suddenly he snapped out of his thoughts of Sindri and realized that he'd been feeling a Dabih since they'd arrived at his house. He'd been so distracted by his feelings for Sindri that he hadn't noticed. It felt now like a Dabih was right across the street.

He went out his back door, walked quietly across his neighbors' dark yards, and glanced around a porch two doors down from his own house. Just outside the glow of a streetlight, there was a man who seemed to be staring at his house. He couldn't see enough to identify him, but he kept watching.

He sensed that this man was Dabih, but didn't really trust himself after the business with Gelar. And Sindri would surely have known if a Dabih had been following them. Something had changed his sensing and, no matter what Sindri and Balere said, there was still that nagging feeling that this may mean that he was changing.

As he watched, the man walked between two houses, still avoiding the streetlight. A few seconds later, he felt a surge of power that signaled the Dabih teleported. He watched the man disappear. With that, all of his doubts were gone. This was not another false sensing like the one with Gelar. This guy was Dabih. But, for some reason, even Sindri hadn't sensed him.

* * *

Gelar returned to his quarters and contacted Yara. Once she arrived, he told her everything that he and Nomarr had said. At this point he knew he had to convince Yara they were working together while he still acted like Nomarr's puppet. The reality of the situation, though, was that he was now on his own.

Yara had acted like she was very pleased with how things had turned out. She even congratulated him and called him 'Council member.' But he had no doubts that she was already plotting his death.

Once she left, he sat at his table and stared at the container of cookies he'd brought home from the coffee shop. There were so many things to balance; keeping his true identity secret from the Mirans, assuring that Nomarr still believed he was nothing but a mindless servant, and keeping a careful eye on Yara.

He may still need to tell Nomarr that she'd been involved in Adam's escape, but not yet. He'd been working with Faru for many years and realized that things would be much more difficult without him as a coconspirator. Faru would be missed, but he had no time to mourn.

If he moved too soon against Yara, Nomarr may start to believe that he had lied, and that he'd actually killed Faru to be appointed to the Ruling Council. Nomarr would kill him instantly if that happened unless Yara killed him first. Neither of them would hesitate to kill him. His safest course of action, then, would be to do away with them at the same time.

More than anything, he knew it was finally time to move swiftly and decisively. After fifty years, the time to attempt a takeover had finally come. To accomplish that and establish himself as the head of the Ruling Council, he would need supporters.

He knew those who had aligned themselves to Faru. There were several military officers who felt their centuries-old plan for taking over this planet needed to be modified. Now that Faru was gone, he needed to meet with them, gain their trust, and convince them to find others that also wanted change.

The first one he'd need to contact was General Kalti, who many, including Faru, trusted. If he could win the trust of Kalti, the others would follow. Without Kalti's alliance, anything he planned would eventually fail. But first, he had to find a meeting place off the ship. Nowhere on board would be safe for the conversation he needed to have with Kalti.

After getting these plans formulated in his mind, he tried unsuccessfully to get some sleep. Each time he closed his eyes, he felt the weight of these conspiracies closing in on him. Until he was able to align himself with Kalti, he was alone. There was no one else he could trust, no one he could be honest with.

He realized he was more honest with the Mirans and Humans than with his fellow Dabih. Sure, he hid the fact that he was Dabih–and that was a significant thing to hide–but otherwise he treated them as friends, and they treated him as a friend. He had actually started to like Adam, Lexi, Sean, and Betsy.

And Emily. No matter how much he told himself he couldn't pursue any relationship with her, he still couldn't get her out of his mind. He could easily convince himself that seeing her again would help him get closer to the Mirans, but the reality was that he wanted to see her. He needed to see her.

He wanted so badly to kiss her again, but he'd also started thinking of her as someone he didn't have to fear. He had to consider every Dabih as someone who may plot against him and every Miran as a dangerous enemy. Emily was safe, and he so needed to feel safe. If only for a little while.

* * *

The time for the meeting about the Dabih spaceship came and Ted met everyone at Lexi's apartment. Without any more than simple greetings, Adam and Lexi changed to their Miran forms. Lexi held her arms wide to hug him for teleporting.

He looked into Lexi's eyes and hesitated.

"Ted," she asked gently, "are you uncomfortable with my Miran form? I can stay Human to teleport if you'd like."

"No," he said quickly, "I love seeing your Miran forms. It's nothing, really."

He moved into her arms so they could teleport. He really did love seeing their Miran forms, but seeing Lexi about to hug him had made him think of Sindri. He'd only hesitated for a second as he remembered how Sindri had felt in his arms. Hugging Lexi was just a hug. Hugging Sindri was so much more.

They gathered in the conference room and settled around the table. Sindri introduced Cascadia and then got down to business.

"You all know the basics of what was discovered at the bottom of the Atlantic," Sindri started, "but we've had a chance to analyze the data and come to some conclusions. Cascadia, would you tell everyone what we've found?"

"Yes," Cascadia said, "I'd love to. First of all, the data supports our original conclusions. That is a Dabih ship resting on the sea floor. It is made of materials that are not available on Earth, so it must be the craft that brought them here.

"The passive sonar revealed quite a bit of energy being used, but we couldn't determine the source. There was also a lot of noise from movement, both mechanical systems and Dabih. But it was the active sonar that gave us a representation of the overall shape and position of the craft."

Cascadia used a remote control to activate a large monitor mounted on the wall and continued speaking.

"As you can see from the display, it is roughly oval in shape, almost like a flattened American football. It rests on a plane that is part of the Continental Rise. The slope of the rise is rather steep above it, but falls off quite sharply below. That implies that the spot was chosen carefully. This doesn't seem to have been a crash or an emergency landing.

"The next images are from the cameras. We digitally enhanced the pictures to get as clear an image as possible, but it is still difficult to see much detail. What is surprising about the craft is that there is no sea life on it.

"Any object left in the sea for even a short time, becomes covered by life, but something is keeping it from settling on the ship. We don't know if that is some kind of energy through the hull, or if it's the material the ship is made of. There is, as you can see, a great deal of sea life on the natural rocks around the ship."

"The question now becomes, what do we do with this new information?" Sindri asked the room.

"Have we discovered any way to contact them?" Erik asked.

"No," Cascadia answered him. "It's just too deep."

"Was there any indication that they know they were detected?" Ted asked, twisting in his seat to look between the display on the wall and Sindri. Sindri, he noted, looked regal in her Miran form. She looked regal in her human form too. He pulled his thoughts back to the topic.

"Nothing that we can determine," Cascadia said.

"If they know we found them," he continued, "they would expect us, I mean you, to attack. That's what they would do."

"Yes, but we won't do that," Sindri said.

"Oh, I know you won't," he said shaking his head, "but I'm concerned that they may feel a need to launch a first strike against us or, you I mean."

Lexi laughed at him. "Us is fine, Ted."

He felt himself blush.

"But they don't know where we are," Cascadia said.

"They know where some of us are," Ted answered.

"I've had some of the same concerns," Balere said. "I've been wondering if there's a way we could go aboard their ship, just a few of us, and attempt communication with them. Since you're the only one who has walked through the corridors of that ship, would you be willing to work with me on seeing if anything like that might be reasonable?"

He shuddered.

Balere raised an eyebrow in question.

"There's a lot of water between that ship and the surface, and I didn't see any easy exits."

Balere started to say something, but Ted held up his hand to stop him. "I'm in, especially if we have teleportation backup. With our power-blocking weapon, we might be able to come up with a satisfactory plan."

"I'll contact you and we'll work on something."

He nodded.

"Another situation has arisen that most of you don't know about," Sindri continued in her usual businesslike way. "As you do know, we've been sensing no Dabih activity recently. That changed last night. Ted sensed a Dabih outside his home, but thought he may be mistaken like he was when he sensed a Dabih in the coffee shop. He became certain that this was a Dabih when he felt a power surge and saw the Dabih teleport."

"Did the Dabih do anything?" Erik asked.

"No, he was only there a few minutes. Seemed to be watching my house."

"What concerns me," Sindri continued, "is that I teleported away from Ted's house just moments before he became aware of the Dabih. I sensed nothing."

"Is it possible the Dabih materialized after Sindri left?" Adam asked, looking at Ted.

"I don't think so," he answered. "I realized I'd been feeling a slight buzzing for some time, but … I guess I was distracted." He knew there was no hope of hiding his embarrassment from the Mirans.

"That's alright, Ted," Sindri smiled. "Everyone here has sensed that our relationship is more than just business."

That really didn't help his embarrassment one bit. He was still working on the idea that they had any kind of a relationship, but now he finds out that all the Mirans were already comfortable with it. He didn't know how they lived with sensing each other all the time.

"I should have sensed that Dabih miles away," Sindri continued. "What could have kept me from sensing him?"

"They've been able to block our powers," Lexi spoke up, "and we're able to block theirs. Is it possible that they could have developed something that would keep us from sensing them?"

"Something that is designed for Mirans," Erik added. "Not Humans," he nodded toward Ted.

"If that's the case," Ted said, looking at Adam and Lexi, "then I think we have to consider the possibility that Gelar is a Dabih."

Lexi paled. "You're probably right."

"That changes everything," Adam added.

"We can't let him know we're suspicious of him," Balere said. "We need to know for sure before we make any move."

"We could use the power block. We'll know right away if we surprise him with it," Adam suggested.

"But we may not be able to get him to tell us what he's doing," Balere answered. "I'd rather we watch him for a while to see if he gives anything away."

"We'd be glad to watch him, but what should we watch for?" Lexi asked.

"Why don't you try to get some personal information, and we'll see if he has legal records and that kind of thing."

"We know some of it," Lexi offered. "He says he was born in Pinehurst and lived there all his life. And I know Sean wouldn't hire someone without the right paperwork."

"I can run a background on him from the station," Ted offered.

"Aren't you still on vacation?" Lexi asked.

He shrugged.

"Good, we can start there," Balere said nodding. "We'll check deeper than an employer would. If he's Dabih, Ted and I should be able to find out if his records are fakes."

"Meanwhile," Sindri looked at each of them, "be very careful. Try not to be alone with him. Even Humans can protect you. He won't want to reveal himself in front of them."

CHAPTER 35

It was so frustrating to always be waiting for the Dabih to do something. Before Lexi's change it had been the same pattern for years. Dabih tried to abduct college girls, and Mirans tried to stop them. That was scary, but it all changed when Gretchen escaped. This was much worse because they were now targeting Mirans.

Worry about what they might do was always in the back of her mind, but that was mainly because all their activity had settled around Adam and her. She decided, though, that worrying and fretting weren't going to change a thing. She was determined to concentrate on her life with Adam.

The semester had finally ended. Neither of them had to work on Monday, they had no classes, no studying, and summer classes wouldn't start for two weeks. They also had no plans for the day. Lexi was doing some cleaning while Adam was doing laundry in the basement when she was struck with the most horrendous feeling she'd ever experienced.

She suddenly felt a deficit. Something was missing that she couldn't identify. It wasn't anything with Adam or anyone else she cared about, but it was so intense, it almost became painful. She tried to sort through what was going on. Adam ran up from the basement.

"Lexi, do you feel that?"

"I sure do. What is it?"

"I don't know. I'm calling Erik."

Erik answered on the first ring. He and Aricia had the same feelings, but also didn't know what was going on.

"We've never sensed this before," Erik told Adam. "I can't help but think something horrible has happened. I'm calling New Mira and I'll get back to you as soon as I can."

The phone finally rang about ten minutes later, but it wasn't Erik. It was Balere, summoning them to New Mira. They teleported instantly.

They materialized in the room where they had their joining ceremony. That day, the room had been filled with joy, but today was very different. Lexi sensed worry, confusion, and profound grief from the many Mirans around the room. Erik and Aricia hurried over, but said nothing.

In the center of the floor mural that represented Mira, six Mirans stood in a tight circle with their heads bowed. The eight Originals stood in a larger circle around them and faced outward to all the Mirans who had gathered in the room. It looked almost like the Originals were protecting the six in the inner circle. The room was silent, emotions were dim, and everyone was waiting with fearful anticipation.

Sindri raised her head to begin speaking to those grouped around the circle of Originals. From where Lexi stood, she could see her eyes. The beautiful dots of light that usually twinkled and danced were still and dim. The rest of the Originals kept their heads down, but she had no doubt that their eyes were the same.

"We have grave news," Sindri spoke quietly and almost reverently. "You all sensed what happened, but I know you have no explanation for it. Only the eight Originals and a few of our first children have felt this before. I regret having to tell you that what you sensed was the death of five Mirans."

A loud gasp went through the room as they heard this news. When the silence returned, Lexi sensed a wave of overwhelming grief and sorrow from every Miran present.

"Eleven Mirans from the Chicago area were gathered for a simple social event when they were attacked by fifteen Dabih. The Dabih struck quickly and five Mirans were killed before anyone realized what was happening. The six Mirans in the center of our circle fought back and killed all the Dabih. They acted with bravery and decisiveness and we commend their actions.

"Before the Dabih bodies were disposed of, they were searched. Each of them carried a small device that we think keeps us from sensing them. Without this device, the Dabih would have gotten nowhere near the Mirans.

"While we grieve deeply those who have died, we must also acknowledge that this was probably a first strike in an all-out war between Mira and the Dabih. They may be planning other attacks at this very moment, so we all must be aware of the danger.

"We will notify everyone as soon as we formulate a plan to deal with this threat. Meanwhile be assured our engineers are working on a way to counteract this new Dabih device. We hope to develop something that will make it ineffective.

"All of you are welcome to stay here to comfort each other and the six survivors of this attack while we Originals meet. Any of you who feel unsafe returning to your homes may also stay as long as you wish."

After saying this, Sindri and the other Originals moved toward the conference room. Lexi and Adam still stood with Erik and Aricia silently sensing all the emotions around the room when she noticed a Human mind approaching. Ted had been standing along the wall trying to be a part of this while not intruding.

"I'm glad you're here," Lexi said, hugging him.

"I was visiting Sindri when it happened. She was devastated when those Mirans died. I guess I didn't really understand that none of you had died for centuries. Since the Dabih killed the ones that tried to communicate with them."

"That's why none of us recognized what we were sensing," Erik said.

"Sindri explained that to me. She asked me to bring you four to the Originals' meeting."

"Then let's go before they get started," Aricia said.

Sindri began speaking as soon as we were all settled. Emotions were very subdued, but everyone shared in the grief.

"I wanted the five of you to be here because Balere and I think Pinehurst may be essential to our reaction to the Dabih. It is obvious that we are now dealing with the Ruling Council as Dirac warned us. Balere, would you like to explain the conclusions you have drawn?"

"Thank you, Sindri," Balere said. "If we look at recent Dabih activity I think we can infer what they have planned. First, when they held Adam, their main concern was the location of New Mira. Second, we observe them actively trying to sense us. Then, Ted detected a Dabih that none of the rest of us can sense. Finally, this group of Mirans is attacked without sensing the presence of Dabih.

"Putting these incidences together, we have to conclude that they are acting on a plan directly targeting us and they have a device that keeps us from sensing them, even at close quarters. The fact that they found the group of Mirans makes it obvious they have another device that enables them to sense us at a distance.

"To blatantly attack us as they did, they must have a high degree of confidence that they can defeat us, but it could also be a reaction to the fact that we just found their ship. We just don't know if they're aware of our discovery or not. The Mirans that survived the attack killed the Dabih easily. Hopefully that will convince them that we are still stronger than they are.

"So what should our reaction be to the Dabih attack? Most of us feel it is inappropriate to attack them. Our refusal to retaliate may finally convince them that we do wish to live with them in peace. On the other hand, if we do nothing, we may be showing a weakness that will invite another attack.

"Assuming that Ted can sense Dabih because their device isn't designed for Human brain waves, we have to accept that the one named Gelar is Dabih. I think we also have to assume that he was placed in the coffee shop to observe and gather information about the only Mirans the Dabih really know, Adam and Lexi.

"That places them in great danger, especially after this attack. But this Gelar remains the only Dabih that we can contact. Ted proposed earlier that we use our power-blocking device on him to test if he is Dabih. I think that's just what we now need to do."

"I wonder," Ted said as Balere finished, "if it might have been Gelar that I sensed outside of my house. He may have shown up there because he sensed Sindri, or sensed something in me and knows we're aware of him. If he suspects anything, he may not be back."

"That's a possibility," Balere answered. "Adam, Lexi, do either of you know his work schedule? Is he supposed to work tonight?"

"Yes," Lexi answered. "Adam and I both have today off, so he'll work tonight, probably until 10:00 p.m. I work with him tomorrow night."

"Then we'll need to get to him after work tonight. If he shows up," Ted said looking at Balere.

"We'll know," Adam said. "If he doesn't show up for work, Sean will try to call one of us in."

"Ted," Balere said, "we'll need to continue the charade of being friendly with him and drop in for some coffee. If we don't go in, he'll sense me outside and become suspicious."

"Good idea," Ted answered. "We can go about 9:30, have a snack, and leave right before his shift ends. We'll wait for him outside."

"Adam, Lexi," Balere said as he turned toward Lexi, "we'll block his powers, lightly stun him, and bring him to your apartment for questioning. The four of you and Sindri can be there waiting for us."

"This is the only way," Sindri said, "we might have of convincing them that we don't want to kill them. Hopefully, Gelar will return to the Dabih as evidence that we want peace. If this doesn't work, I don't know what else we can do to avoid an all-out war."

When they left New Mira, Erik, Aricia and Ted returned with Lexi and Adam to their apartment. They spent the afternoon talking, watching TV, and waiting. They didn't talk much about the Dabih attack because there wasn't anything else to say. She could even feel how sad Ted was about these developments, but he seemed to be dealing with it better than the rest of them. She figured he had much more experience with death.

About 4:30, Sean called. Gelar hadn't shown up for his 4:00 shift and he couldn't find him. Adam offered to go in to work Gelar's shift.

Ted immediately called Balere. Lexi didn't have any idea how they should proceed if Gelar never came back, and they were all sure, at that point, they'd never see him again. Since Ted was the only one that could sense them if they were using the new device, he offered to do some patrolling. Balere teleported over and went with him. It was the only plan they had, but none of them had much hope for that plan's success.

CHAPTER 36

Gelar was very pleased. He'd approached his meeting with Kalti that morning, not knowing if he would find a supporter or another enemy, but he'd come away with more support than he'd ever hoped for.

Faru had always told Gelar that Kalti and his followers knew and approved of their plans, but he was never completely sure of Faru's truthfulness. He felt rather sad that it took Faru's death to finally convince him that their alliance was genuine.

Kalti came to the meeting at an abandoned house near some train tracks outside of Pinehurst with another general that Gelar had never met. General Mada had worked with Kalti and Faru for decades. They both believed that Nomarr and Yara were more interested in their own power than in the good of the Dabih.

He led them to the living room area where they made themselves comfortable on some milk crates and a dilapidated chair. He started his meeting by telling Kalti and Mada everything he knew about Nomarr, Yara, the Mirans, and Humans. If there was ever going to be any significant change to the way the Council ruled the Dabih, it had to start with truthfulness among those who were conspiring to take over the Council.

He hoped to someday end the conspiracies and backstabbing methods that had plagued the Ruling Council, and the time had come for him to accomplish his goals or die in the attempt. If Kalti and Mada agreed with him, the three of them could start a new age for the Dabih. If they didn't agree with him, they would kill him and continue their own plots to take over the Council.

"Faru was correct in placing his trust in you," Kalti said when he finished telling them everything he'd discovered. "Faru, Mada and I, along with dozens of other officers that follow us, have watched for too long as Nomarr and Yara accomplished nothing but building their own power. Your information may be what we finally need to depose them."

"We will need to move on our plans soon, before Nomarr starts killing Mirans," Mada added. "And you are correct, Gelar, it will be best to destroy them both at the same time."

"I will keep gathering information on the Mirans and Humans as I have been," he said. "Nomarr will notice nothing, and we will make our move before he makes his."

"We have some followers who are in place to keep an eye on Yara," Kalti added. "She can be very dangerous. She knows you'll eventually go to Nomarr with the information about her allowing a Miran to rescue Adam."

"Does she suspect that you and Mada have worked with Faru?"

"We don't think so, but Yara has many ways of gathering information and she never did trust Faru. But as long as we watch her closely, she won't be able to do much. She may make it necessary for us to move sooner than we plan, though."

"I will stay as close as possible to Nomarr," he said, "and try to find out when he plans his first attack on the Mirans."

"Good," Kalti said. "We'll get back to the ship and inform our followers of our plans. They will look forward to following you as the new head of the Ruling Council, as we do."

"I look forward to the three of us forming a new Ruling Council that will accomplish great things for the Dabih," he said.

"You should return first, and I'll follow later so no one becomes suspicious that we were together."

He watched them leave before teleporting to his quarters. Once he got back to the ship, he sat alone, thinking. For fifty years he'd looked forward to the time when he could destroy Nomarr. Finally, that time was upon him.

Once he took over the Ruling Council with Kalti and Mada, he knew it would be a struggle to make any significant changes, but the struggles would be worth it. He would find a way to create a world for the Dabih where no more innocent victims like his wife would die to increase someone else's power.

He had never planned or hoped that he would rule the Dabih. He'd started his alliance with Faru to avenge his wife's death. Things had grown way beyond that. He'd get his revenge, but he'd also honor her by creating a better life for all Dabih. Even for those who had no power or influence.

In a few hours he would need to return to Pinehurst for his shift at the coffee shop. In some ways he looked forward to his time there and its safety. Maybe he'd call Emily when he had time for a break. This was a dangerous time to become more involved with her, but maybe he could try to have a casual relationship. Maybe having her as a friend would be what he really needed.

Kalti and Mada materialized in his room, causing him to jump. One look at them, and he knew they were furious. Something had happened.

"Nomarr's men have just killed some Mirans in Chicago." Kalti shook his fist.

"You're two of his generals," he said as his own anger flared. "How could he do that without informing you?"

"He obviously doesn't trust us," Kalti answered. "We might not have even known he'd acted on his plans if his soldiers had been successful, but none of them returned. It is assumed that the Mirans killed them."

"How many Mirans were killed?"

"We have no way of knowing, but many are saying that his plan was ill-conceived and bound for failure," Mada answered. "We need to move against him immediately. If we wait, we give Yara the chance to claim she knew nothing of his plan and gain followers. She will move against him as soon as she can, and we will be left with no way of overthrowing her."

"How many can you gather right now?" he asked Kalti.

"About two dozen are ready to move with us."

"Gather your supporters. We should kill Yara first, then immediately attack Nomarr."

Kalti and Mada left to quickly gather their men. Gelar reached out mentally to find Yara's location. She was in her quarters and alone. He knew she would be making her plans to move swiftly, so he would have to move faster.

Kalti and Mada returned within minutes. They gazed at each other with determination, nodded their heads, and teleported.

As Gelar materialized in Yara's quarters, she quickly assumed he was there to join her and she actually smiled. The smile quickly turned to a look of confusion, though, as Kalti and Mada materialized behind him.

"I've come to demonstrate how much you can trust me, Yara," he said, not smiling. "Not at all." With that, he let his powers surge and struck Yara with as much force as he could. Her shocked expression only lasted a moment before she slumped in her chair. He sensed her hatred as she died.

"Our men wait outside Council chambers," Kalti said.

They teleported to join their men, glad to see that more than thirty of them had gathered. He told them briefly of their plan before the whole group teleported into the Council chamber to confront Nomarr. He went in first with the others teleporting just seconds later.

He found Nomarr alone, fuming.

"How dare you enter unannounced? What is the meaning of this?"

He could feel Nomarr gathering his strength to strike him and smiled as the group of over thirty Dabih appeared behind him. Nomarr was confused.

"You're just a follower," he stammered as Gelar's power overwhelmed him.

"Before you die," he said, "know that I've been plotting against you and waiting for this moment for fifty years. Your greatest oversight, Nomarr, is that you underestimated me."

Nomarr's disbelief turned into fear, and then nothing.

CHAPTER 37

When Sean let Adam and Lexi know that Gelar couldn't be found, the disappointment that their only link to the Dabih was gone put them even deeper into the emotional dumps. Erik and Aricia had continued hanging out with her while Adam went to work and Balere and Ted patrolled the streets. By 10:00 p.m., everyone was back at the apartment. Sindri joined them.

"According to the IRS and the state of Massachusetts, Gelar Davis is who he says he is," Ted reported. "But I was unable to find any pictures of him before his current driver's license. I called his high school and none of the teachers remembered him. The apartment he listed on his application for employment at Sean's Coffee Shop is actually rented out to a nice couple from Taiwan."

No one seemed surprised by that.

"Ted and I discussed finding a way to go to the Dabih ship, but we decided it would just be too dangerous," Balere said when none of them could think of any way to contact Gelar. "Now, we may have to go there despite the danger."

"If enough of us go in with power blockers, we won't be in that much danger," Ted said. "They can't attack us, so they'll have to listen."

Balere looked at Ted and shook his head, "We can't let you go. You have no defense against them."

"I'm the only one who's walked around in there," he said, sounding irritated. "They didn't notice my human mind and they won't notice me if I show up again. I'm probably the one that's safest in there."

Sindri, sitting next to him, put a calming hand on his leg. "He's right, Balere. He probably is the safest one to go to their ship."

Ted linked his fingers with hers. "Don't worry, Sindri, we'll all get out of there. And we'll make the Dabih listen to us."

"I know you will," she said, "but, before anyone is ready to materialize on that ship, we need to have detailed plans. I would like to see a definite time limit, Mirans in several locations ready to beam you out, and armed Mirans. We may have to shoot Dabih if they stun us and we can't get out any other way. We need to go in to talk peace, but be ready to be ruthless if necessary."

"I completely agree," Balere said. "We will spend the day tomorrow making plans and be ready to go by evening."

"We haven't discussed who will go," Adam said, "except Balere and Ted. I want to be included."

A shot of fear made Lexi almost drop her cup. "No, Adam. I couldn't stand that."

"Lexi, babe, think about it," he said looking into her eyes, "they abducted and tortured me, yet I go back to talk to them about living in peace. What could be more convincing that we really mean it?"

Sindri sighed and slowly shook her head and exchanged a look with Balere. "How can we send any of our children into such danger, especially our youngest? We can't move on this until we're sure there's no other choice."

As Balere was assuring her that they would continue to think of alternatives, Adam's cell rang. He stepped into the kitchen to answer. Lexi couldn't imagine who might be calling this late because everyone that it might be was already sitting in the apartment.

He came back to the group looking amazed and a little frightened. "You won't believe this," he said shaking his head. "That was Gelar. He wants to come over to talk to Lexi and me."

"What did you tell him?" Balere asked as the rest of them stared in astonishment.

Adam shrugged, "To come on over."

* * *

After disposing of Nomarr's body, Gelar, Kalti and Mada took their seats at the Ruling Council table with Gelar in the center seat as the Head of Council. Their Dabih followers cheered and congratulated them, but the celebration could only last a moment. There was still much to be done.

It wasn't enough for them to just take over the Council chambers. They had to announce the change in leadership to all the Dabih while watching for and putting an end to any possible uprisings from Nomarr's or Yara's factions.

Gelar sent the group of Dabih that had joined them in the chamber out among the most powerful of those supporters to watch and listen for any trouble. Once they were gone, he announced his self-appointment as Head of the Ruling Council through monitors that were in every room and area of the ship.

He explained Nomarr's crimes against the Dabih, first. He went back to his weakness in allowing Dirac to break away from them fifty years ago and ended with his failed plan to attack the Mirans. Then he declared Yara's crimes of hiding how she had endangered them all by allowing a Miran to escape from their ship and her illegal murder of Faru.

He then announced his fellow members of the Ruling Council, General Kalti and General Mada. Finally, he assured the Dabih that this change in the Council had been accomplished without harming any innocent Dabih and promised that they would continue to protect them from the Mirans.

The new members of the Ruling Council received reports from their supporters who were out among the other Dabih. They were somewhat surprised to hear that, while there was quite a bit of talk about the takeover, there was very little discussion against it. And that discussion seemed to stem from a fear that the Mirans would retaliate.

Over the next few hours, they came to realize that no one really believed in Nomarr and Yara. They were supported for decades out of fear. Most of the Dabih had been hoping that someone would move against them and felt fifty years of Nomarr and Yara had been too long.

Once they felt secure in their new positions, the three new members of Council moved to a discussion of the Mirans. Like the rest of the Dabih, neither Kalti nor Mada had ever met a Miran, so they willingly deferred to Gelar's knowledge.

"We can't ignore the situation Nomarr has put us in," Gelar started, "even though I really don't believe the Mirans will attack us. Open warfare is not their style, and it is possible that no Mirans were harmed. All we really know is that our soldiers did not return from the attack, so they were either killed or captured.

"If the Mirans killed them, they would probably be waiting for our next move. If the Mirans captured them, they would probably send at least one of them back to us with a message. Since we've received no message, I have to presume that the Dabih were killed."

"Your reasoning is very sound," Kalti said. "So, if the Mirans are waiting for our next move, what will that move be?"

"We need to talk to the Mirans," Gelar said with assurance.

Uprising

CHAPTER 38

To say that Lexi was in shock that Gelar had just called and asked to come over was a gross understatement. All of their minds were blank for a few seconds before they started talking about how to handle this.

"We're going to have to be very careful," Balere finally said. "Sindri and I will do most of the talking."

"Should we all be here?" Aricia asked.

"If we're right about them being able to sense us from a distance," he answered, "he may already know how many of us are here, so there's no point in anyone leaving."

Sindri dialed her phone. "Ibon, be ready to teleport us immediately if we reach out to you. We are about to meet with Gelar. I hope not, but be ready in case."

Looking at Balere, she said, "He'll have everyone ready."

"Do you think Gelar will reveal himself to us?" Lexi asked Balere.

"I don't know," he said shaking his head. "Ted, do you have your power blocker?"

"Yeah, I've started carrying it all the time," he answered. "He won't sense me. Should I hide in the bedroom in case we need to catch him by surprise?"

Balere thought for a moment. "No, let's not hide anything from him. He'll need to see us as being completely honest if he's going to believe us."

Ted winced slightly as the buzzing started in his head. "He's not alone. I sense more than one of them, but I'm not sure how many."

The rest of them felt nothing, so either Gelar was still using something to keep them from sensing him, or they were completely wrong and he wasn't Dabih, but that wasn't likely. Lexi knew they were about to find out. Adam hesitated for just a second before going to answer it. As the door opened, they could all see Gelar standing outside with two other men.

"Hi, Gelar," Adam said. "We've got some friends over tonight, but I think you know most of them. Come on in."

* * *

Gelar had sensed the six Mirans and one Human before he'd knocked on the door. As he walked in, he mentally reached out to sense their emotions. They were very apprehensive, but he didn't sense any aggression. He was determined to reveal himself to the Mirans and confident they would not attack. Kalti and Mada sensed the same thing, but their own uneasiness and inexperience didn't allow them to be as comfortable walking into a room full of Mirans. He felt their emotions also and glanced quickly at them to let them see his confidence.

They stood in a semicircle in the living room. No one offered them a seat.

"Gelar, I think the only person you don't know is Sindri," Adam said while extending his arm toward her. "Sindri, this is Gelar. He works with Lexi and me at the coffee shop."

"I'm glad to meet you." She had a calm voice and green eyes that sparkled like light falling on water.

"I'm certainly glad to meet you, as well." He knew immediately that she was the powerful Miran he had sensed teleporting away from Ted's house and was glad that she was present for the conversation he needed to start. "But, I'm afraid

Adam's introduction was, let's say, somewhat incomplete. I have some things to tell all of you about myself. I'm concerned, though, that what I have to reveal to you might cause problems between us."

Sindri looked deeply into his eyes and gave him a slight, knowing smile. "We feel that the truth usually solves problems instead of creating them. You have no reason to fear us."

He smiled back at her. He now understood that the Mirans had somehow discovered that he was Dabih. How had they gotten through his blocking device and how long they had known? However they discovered him, though, he also understood that she was letting him know that they were not a threat to him. At least not right now.

"My title is actually Head of the Ruling Council. My friends are Councilmember Kalti and Councilmember Mada." He indicated the two men accompanying him. "The three of us make up the governing body of the Dabih."

"Thank you for your honesty," she said. "I should reveal to you that we had already suspected that you are Dabih. Dirac told us of the Ruling Council's existence, but we had no idea that you were the head. Was he truthful when he said the Ruling Council abducted Adam?"

"Yes, but the Ruling Council was headed by Nomarr at that time. It was Councilmember Yara's strategy to use Professor Carpenter to abduct Adam."

"So Nomarr and Yara are no longer members of Council?" Sindri asked.

"No. We deposed them several hours ago, right after we learned Nomarr ordered his soldiers to attack Mirans in Chicago. Are those soldiers dead?"

"Yes." She seemed sad.

"What of the Mirans?"

"Five Mirans were killed before they knew they were under attack."

An upwelling of sorrow filled the room. It reminded him of the loss of Faru. He shook his head and changed the subject.

"I get the impression that you are the head of the Mirans."

"Balere and I are leaders," she said, indicating the Miran next to her. He remembered him from the coffee shop. "Others also have leadership roles."

"As leaders of Mira," he continued, "I'd like to assure you that the attack in Chicago was conceived and carried out by Nomarr. It was not by the Dabih as a whole."

"Are you saying that your policies change at the whim of one Dabih?"

He thought for a moment. "In a way, that is, or at least has been, true. For decades you fought Dirac and his followers as they kidnapped and experimented with Human women. Those who survived your attack were killed by Nomarr. Terazed kidnapped Lexi. He was under Dirac's control and was also killed by Nomarr. Yara and Nomarr plotted to kidnap Adam. We killed them. The old Ruling Council and Dirac are gone. You are now dealing with the three of us."

"Are you offering peace between Dabih and Mira?"

"We are conquerors. The Dabih have always moved ahead through aggression and violence. I can't promise peace. I can, however, offer nonaggression for the time being."

The Miran leaders considered that for a moment. Lexi fidgeted and clung to Adam's hand. Ted, the Human, leaned against the wall, his arms crossed. The other two hovered behind the leaders.

"That is at least a step forward." Sindri said. "We would prefer living in peace with the Dabih and Humans, but we will gladly honor a nonaggression pact. There is one thing, though, that may make it difficult for us to trust such a pact."

"What is that?"

"We still can't sense you. Why is that?"

"We developed a device that blocks us from you. I apologize for not turning them off sooner. We will agree to no longer use them." He nodded to Kalti and Mada as he reached for the object at his belt. As they manipulated the devices, he could tell the Mirans sensed them by their sudden alertness.

"Thank you," she said. "To demonstrate our desire for peace and honesty between us, I'd like to reveal a device we have developed."

She looked at Ted and reached out her hand. He handed her a device that looked like a television remote control. She tilted her head and pushed a button. Gelar was suddenly frozen. He blinked and rubbed his face. His senses were gone, no longer feeling the Mirans or the other Dabih. He couldn't even sense the human, and that frightened him. He glanced at Mada and saw that the general had tensed and seemed ready to strike. Kalti put a restraining hand on his shoulder and nodded.

Sindri pushed another button and released their powers.

"And we will agree to no longer use this device," Balere said.

Gelar's power flooded back. He shuddered. "That is an interesting weapon. Is that what you used against Yara's guard when you rescued Adam?" he asked quietly, trying to hide his fear.

"Yes, it was used," Sindri answered.

"May I know which one of you was able to infiltrate our stronghold?"

The Mirans looked at each other or at the floor. None of them would look at Ted and give away the fact that he was the one to rescue Adam. Ted glanced at the leaders and shrugged.

"I rescued him."

"You're Human." Gelar couldn't help but let the surprise show in his voice and on his face.

He simply smiled.

"Ted is not your average Human," Sindri said.

"What does that mean?"

Sindri exchanged a look with Ted. It seemed like they were communicating without speaking. Perhaps he wasn't the average Human, and maybe the Mirans had been doing their own Human experiments? Maybe collaborating with humans for years.

"Ted," Sindri said, "it is your decision whether or not they know about you."

He nodded and cleared his throat. "I'm a police detective and discovered the Mirans while investigating Gretchen Wagner's death."

Gelar recognized the name, but Ted had said it purposefully, hoping to discover if Gelar knew about her death.

"They realized the strange buzzing in my head was my ability to sense Dabih. Rescuing Adam was a simple case of taking advantage of an opportunity. I sensed the guard who was taking Carpenter to Yara and touched him so I could teleport with them. I found Adam, destroyed the pain thing in the ceiling, and he teleported us home."

"How can you sense Dabih?"

"That's the really fun part." His sarcasm seemed so Human. "Seems I have some Dabih DNA. Guess you could be my great-great grandpa."

"What?" He looked at Kalti and Mada. They had no idea that was possible either. "We know some Dabih have mated with Humans, but never knew of any surviving offspring."

The Human made a wide gesture with his hands. "Well, you know of them now."

"Are there others?"

"None that we know of," Sindri answered.

Now it was Gelar's turn to pause and consider. A Human with Dabih genes. Perhaps Dirac's dream of reproduction hadn't been a total waste.

"Would you be willing to let us study your DNA and your abilities?"

"No." Lexi's emphatic answer was echoed by Ted's "Not a chance." He shook his head and added, "I think I'll stick with the Mirans."

"I hope you someday change your mind. Your DNA could be very important to the Dabih."

"Don't hold your breath."

CHAPTER 39

There were a few moments of awkward silence after that.
Both sides had revealed many things, but there were still
questions in Lexi's mind. She didn't want to interfere with
anything Sindri and Balere wanted to say, but she just couldn't
let this opportunity pass without trying to get some answers.

"Gelar," she said as every head in the room turned toward
her, "I couldn't help but notice that you seemed to recognize
Gretchen Wagner's name when Ted mentioned her. Did you
know her?"

Gelar actually seemed sad as he looked at her. "Yes, Lexi, I
knew her. For several years I was Dirac's lieutenant while
actually spying on him for Nomarr, so I was Terazed's
supervisor. He forced Gretchen to tell him about you and then
killed her. We left her body for you to find so you would not
come looking for her."

She wanted answers about Gretchen, but wasn't very pleased
now that she'd gotten them. She hated the idea that Terazed had
tortured and killed Gretchen. He was so cruel, and Lexi knew
first-hand the pain she must have endured before she gave him
the information he wanted.

Overwhelming her hatred of Terazed, though, was her guilt.
Gretchen was tortured and murdered for information about her.
Gretchen trusted her and asked her for help. Her hatred of
Terazed expanded into a hatred of Gelar for the role he'd played
in the tragedy of Gretchen's death.

"I was also the one, Lexi," Gelar continued, "who called you
asking why you didn't kill the Dabih in Oregon. And also the

one who called to reveal that Terazed held you in San Francisco."

Was he saying that he'd tried to do the right thing while forced to be cruel and merciless? Was he trying to justify his brutality? She just didn't know. He was a Dabih, but he had saved her from Terazed. She didn't know if she wanted to punch him or thank him.

"Gelar," Sindri finally said, "can you guarantee that no more Humans will be abducted?"

"Kalti, Mada and I can only tell you that we are concentrating on the Dabih. We have no plans to harm Humans or Mirans."

"Do the rest of the Dabih agree with these plans?"

"At this point, no one is opposing us."

Sindri sighed. "Quite frankly, Gelar, that disappoints me. All Mirans share the same goals and desire for peace. The three of you could be deposed at any time and the goals of the Dabih could change drastically. How can we ever know what we're dealing with?"

"We are conquerors. I will not apologize for our culture or our system of government. As I said, you are now dealing with the three of us as the present Ruling Council. You either accept that and our nonaggression pact, or you don't."

"We accept it and welcome it. But we also hope that all the Dabih will someday find a desire for true peace."

There seemed nothing more to say.

"Thank you for allowing us to come here tonight," Gelar said and nodded. The three of them teleported away.

Lexi got up and pulled Aricia into the kitchen. It seemed like there would be a lot of talk now and she had to do something, anything. Aricia helped her make more coffee and set out chips and dip to tide them over until the pizza she ordered came.

She returned to the living room. Everyone had taken a seat. She passed out coffee and sat on the arm of the couch near Adam. He put his hand on her leg and squeezed.

"We have waited so long to talk to the Dabih," Sindri said looking at Balere. "Now that it has finally happened, I have to wonder if it will bring about any real change."

"I don't know," Balere answered, "but I didn't sense deception or trickery. I wonder about his statement that they're going to concentrate on the Dabih instead of worrying about Humans and Mirans. Maybe they're having problems we know nothing about."

"You know," Ted said with a curious look on his face, "that's interesting. One of the things that I noticed on that ship was that it seemed so big and empty. We've been killing them, they've been killing each other, maybe they've lost enough people they're afraid of going on with this war."

"That's a good point," Balere said. "We have no idea how many they've lost over the centuries."

"Part of me wants to believe that Gelar really does want peace," Adam added, "but maybe the other two don't. Or maybe some other Dabih don't and could overthrow them."

"Or maybe they're just not sure," Lexi said after passing the bowl of chips. "Their whole culture is based on conquest and aggression. Changing a culture isn't an easy thing."

"We may not hear from them again for years, maybe centuries," Erik sighed. "When will we ever be able to trust that problems with the Dabih are over?"

"We'll be analyzing every word Gelar said for quite some time," Sindri said, "but no more tonight. I'm grateful that we have some assurance that there will be no more killing. At least not in the near future." The pizza came and everyone ate some.

Afterward, they said their farewells, Erik and Aricia teleported home, and Sindri, Balere and Ted teleported to New Mira. Adam and Lexi were finally alone after another late, tension-filled night.

"Oh, Adam," she said as she put her arms around him, "I don't know how to feel about any of this."

"I know, babe," he answered, holding her tightly. "Part of me wants to rejoice that the attacks are over, but most of me just can't really trust anything a Dabih tells us."

"We were getting to be friends with Gelar, but he was deceiving us all along."

"He sure was, but there is one thing I'm sure of," he said, giving her a mischievous smile. "If we keep having these meetings, we'll need to get a bigger apartment."

* * *

Ted, Sindri and Balere materialized in Sindri's quarters.

"I get the impression you two want to talk to me." He grinned at her.

"Either that or we just kidnapped you," Sindri smiled back as she led them to one of the cozy conversation areas so they could all sit comfortably.

"I could live with that." He winked at her. He caught Balere giving them a knowing grin, but Ted was more interested in Sindri's coquettish look.

"We have a proposition for you," Balere said, clearing his throat.

"What about?"

"There are times when we could use a good private investigator, but very few Mirans have the skills and background to do the job. There just aren't many of us that lean toward police work."

His interest peeked. "What do you need investigated?"

"There are different things. A situation we had recently involved one of our chemists being offered a job with a small drug manufacturing company. We investigated the company and CEO to make sure they ran their business legally and ethically.

"Our biggest concern, though, is with young Humans who will become Miran. We try to watch them carefully. We watch to make sure they're safe and not getting too involved with anyone that could seriously harm them, but without intruding. We have plenty of Mirans who are willing to become part of their lives if necessary.

"But the Human world seems to be more dangerous, and young people are exposed to things that could cause great harm. We need to investigate their families, schools, clubs, even social networking sites on the Internet, anything that's got an influence on them and their safety.

"Quite frankly, we're not that good at that kind of investigation. We need someone like you to not only investigate for us, but to also train some of us. You have an expertise that we need. Would you be interested in working for us in such a capacity?"

"Are you talking about full-time? Working as a PI for you guys?" He was astonished and excited.

"Yeah. You'd have to quit your job and work full-time for us."

"I'm blown away. The best part of my job has always been digging for information and answers. Keeping people from being victims by finding out what was really going on. Doing that for Mirans would be unbelievable."

As he spoke, he looked at their tall, Miran bodies and bright eyes. Spending time on New Mira with Sindri, he'd gotten used to seeing their natural forms, but usually felt so out of place. He often tried to stay out of sight and sometimes thought of himself as a rat slinking around a luxurious ship. But they wanted him here. They wanted him to be a part of their marvelous, secret lives. How could he say no?

"Do I hear you saying yes?" Sindri asked.

"Big time," he declared with joy pouring out of him. "Thank you so much. I can't believe it."

He reached up to give Balere a high-five. He looked over at Sindri and stood up to hug her and kiss her cheek. As he sat back down, he got more serious. His life in Pinehurst had been good before the aliens, but it had been missing something. He'd been the lonely, third wheel. Now he had Sindri and what seemed like a whole family. Yeah, they were lavender aliens with sparkling eyes who could tell his every feeling, but he didn't have to hide anything now. He felt like he belonged.

"You guys have been the best thing that ever happened to me. I can't tell you how much it means to hear you say you want me to help you. That really means a lot to me. And I'll also be helping to protect the whole human race. Amazing," he sighed. "I promise I'll do my best in anything you need me to do."

"We're thrilled, too," Sindri said reaching over to touch his hand.

"I suppose you'll have to give the police department a couple weeks' notice," Balere said, "so we'll have plenty of time to figure out the details. From now on, though, you're working for us."

-End-

ABOUT THE AUTHOR

Ellen Fritz is a retired teacher and high school counselor. Over the years of teaching Reading and English to students in grades seven through twelve before becoming a counselor, she had the great opportunity to discuss numerous favorite books with students and also took their recommendations for her own reading.

She finally found herself with the time to give life to the stories that have always been patiently waiting in her head for an audience.

Ellen wrote *The Second Birth Chronicles* to appeal to those readers that she found so inspiring through her career as an educator.

Tell-Tale Publishing would like to thank you for your purchase. If you would like to read more by Ellen or other fine TT authors, please visit us at:

www.tell-talepublishing.com